THE
ORCHARD
ON FIRE

A Novel

Also by the author:

A Bowl of Cherries

Dunedin

Dreams of Dead Women's Handbags: Collected Stories

THE
ORCHARD
ON FIRE

A Novel

By Shena Mackay

MOYER BELL
Wakefield, Rhode Island & London

Published by Moyer Bell

Second Printing, 1996

**LIBRARY OF CONGRESS
CATALOGING-IN-PUBLICATION DATA**

Mackay, Shena.
  The orchard on fire / Shena Mackay.

  p.   cm.
  1. Divorced women—England—Psychology—Fiction. 2. Girls—England-Fiction. I. Title
PR6063.A2425073   1996
                           96-8420
ISBN 1-55921-175-X   CIP

Printed in the United States of America
Distributed in North America by Publishers Group West,
P.O. Box 8843, Emeryville, CA 94662, 800-788-3123 (in
California 510-658-3453)

THE
ORCHARD
ON FIRE

A Novel

One

I chose this place to live, believing that I would find anonymity
among those who did not care if the plaster and glass and
paintwork of rented houses splintered and decayed, who were
not reproached by gardens gone to seed and rotting sofas. In
that hope, as in most things, I was proved wrong. People in
the shops, who are living their real lives, even if you aren't,
soon start to recognize you. These are blowzy houses divided
into new conversions that generate ancient dust, and next door's
great gorgeous crimson full-blown roses pouring over the Rus-
sian vine and honeysuckle that holds up the fence, unpruned
like my own friable yellow, pink-tinged roses, are persistent
reminders that the gardens were loved once.

Usually, I stay inside trying to forget that there is a summer
going on out there, but tonight, at eight o'clock on a July
evening, I am watching swifts flying in the transparent space
between the treetops and roofs, and a vaporous blue white-
clouded sky. I have cut back rosemary and lemon balm to make
a space for a chair and my arms and hands, scented from their
aromatic work, are tingling with stings and scratches and the
invasive tiny barbs of borage. It is a narrow London garden,
where plants must grow tall or sprawling to survive, bordered by
lime trees behind the back wall and tangled elder, philadelphus,
forsythia and pyracanthus. Pheasant berry seeds itself every-

where, leaving dead canes where it cannot stand the competition, that rattle and creak. One of the cats, tired of leaping and pouncing on falling foliage and exploring exposed secret places, jumps onto my lap and settles there, and I see that the summer has tinged her almost sage-green ears ginger, and I feel a stillness of spirit and an intimation of a sensual, visual intensity that I thought I had lost for ever. It is as if I am in that airy insubstantial zone where the birds are flying, between the past and the future.

'Been doing a spot of ethnic cleansing, I see.'

It is my upstairs neighbour, leaning out of the window, the author of several unpublished novels of the depilatory school, about whose manuscripts I am sometimes called upon to dissemble in my capacity as an English teacher. I have a copy of the latest in my possession now.

'You've ruined my view,' she says, activating a yelping police siren, thudding music and barbecue smoke beaded with burned fat.

'Sorry. How's the work going, Jaz?'

The chopped and broken branches are wilting in heaps under the bushes. The cat disappears.

'For goodness sake. In no other profession is one called on to account for oneself a thousand times a day by every Tom, Dick and Harry.'

'Sorry. Rather poor taste though, your remark about ethnic cleansing.'

Truth to tell, a need to escape the television news as well as restlessness has brought me outside.

'Sense of humour failure?' asks Jaz. 'Well, you've got to laugh, haven't you, or else . . .' Her voice tails off, and rallies. 'Tell you what, April, I've got a couple of cold beers in the fridge. I'll bring them down.'

I don't want Jaz in the garden, which technically belongs to me as tenant of the downstairs flat, and I see now, dully, that it looks mangled and bereft. I don't want a cold beer. I was born into the licensed trade, and a brief froth of happiness, bursting in bubbles, evanescent as elderflowers, is the last thing

2

I want, but the bitter-sweet smell of moist green hops that stain the fingers comes to me, from wiry bines entwining in the rafters of a saloon bar or the rood screen of the church at Harvest festival, and I almost glimpse the gate, far away and cloudy, that leads into the orchard before you come to the hop gardens.

The only access to this garden is through my flat and Jaz is banging on my door. 'So, you're on holiday now, you jammy so-and-so.'

She sprawls, in shorts and vest, on the chair, sucking beer through a wedge of lemon rammed into the bottle's neck, while I drop a cushion onto what had once been a little lawn.

'Cheers,' she says, in her delusion of youth, 'I should've gone into teaching – a writer doesn't have holidays. Still, you know what they say, those who can do, et cetera, et cetera.'

And there are those who can neither write nor teach. Her shoulders, arms and cleavage are so moist that I feel like a bundle of dry elder sticks, snappy and hollow, and I think of our camp, where a spring welled up under the roots of a elder tree.

'Penny for 'em, you're staring into space again, and it's most disconcerting.'

'Sorry. I was miles away.'

'Where? Where miles away?'

'Oh, in Stonebridge, the village where I grew up. In the fifties.'

'That drab, grey and repressive decade. Thank goodness I was a child of the sixties.'

'It wasn't grey. That's not how I remember it at all.' It was politically, intellectually and artistically exciting. I see the Iron Curtain, as I saw it then, rusting corrugated iron hung with white convolvulus.

It was the time that coloured everything for me, that set my weakness for the gawdy and tawdry and ephemeral, for the veined gold and silver paper from cigarette packets. Today, my favourite restaurant in London is a little Greek-Cypriot place with lace curtains, hanging spider plants and fairy-lights.

'Oh come on, don't give me that Festival of Britain stuff,

and don't forget I did my thesis on 50s children's books. By the way, April, most people have gooseberry bushes in their gardens but you've got a gooseberry tree. You'd better watch out, you might find a very tall baby under it one day.'

The gooseberry is a poor skinny thing, some nine feet tall with leaves turning red, which bears no fruit.

'So, what plans for the hols?'

All my postponed dread of the school year's ending engulfs me. Empty days. Hot pavements blobbed with spit and melting chewing gum. The walk down to the shops and back. The little park with its fountain, and loneliness sitting beside me on a bench.

'Actually, I'm going down to Stonebridge tomorrow, and I may stay the night. I've been meaning to ask you if you'd feed the cats.' My heart starts racing as I speak.

'Of course I will,' Jaz says. 'If I'm around,' knowing, as I did, that she would be. 'Got family there, or will you be staying with friends?'

'No. My parents are both dead, and my brother's in London.'

After a time you can say quite levelly and conversationally, 'my parents are both dead', and yet 'dead' is stamped in black letters on the air, like newsprint. Lightly spoken words come back to me, from a summer afternoon, and hurt, like a piece of grit sticky with melting tar.

Two children are walking barefoot up a gravelly road, a girl of ten holding her baby brother's hand, and a woman, passing with her shopping basket, calls out, 'My, Peter, those are smart shorts!' Her voice, as bright as nasturtiums, and his orange-bordered new green shorts, lodge in my memory, for ever, and will probably come to me through mists of senility, pointlessly evoking a summer's day, when I am slumped sightless and speechless in a vinyl chair in some geriatric day-room waiting to die.

A black mongrel, Trixie, comes scraping along on her haunches downhill towards us and, overtaking her, runs the Jack Russell, Nip. I know now that Trixie was a misshapen old dog and is dragging herself on her bottom like that, grinning or grimacing, because she has worms, but then I loved animals

4

with the physical passion that little girls feel, and I knew all the dogs in the village by name.

Nip and Trixie belong to old Mr Annett whose legs bow outwards in an almost perfect arch above his wellingtons, so that you think he would fall over if he took them off. I see him carrying a bucket of crayfish home from the river one evening, treading down with a contemptuous boot the tripwire which Ruby and I have stretched across the road. Ruby Richards. Ruby Richards, the Rising Sun, Stonebridge, Kent.

'So where will you stay?' Jaz sounds impatient and a bit envious. 'Some bijou B and B?'

'No. I'll be staying with my oldest friend Ruby at the Rising Sun. We've known each other since we were eight.' It isn't true that I shall stay there, but then I spend my life dealing with fiction of one sort or another.

'Ruby at the Rising Sun. You've got two songs there.'

'Neither is appropriate,' I say before she can burst into song, regretting having given her the names that flash fire from a Woolworth's ring and a sharp-edged bracelet made from the gold seal of a jar of fish paste. 'Actually there are others, but you couldn't be expected to remember the Hit Parade of 1953.'

'Hmm. Going back to your roots.' She, a damp fungus grown from a spore blown onto London plaster and I, a brittler accretion but as rootless, sit on in silence. I know, from picking up the post from the hall in the mornings, that Jaz has a mother in Northumbria who thinks her daughter's name is Janette. That jaunty z is but a wedge of lemon stuck into a bottle of beer.

'So what do you think of it so far? My opus?'

My silence on the subject has forced Jaz to enquire about her manuscript, *The Cruelty of Red Vans*, which lies half-heartedly half-read on my desk. I like the title and I tell her so. I can see how red vans could be cruel, always bringing presents and mail-order goodies to other houses and delivering returned manuscripts in jiffy bags to hers, and pulling away from kerbs beside pillar boxes to tell you you have missed the post, if you had any letters to send. Something prompts me to speak honestly for once.

5

'Let me give you a little Tippex, dear,' I begin.

'What?' She is affronted.

'Sorry. *Lapsis lingae*. A little tip, I meant to say. Try writing about *nice* people for a change, *pretty* people, people who at least *aspire* to being good: a touch less solipsism, a bit more *fiction* . . .'

'Bloody teachers!' Jaz is a mutinous schoolgirl about to snatch back a poorly marked essay.

'I myself keep a journal, I have for years, in which I write down something good, however small or trivial, about each day. Look at those hydrangea flowers, for example, how they float, each flower on its tiny stalk, so delicately on the dusk, or the stars.' My words sound as prissy as my Liberty Print shirt-waist dress.

'Dreary municipal flowers. Light pollution. You can't see any stars nowadays. There aren't any.'

In fact, we are quite high up here, and you can see the stars quite clearly, not strewn like seeds or pollen as in the country sky perhaps or as bright, but they are there.

'Keep a journal!' says Jaz. 'Nice people! Stars! Get a life, Miss Harlency.'

Oh, I've got a life. I've got my work, and I go out sometimes, and fly home again, a bittern without a mate booming over the desolate fens, sitting on the tube with my nose in a book. A lone peewit. Possibly dustbin day is more of an event for me than it might be for some, but I have visitors; sometimes in the evening the doorbell rings and it's a delivery boy, with a pizza for somebody else in the house. 'You've got the wrong bell,' I tell him. 'It's not for me. I ordered the dust and ashes special, with extra acrimony.'

When at last we go inside, followed by both the cats, my calm kitchen gives a moment's reassurance, then out of the blue comes my grammar school geography teacher Miss Tarrantine, who must have been about the age I am now, closing an ancient blue reptilian eyelid in a monstrous wink as she tells us, 'I've had my moments, you know!' We nearly died.

As I leave in the morning, while the cats' little faces are busy in their bowls, a red van pulls up at the kerb and postie climbs out holding a brown package. I had vowed never to have another cat after my last one died but when a colleague brought these two into the staff room in a basket I succumbed, intending them to be workaday cats, Tibby and Tabby, independent creatures with a talent to amuse when it suited me. However, the little swine have ways and means of getting their claws into your heart, and their fur is graduated like the coloured sands of Alum Bay, like pencil sharpenings.

July is purple and green and white in the railway banks as the train leaves London behind. The first time we made this journey, Betty, Percy, and I, was in a smoking compartment with leather straps to let the windows up and down, and string-mesh luggage racks and framed photographs of seaside resorts on the walls; buddleia and willowherb burned on glittering bomb sites and white convolvulus rambled everywhere. I was never a particularly balletic or acrobatic child, but sometimes when I was happy I could see another self slip from my body and run leaping and doing cartwheels, somersaulting through the air beside me. I almost glimpse her now, running along an undulating hedge and telegraph poles' tightropes, as we travel, our journey so pathetically short and yet its destination so far away as to have made it inconceivable until now.

Now that I am here, in Stonebridge, in the hot still breath of cornfields and the took-took-took of hens and whirring woodpigeons, I don't know where to go. I walk, a self-conscious stranger, through the village to the church of St Michael and All Angels and up the path, petalled with confetti. If Mr Seabrook were still the verger, nobody would have dared to throw it.

The only sign that Mrs Greenidge's grave has ever been disturbed is the addition of Mr Greenidge's name to the stone, in 1964. As I stand in the feathery summer grasses, tracing a coralline fan of lichen with my fingers, I am jolted by an image of Mrs Greenidge, woken from ten years' sleep, sitting up in a flowered nightdress and stretching out her arms to welcome her husband to the wormy marital bed. Mr Greenidge, rigid

7

in her embrace, is wearing the linen suit I know so well, and I am startled by his eyes, bright as blue glass. I know that I could summon then every feature and line of his face, which had faded until Mr Greenidge was just an empty suit of white clothes hanging in my memory.

Two

The village of Stonebridge, set in a loop of the river Cray, has attracted many visitors over the years, hop pickers, painters, ramblers and cyclists, and settlers such as some of the residents of the council houses in Brewers Road and Manor Way. Back in 1927 a commercial artist had come to Stonebridge, attached wings to the shoulders of village children and antennae to their foreheads, and photographed them as fairies for a series of glossy sepia postcards tinted with acid yellow, pink, blue and green, that he called 'Elfin Revels'. The names of elves can be found on the war memorial today, and the 'Elfin Revels' cards are prized by connoisseurs of kitsch. Stonebridge's orchards and hop gardens, woods and hills are illuminated, their autumnal leaves enamelled by magical light, and sometimes in the evenings a white mist rises from the river and lies in layers of vapour over the fields. In 1953, the year of the East Anglian floods and the ascent of Everest, coronation year and the year of the Rosenbergs' execution and Stalin's death, when we came to Stonebridge, there were a dozen or so commuters whose bowler hats bobbed up and down Station Hill under the massive horse chestnuts and beeches on either side. None of the village girls would have dreamed of walking down Station Hill at night, or, if they did, their dreams were nightmares, because everybody knew there was a man with a sack and a knife

9

waiting to jump out on you. Even by day the hill was long and silent under the heavy leaves.

My parents, Percy and Betty Harlency, were brought up in the licensed trade and met and married in that profession. After Percy's demob from the Catering Corps, we lived above a series of public houses which time has condensed in my memory into one bleak establishment with cold, stained-carpeted rooms too vast for our few pieces of furniture and a green linoleumed kitchen smelling of gas. We had left the last of the pubs, a gloomy gin palace in Streatham, after some disagreement with the brewers, and were living in a rented room in Tooting, while my parents were negotiating the lease of the Copper Kettle Tea-room in Stonebridge. The country, and a café, were a new venture for us Londoners. The Copper Kettle was a bargain, going astonishingly cheap, that it seemed we could just, with judicious borrowing, afford. I think now that my parents' falling out with the brewers must have been connected with their politics. Unusual for publicans, Percy and Betty were strongly left-wing and they had pinned up a petition to President Eisenhower to save the Rosenbergs on the wall of the public bar. Their petition attracted as many perforations from darts as signatures and the President never acknowledged it. Or it might have been that they chalked up too many drinks on the slate. There is nobody to ask now. We were a scattered, deracinated family, not buyers but tenants who took out short leases on life. Grandma and Grandpa Harlency had both paid the price of their profession by this time, although Granny and Grandpa Fitz, Betty's parents, the Fitzgeralds, were still the genial hostess and host of the Drovers Tavern, Herne Hill.

The rain started when we were in the train, and our first impression of Stonebridge was of a green, stinging, miserable place. We took the wrong turning out of the station and sheltered in a midgy, nettly little wood. Betty's light brown hair darkened by the rain, drips from the tortoiseshell combs that hold it off her face: her red lipstick matches her red and white patterned dress. Percy takes off his jacket and drapes it over her shoulders. His white shirt, belted into flannels, and his curly hair are soaked. I'm the one in tears between them, eight years old. Hindsight blobs a blister onto a pink heel above a fallen-down sock and unplaits one brown pigtail from a lost ribbon.

We went on after a while and found the village, and the Rising Sun, a pretty little pub with a thatched porch, hung with green Virginia creeper. 'Civilization!' said Percy. He looked at his watch. 'Time for a quick one I think.'

'Give us a chance to dry off a bit,' Betty agreed. 'We don't want to arrive looking like a bunch of drowned rats.'

A bag of crisps was handed to me, shivering under the porch. I took out my comic from my blazer pocket and found that it was a soggy mass with all the colours run together. Then my heart sank into my wet sandals as a piano struck up and my mother's rich contralto rolled out 'The Kerry Dancing' into the rain. Oh to think of it, oh to dream of it, fills my heart with tears. I decided to find the toilets, following a sign pointing to a yard behind the pub and as I approached I could smell burning.

I saw a flash of red and green and blue and yellow flames through the half-open door of the Ladies and realized that a girl of about my own age had set fire to the roll of toilet paper. Noticing me, she tore off the burning sheet and threw it into the bowl and came out, pushing a box of matches into her pocket. I stared at her. She wore an emerald-green dress and her hair, in long pigtails with curly ends, was so red as to be almost scarlet, and the sun, suddenly blazing out, struck a fuzzy aureole of red-gold round her head and lit the freckles scattered like seeds over her face, arms and bare legs. Black, laceless plimsolls were on her speckled feet. I went inside and closed the wooden door with its big iron latch. When I came out the girl was waiting.

'Why were you setting the paper on fire?'

She shrugged. 'I like it. Do you want a go?'

She gave me the matches and I struck one, holding it to the burned edge of the shiny paper and stepping back in alarm as it glowed and the flames licked upwards. We watched it for a moment and drowned it.

'What's your name?' she asked.

'April. What's yours?'

II

Her eyes were green, like her dress and a glass ring on her finger, and her eyelids pink as if she might have been crying recently.

'Ruby. We've got some piglets. Do you want to see them?'

Inevitably, one of the curly-tailed darlings was called Percy, and there were Peter, Petunia, Primrose, Pauline, Paul, twelve of them, with perfect little snouts and hoofs and their enormous mother Pansy.

'Can I stroke them? Can I pick one up?' Melting with love, I wanted to clasp a piglet to my chest and tuck it in my blazer and take it home to Tooting. I wanted a piglet more than anything in the world.

'No. You mustn't touch them or Pansy might go for you. She could take your arm off right to the elbow with a single bite.'

'April! Where've you got to?'

It was my mother's voice.

'We're going to live here. Probably. I'll come and play.'

I ran to join my parents, Ruby following slowly and staring after me.

'Making friends?' said Percy. 'Proper little carrot-top, isn't she? Temper to match, I'll be bound. You'll have to mind you Ps and Qs with that one.'

'Red and green should never be seen, except upon an Irish queen,' Betty remarked. 'Do you know, when I popped in to pay a visit the paper was all charred as if somebody had set it alight. Charming!'

I opened my mouth to speak, and closed it again. It was as if Ruby and I were already conspirators.

A giant's tarnished copper kettle was suspended over the door of the tearoom, which was of frosted glass hung with a dingy lace curtain. Inside, the parchment shades of the electric candles on the walls above the dark oak tables and chairs were cracked and splintered: a single pink iced fancy had fossilized on a tiered cake stand and from the central light fitting a flypaper dangled, clotted with flies and bluebottles. To the left was a tiny private sitting-room, and squatting behind the tearoom, the kitchen was freckled and speckled with the dusty grease of years and led out to a garden where a smelly toilet, with rough-cut slices of newspaper impaled in a nail, and a wooden shed stood among tall mildewed weeds thick with the red insects children call bloodsuckers, and broken chairs and tables. On a shelf in the shed was that mouldy suitcase you always find, whose rusted locks threaten to spring open on something unspeakable.

Upstairs, the larger bedroom with an adjoining boxroom, filled with stained mattresses and bits of crockery, overlooked the street. In the bathroom an ellipse of pink, black-veined soap lay on the basin and a perished rubber ball hung from the end of the chain. The smaller bedroom's window would have opened above the garden, had it not been sealed with gravy-coloured paint and throughout the living accommodation tones of meat and two veg prevailed. All in all, the Copper Kettle was a disgrace. We took it.

In the train on the way home I pictured Ruby and myself side by side in a class-room sitting at polished desks with inkwells. When we arrived at the Peggs', where we were lodging, Rodney Pegg, the son of the house, twenty-one with bad skin, bumped his bicycle into the hall behind us.

'Been out for a spin?' Percy tried a friendly overture which fell flat on the lino. The Peggs hated us, and we hated them. I had been sleeping with a knife under my pillow ever since Rodney Pegg had threatened to strangle me with one of my mother's stockings if I told anybody how he had trapped me up against the wall with his bicycle and kissed me. Mrs Pegg was in the kitchen frying mince, with her hair, not yet released for the evening, snarling in a row of pipe cleaners across her forehead.

'Oh for a kitchen of my own,' Betty sighed. Percy went out for fish and chips which we ate in our room, against house rules, but we didn't care because soon we would be shot of the Peggs for ever.

When we left their house for the last time, before we were out of the gate, Mrs Pegg was hanging a notice in the window: Vacancy. No Blacks. No Irish. No Pets.

Three

The kettle had been taken down, burnished and rehung over the door, which was draped with a new lace curtain gathered at the waist, where it caught the sun, flashing and winking an invitation to the ladies of Stonebridge to take morning coffee and afternoon tea. Inside, a warming pan was a lesser sun and a belt of horse brasses, taken from the Princess of Teck, Streatham, hung down on either side of the fireplace, framing a screen embroidered with a crinoline lady watering hollyhocks. Percy had replaced the cracked parchment with pleated shades of stiff pink paper. Our hands were sore from sugar soap and my parents' fingers pricked from sitting up all night sewing tableclothes and there were specks of paint in our hair.

We had warm scones steaming in a tea towel, jam and thick yellow cream, fan-shaped wafers and napkins folded into fans, a buzzing fridge full of ice-cream, and false knickerbocker glories and peach melbas and banana splits that looked more delicious than the real thing, a little pot of wild flowers on every table. Nobody came. It was a long, hot day of false hopes and humiliation.

At half-past five Percy was turning the sign on the door to 'closed' and Betty was crying in the kitchen when the bell above the tea-room door jangled, and a fat, middle-aged woman with long grey hair caught back in a dirty ribbon and a variety

14

of coloured slides stood, looking round, with a sneering expression. No doubt it was the day's disappointment as much as her appearance that made Percy say 'We're closed' to our first customer.

'Never mind about that,' the woman said. 'I've only come to have a look. Mrs Vinnegar, late of the Copper Kettle, and happy to be out of it. Got my own council house now.'

Mrs Vinnegar took cigarettes and matches from her dress pocket and lit up, and exploded in a fit of wet coughing.

'Is this the kiddie?' she spluttered. I backed away. 'I've got seven of my own.'

'They never should have closed me down,' she said. 'Whatever anybody might tell you, I've been catering functions for twenty-five-odd years with never a complaint except from certain spiteful busybodies, but you have to expect that.'

'Closed you down?' Percy stared at her.

'Next time they want a Coronation Party in the Village Hall, they can do it themselves, I told them. Food poisoning, my eye! Greed, I call it.'

Mrs Vinnegar waddled out, giving our 'Under New Management' sign a contemptuous twirl and spraying ash over a tablecloth and its little vase of flowers.

'I'd get rid of them weeds if I was you, unhygienic.'

She squashed a greenfly with a fat fingernail rimmed in black.

'How on earth did they all fit in?' Percy asked me.

'April! Someone to see you,' my mother called.

It was Ruby at the back door in a pink dress with the hem coming down. We sat at a table in the tea-room and Percy served us a cream tea.

'The full monty,' he said, piling scones, jam, cream, cakes and ice-cream on the table.

'Mr Harlency, this is the best tea I've ever had and this is the most beautiful room in the whole world.'

Ruby went as red as glacé cherry and Percy gave a little bow, like a waiter with a tea towel folded over his arm. I couldn't be perfectly happy because Betty was lying on her bed upstairs, but almost. Because I was so delighted with my new first, best friend and my funny father. After tea we went out to play, Ruby with a paper lace doiley folded in her pocket.

'Oi, Rube, oo's that queer gink?' one of the boys sitting on the steps of the rec called out as we went past.

In reply Ruby picked up a stone from the road and aimed it at him, causing a yelp.

'That's Titchy Vinnegar,' she said. 'He tries to pull the girls' knickers down in the playground.' My suppressed fear of school resurfaced. We were walking along the High Street and Ruby stopped outside a shop, T. D. Boddy, Butchers and Purveyors, it said in gold letters, and on the windows was painted Poulterer and Grazier. Home-killed meat. Sausages a speciality. It was there I learned the fate of Pansy Pig and all her pink litter and burst into tears.

'I hate my dad,' Ruby said. 'He always kills everything. I'm going to kill him.'

She flung another stone, at the window of T. D. Boddy, and we fled.

'But that would be murder, to kill your dad.'

We were safe, lying in the grass beside the river, smoking, choking, on cigarettes Ruby had pinched from the bar.

'He's a murderer. He deserves to die, with an axe, and be hung up on a hook. Doesn't he?'

'Yes,' I said, although I was frightened.

'Have you got an axe?' I asked tentatively.

'There's one in the shed.'

'When are you going to kill him then? Bet you don't, really.'

'You wait,' said Ruby.

And when I thought of the twelve brothers and sisters and their mother, bleeding and skinned, I had to agree that Mr Richards did deserve to be condemned to death, even though I had been brought up to believe capital punishment was wrong. The wireless in our house was always switched off on the morning of an execution.

'I was going to kill somebody once. This horrible man called Rodney Pegg, who said he was going to strangle me, but we moved here, so I didn't have to. I had a knife under my pillow.'

'Have you still got it?'

'No. I had to give it back. It belonged to Mrs Pegg.'

'Never mind. You can get another one. There must be hundreds of knives at your caff.'

'Café. Anyway, I promise I'll never go into that butcher's as long as I live.'

'Your dad's nice isn't he?' she said wistfully.

I remembered the time I had come running home incoherent with grief and horror at a terrible scene I had witnessed. Some boys kicking around a dead cat, swinging it by its stiff tail. Its glassy eyes. Somebody's pet. Percy went charging out and chased them away, and buried the poor cat.

All the talk of knives, though, came to nothing. I met Ruby's father, Lex, the pig killer, a gingery, fleshy, tattooed man in a vest, who had served in the Merchant Navy, and Gloria, her mother, beetle-browed with bad temper and brush and dustpan out of hours, in petticoat and slippers, and sparkling darkly in a black and gold top behind the bar.

'My mum could've been a film star,' Ruby said.

We were not allowed in the pub but if Gloria were in the right mood she would slip us a pickled egg or a packet of crisps. Pubs held no glamour for me, who had been brought up on the smell of beer, and the morning smell of polish and wet ashtrays always induced a mixture of melancholy and apprehension in me as motes of depression swarm in the dusty curtains of a theatre robbed of illusion by cruel sunshine. The cellar where the intestines of the establishment snaked across the floor in tubes, running from barrel to tap, was a dank, fearsome place. Ruby's parents had locked her in the cellar one evening for some misdemeanour and forgotten about her, and she had spent the night crouched in a corner in the dark with ghosts and rats and cobwebs. The Richardses had a television which we could hardly ever watch because Ruby's dad was often asleep in front of it in his vest, with a newspaper rising and falling over his face. Sitting on the green quilt of Ruby's bed was her golden-haired walkie-talkie doll, who wasn't allowed out because she had been so expensive. Ruby, who loved reading as much as I did, had no books except a few old Annuals and those she had borrowed from the library, which was opened one afternoon a week after school in the canteen. I had a bookcase made from an orange box in my bedroom and there was a shelf, in the sitting-room alcove, of green and orange Penguins and a jumble of old books. I never felt at ease in Ruby's home, and I don't think she did either. We both much preferred mine, where we pretended to be sisters, or brothers.

The first day at a new school is like a jigsaw tipped out of its box and scattered on the floor. You think you'll never be able to fit the pieces together. You stand on the edge of the play-ground noise sick with fear, tasting the fried egg with burnt frilly edges and runny yolk, that your mother made you eat. You feel like a fried egg as you see, queasily, whirling skipping ropes and the chains and arches of bodies in some game such as In and Out the Dusty Bluebells, boys zooming round as spitfires, a chanting gang with linked arms, twenty abreast is converging on you, it will crash into you, and then a whistle blows, sharp blasts cutting through the din and sending every-body into lines and you are left alone and conspicuous on the asphalt trying not to cry or run out of the gate. Then the girl nobody else wants to play with claims you as her best friend. This time it was different. Ruby was waiting outside the railings when Betty left me at the top of the road.

My fantasy of sitting next to Ruby in class came true but the inkwells in our splintery desks were repositories of crumbled indigo blotting paper. Our teacher was Miss Fay whose hair was coiled in a dried fig on the nape of her neck, faded from teaching generations of girls to sew a run-and-fell seam and knit kettle holders. The boys did woodwork with the head-master, Major Morton, and we heard the whizz and crash of tools thrown across the class-rooms, and yelps as he lashed out with his cane. Major Morton had a steel plate in his head and was subject to terrible headaches and rages which shook the school. I was in terror of him and of his wig slipping to expose that shining circle screwed into his skull. If anybody was sick or one of the infants 'had an accident' a huge boy, Albie Fatman, was summoned from his desk to clear it up. It was assumed that Albie enjoyed the responsiblity, the smell, and the disinfectant. The Vinnegars had their own peculiar musty odour.

'Piss and biscuits,' said Percy, when I told him, rudely but precisely identifying the scent of poor children I had known in London. The eldest Vinnegar girl, Charmaine, was an assistant at Boddy's the butchers. Sack Vinnegar worked at the sack factory and Twin and Twin went to the secondary modern on the bus.

One afternoon I came home from school to find my mother in conversation with Mrs Vinnegar at our gate.

'. . . bun in the oven,' I heard from old Ma Vinegar Bottle who was licking a dripping Wallsy ice, purchased elsewhere. 'When's it due?'

A smell of baking was coming from our kitchen, an optimistic cake or pie, but for some reason I asked my mother when she came in, 'When's what due?'

'Oh,' she flustered about with a tea towel, red and white checked, 'Christmas. The baker's van. I don't know. There's a gentleman coming through the door. Go and tell him I'll be with him in a minute. I just want a word with your father.'

Percy was at the back, clearing the garden. The idea was to put white wrought-iron tables and chairs out there next summer.

It was the man in the white suit, with the neat salt and pepper beard, whom I had seen several times in the street, with a dachshund on a lead. He took off his panama hat, revealing thick white hair, when I approached, and the little dog was jumping up at me and I patted its squirming, hard yet silky brown body.

'What's his name?'

'Liesel Otter. She's a she. Sit, Liesel.'

'I wonder if you'd mind if this charming young lady joined me in an ice-cream?' he asked my mother when she came to take his order. 'Unless she's too busy, of course.'

The empty chairs and tables answered for me. The man's face was tanned and he had very blue eyes under white eyebrows.

'That's very kind I'm sure. If she won't be a nuisance.'

So I sat at a table with Mr Greenidge and Liesel sitting up so sweetly on a chair with his big handkerchief tied in a napkin round her neck, licking ice-cream delicately from a saucer.

A knickerbocker glory, and a half-promise that I might take Liesel for a walk one day, decided me, in my heart, that I loved Mr Greenidge almost as much as Grandpa Fitz.

'Did you call her Liesel Otter because she looks like an otter?'

He laughed.

'It's Liselotte: German.' He spelled out her name. 'She's my wife's dog really. I should prefer something larger and preferably British, but Mrs Greenidge has a dicky ticker and doesn't get about much. Liesel's her companion. You see, we weren't blessed with children of our own.'

'I'd rather have a dog if it was me.'

A dicky ticker? I saw a mouse running up a grandfather clock. Hickery dickery dock.

After he left Betty said 'What a charming man. He certainly seems to have taken a shine to you, though I can't think why when you look like something the cat dragged in. I don't know how you manage to get so dirty at school.'

Two women in divided skirts and hobnailed boots were waiting for their toasted crumpets. Passing trade, like all our customers so far, except Mr Greenidge.

Four

A path of beaten mud, overgrown with nettles and flowers, ran between fields of blue cabbages and sugar beet and the river, past what used to be our secret camp under an elder tree where an icy spring welled up into a shallow pool of stones bright green with algae and rusty red. If you went under the barbed wire and over the crumbling bridge you were in a meadow edged with willows and alders overhanging the river, where cows graze and you can lift the dried lid off a cowpat with a stick, disturbing a buzzing cloud of yellow horseflies. A notice on a willow trunk says PRIVATE. TRESPASSERS WILL BE PROSECUTED, and you might pass an angler or two or old Mr Annett with Nip and Trixie at his heels and a bucket of crayfish or white-haired May Chacksfield with two heavy shopping bags full of sticks for the fire. Mrs Chacksfield was very deaf and, long ago, she had slept in the same bed as her dead husband for weeks until they broke down the door and took him away. If you offered to help carry her firewood, whose weight bent her almost double, she would reply: 'Yes, it is rather damp down the meadows', or 'I always look nice' or make some such remark and hobble on, head bowed, in her splitting black buttoned shoes.

You might catch the flash of a kingfisher or the scuttle of a crayfish into a glinting tin can on the river bed, or see a water vole on a green island of crowfoot in midstream, before it runs like a shadow along the roots that lace the mud banks dappled with reflections from the water. In the distance, hop poles spiral away into the heat haze over glittering earth and the white conical caps of the oast house are chalky against a sky as pale blue as the scabious that grows with fragile poppies and the scarlet pimpernel sprawling over the marled furrows.

A five-barred gate, to be climbed, not opened, led into the orchard, a dark-green and purple-blue paradise where bloomy plums dropped from the low trees into your hands. The bloom rubbed off on your fingers and you bit into sweet dark-yellow flesh reddening towards a stone set in crimson. Wasps buzzed on pecked and fallen fruit, too gorged on oozing alcoholic pulp to chase you.

What made the orchard miraculous though was an abandoned railway carriage in the far corner, set down as if by magic, its wheels gone, anchored by long grass and nettles, with brambles barring its door. Ruby and I stared at it and at each other. Any enclosed space can inspire a primitive fear, of death or danger, supernatural or human. The orchard became lonely and silent as we gazed.

'Perhaps there's a dead body inside.'

'I dare you to look.'

'I dare you too.'

'I said it first.'

We might have run away then, but the railway carriage, dark-windowed, out of place in a thicket of thorns, was the perfect hide-out, house, the camp of our dreams. We fought our way through and scratched, stung and bleeding, with clothes ripped, peered in the earthy, rain-streaked, bird-squirted, berry-smeared windows. It was completely empty, seats and luggage racks removed, except for one cushion sprouting horsehair on the floor.

Perhaps somebody had intended to live there once, or the farmer had meant to use it for some purpose, but it was evident that no one had been inside for years. We forced open the door and stood in the smell of trapped time. The spiders who had made it their home raced away from our intrusion. It belonged to us now. The headquarters of a secret society with two members. We sealed our pact never to tell anybody about it with the blood from bramble scratches.

In the days that followed we would smuggle out two cups, an army blanket for a carpet, candles, knives, matches and comics and what food and drink we could take from the Rising Sun and the Copper Kettle. There was space inside for a kitchen, a bedroom and a living-room. We could not spend all our time there, as we wanted, because we both had to help at home, and couldn't always go too far afield.

'Where are you going?'

Doreen, Titchy with little Juney Vinnegar, Albie Fatman and Roger Goodenough barred our way to the stile at the path by the river. Nobody could get past Albie Fatman.

'Just down the meadows.'

'So are we then.'

'You're not allowed. It's private property.'

'Well, nor are you then.'

'Anyway, there's a bull in the field.'

'So what you going there for then?'

'It's all right for us, we can run fast and jump in the river if it comes after us, but you've got little Juney.'

'We could tie her to the stile and come back for her later,' Albie suggested. Juney opened her mouth to wail, showing tiny blackened baby teeth. Titchy was unbuckling his snake belt, until Doreen said, 'Nah. Who wants to play with them anyway. Let's go up the rec. Come on, Juney. We know where we're not wanted. Think themselves so cocky. Serve them right if the bull gets them.' Then she added, 'Ruby was *my* best friend until you came along and took her away, Apeface.'

They trailed away and we went on, towards the orchard and the railway carriage where we were perfectly happy travelling nowhere through fields of high summer.

'Did Doreen really used to be your best friend?'

'Nah. I was hers, but she wasn't mine.'

We made little fires of twigs and paper, and beat them out after a few minutes lest the smoke should betray us, but we became habitual smokers ourselves, of Weights, Woodbines,

Gold Flake and sweet cigarettes, or we choked on cheroots of rolled-up newspapers or leaves. I was more of a pipe man myself, preferring to clench an acorn stalk in my teeth, but Ruby really enjoyed taking little sips at a cigarette and puffing the smoke as if she were blowing out a candle.

It had happened that one morning at the beginning of the school holidays we were playing a game called Lady Marlene in Ruby's yard with Doreen and a girl named Sorrel Marlowe who wasn't really supposed to play with us because she went to a posh school. To play Lady Marlene you had to dress up in your mother's old clothes, apply lipstick from a stub found in a cast-off handbag or a red Smartie and parade around in your mother's shoes doing ladylike things. Sorrel proved an unsatisfactory recruit to the game, exposing its fundamental weakness; with questions of 'What happens now?' 'What am I supposed to do next?' Ruby, as befitted the black taffeta skirt she was wearing, was Lady Marlene.

'Say something ladylike' she told Sorrel.

'You ladies are looking very glamorous this morning.'

Mr Greenidge, with Liesel on her red lead, was standing watching us.

'Ruby! What do you think you're doing of? Who said you could have that skirt?'

Ruby's mother was shouting from an upstairs window. We froze, in her clothes.

'Get it off and get in here at once! Well, don't just stand there gawping. And the rest of you, go on, hop it! I've a good mind to come round your houses and drag *your* mother's best skirts in the dirt. Go on, get out of it, the lot of you. You've got no respect for yourselves or anybody else!'

'I say—' bleated Mr Greenidge but the window was slammed shut. I was shaking in my shiny blouse, Sorrel was sobbing loudly as she struggled out of a yellow dress and Doreen Vinnegar was half-way down the street. Ruby's freckles stood out like coins on her white face and arms as, shamed, she stepped out of the black taffeta skirt and pulled her frock over her vest and knickers. I wanted to run away too but started to gather up the clothes and shoes.

'You'd better go,' she said, and walked inside, head bowed, with the slippery heap of garments.

'Poisonous woman,' said Mr Greenidge. I could say nothing, because it was true about Mrs Richards, but she was Ruby's mother.

There was no doubt in my mind that Mrs Richards would come to our house and I could see her crashing into the tea-room, pushing my mother aside and charging upstairs to rip her Gorray skirt from its hanger and drag it round the garden.

'Here, dry your eyes.'

Mr Greenidge handed me his handkerchief.

'Would you like to take Liesel?'

This was what I had wanted so much but the lead in my hand and Liesel pulling me along were as nothing as I imagined the fearful scene at the Rising Sun, and Mrs Richards's revenge.

'Tell you what. How would you like to come to tea with me tomorrow?'

'Can Ruby come?'

'Another time perhaps. One visitor at a time is enough for Mrs Greenidge, I think. Don't forget to ask your mother. About four o'clock.'

I spent the rest of the day hanging round my mother, helping in the tea-room, filling cyclists' water bottles, expecting Mrs Richards at any moment.

'You're very keen on washing up all of a sudden? If I didn't know you better, I'd think you were after something.'

'No I'm not.' I put my arms round her. 'I'm just glad you're my mum, not Mrs Richards.'

'So am I, love.'

She unclasped my hands.

'Listen, April. There's something I've been meaning to tell you.' She stroked my hair back from my forehead. 'You're going to have a baby brother or sister. Won't that be lovely?'

Pink, white-shawled shock hit me. I was pushing a pram along the High Street past the boys on the steps of the rec. I saw a squirming baby kicking in a grey nappy with a big pin on either side and a grey bib encrusted with mashed carrot.

'Aren't you pleased? April?'

I could see she wanted me to be pleased. 'Yes, of course I am.'

There were girls who knocked on people's doors asking to take their babies for a walk. I was not one of them.

'Why?'

'Why? What a question! Remember when you asked Father Christmas for a baby sister or brother?'

'When I was four.'

'Yes, well. We thought you'd be so happy about the baby. Somebody to play with.'

'I don't need anybody to play with now. I've got Ruby. Except she's probably locked in the cellar.'

'What do you mean, locked in the cellar?'

'Nothing.'

It seemed they were getting this baby for me and I didn't want it. I felt ungrateful and knew I should pretend to be happy.

'I'm going to need your help, April. You can help give him his bath and take him out in his pram and play with him when I'm busy in the tea-room. I won't be able to manage without my big girl.'

I looked at her in horror.

'Will it be a boy, then?'

'Oh, I don't know yet. I've just got a feeling. She might be a lovely little girl just like you were.'

Everything she said just made it worse.

'When is it coming?'

'Oh, not for a long time yet. Around Christmas time. A special Christmas present for you.'

'Mr Greenidge asked me to tea tomorrow, can I go?'

'Yes, of course, but April . . . April, where are you going?'

I ran out, colliding with Percy who was coming in from the garden. I hit him hard in the stomach.

'I suppose you knew about this all along!'

Where could I go? I dared not go to Ruby's. I set off for

the orchard, by myself for the first time. As I climbed the stile that led to the path along the river I suddenly felt afraid, as if somebody or something was waiting to leap out on me. I jumped down and ran all the way home. In our garden shed, in the smell of sun-warmed wood and earth and creosote, I started to feel a little sorry for this baby whose sister didn't want it. I knew a boy whose birthday fell on Christmas day and he only got one lot of presents. It might be the same for the baby. I didn't know if I was pleased or sorry about that. I went inside to pretend to be excited and to apologize to Percy, and everything was all right, only I felt already that nothing was quite as it used to be.

That night, I woke from a dream of terror, of running, in high-heeled shoes and a long black skirt, with a pram through a dark wood trying to save a piglet or a baby and Ruby's father crashing behind me with an axe, and Rodney Pegg stepped out from behind a tree with a stocking stretched between his hands, and Mr Greenidge was there somewhere. I lay in bed feeling my heart thumping, saved, so glad it wasn't true, but oppressed and still trembling from the nightmare. My parents' voices rose and fell reassuringly below and I could hear faint music from the wireless. It was hot in the tangled sheets. I pushed back the covers and knelt up on my bed to open the window. The beam of a torch dazzled my eyes. I screamed.

Percy and Betty came running upstairs.

'There's a man in the garden with a torch.'

Percy rushed down while Betty held me tight.

'Get back into bed, you're shivering.'

'There's nobody there, pet. I looked all round. You must have been dreaming,' he said when he came in. He sat down on my bed, tucking, Bobbity, my toy rabbit, in beside me.

'No more bad dreams now. Daddy's here, and Mummy. Nothing can hurt you.'

'Snuggle down,' Mummy said, and she sang softly, 'My curly-headed baby.'

Then I sat bolt upright.

'Mrs Richards. It could've been Mrs Richards in the garden with a torch.'

'Go back to sleep.'

The Greenidges' house, Kirriemuir, was of red brick. The gate in the tall variegated privet hedge opened onto a paved path leading through a gravel garden of periwinkles among dark green leaves, sharp shiny shrubs and heathers and dwarf conifers. To the left of the front door stood a statue of a deer with a fawn, Bambi and his mother in grey stone, on the right-hand side was a tub of scarlet geraniums, alyssum and lobelia, and on the door itself a galleon sailing on a bubbly glass sea.

Barking and skittering claws on a polished floor answered my ring as I stood on the step with the flowers I had picked on my way, taking a short cut through the allotments. Betty was always delighted by a bunch of flowers although Ruby's mother scorned them.

'Ah, April, come in, come in. Liesel, basket!'

Mr Greenidge led me into a panelled hall where dull silver figures of knights in armour stood in alcoves, and the dicky ticker was there, with a motionless brass pendulum, and the sun and moon on its face beneath stopped hands. Dark brown staircases on either side of the hall met on an upper landing with closed bedroom doors visible behind the wooden railings.

'Our minstrels' gallery,' said Mr Greenidge. Overawed by all the poshness and polish and panelling, I followed him through to a brown room with heavy dark furniture and a blaze of crossed swords above the fireplace, and there, in sunshine under glass, was Mrs Greenidge in the built-on conservatory, half-lying on a long green wicker chair with her head on a chintz cushion.

'Are these for me?'

She stretched out a hand for the flowers.

Mrs Greenidge was in pale blue, like a faded flower herself, a periwinkle bleached by the summer, tall with soft grey hair and a pretty face that would have been young were it not gathered and pleated in a thousand tiny tucks.

'Dahlias. Already. They always make me think of autumn.

And poppies, I do wish they wouldn't drop their petals so. Nicotiana and nightshade, how nice. Put them in water, Clem. Come and sit down, April, and tell me all about yourself.'

I sat on a creaking chair that scratched the back of my legs and stroked Liesel who had ignored the command to go to her basket. Mrs Greenidge picked up a piece of embroidery in a circular frame and pricked a needle threaded with pink in and out of the stretched linen.

'Do you like school?'

'Not much, but I've only been there a little while. It's the holidays now. I don't like Major Morton.'

'The less said about that unfortunate gentleman the better, but one has to remember that he was wounded in the service of his country and make allowances, don't you think?'

I didn't know if she were telling me off or not.

'He hit Roger Goodenough so hard that his mum came up the school. She said if he did it again, she was going to report him to Mr Cox.' Our local constable.

'That boy with the cotton wool in his ears?'

'Which one do you mean?'

Mr Greenidge returned carrying a heavy white wicker tray with tea things sliding about on glass and set it down on the white table of embroidered flowers under glass. Brown buttered bread and iced cakes and chocolate biscuits glistened in the heat. Points of light danced on a pond in the garden.

'Bless me, I've gone and forgotten the sugar!' Mr Greenidge slapped his forgetful forehead playfully.

'April, would you run along to the kitchen and get it?' he said.

With no idea where the kitchen was, I rose obediently and crossed the room and went into the silent hall and made hopefully, past the knights in armour and the clock, for an open door, in a mild panic that I would fail in my quest, get lost, make a fool of myself.

It was the kitchen. I looked round dark shelves for the sugar. My flowers were in a vase on the table. There was a huge stove with a dishcloth draped on the handles of its oven doors, an enamel dog's dish and water bowl on newspaper, a brown radio, a pulley hanging from the ceiling dangling socks and stockings and old people's underclothes.

'Ah, there you are. Thought you'd got lost. Silly of me, I didn't tell you where to find it.'

Mr Greenidge, to my relief, was smiling, making it his fault not mine.

'The sugar lives in here,' he said, opening a cupboard and taking out a silver fluted bowl and tongs resting on white cubes. 'Here you are.'

As I took it, his arms went round me pressing me hard against his shirt, squeezing me and his lips were kissing my face, and his beard tickled like a soft shaving brush. I was rigid with surprise, and fear that Mrs Greenidge would walk in.

'You didn't mind that?' he whispered, out of breath, letting me go. 'You didn't mind, did you?' His brown face had turned dark red, like Colonel Beetroot's in the comic. I shook my head. I knew it was wrong because Mr Greenidge was married to Mrs Greenidge. My own face was burning from guilt and the brush of his beard as I carried the sugar back to the conservatory. I felt as though I'd been gone for hours. Mr Greenidge came bustling in behind me, and poured the tea.

' "April, April / laugh thy girlish laughter; then the moment after, Weep thy girlish tears," ' Mrs Greenidge said. 'I suppose you know that poem, April? People must quote it at you all the time.'

'No.'

'And how are your parents? I must say the Copper Kettle's looking greatly improved these days.'

'Thank you. They're very well, thank you. We're going to have a baby.'

'How splendid. You'll have to call it May. "After April, when May follows . . .".'

I couldn't tell if she were teasing. My name sounded silly, and a sense of foolishness came over me making my whole body, my self, feel somehow silly and uncomfortable in my cotton dress.

'Are you too hot? Would you like to play in the garden?' Mrs Greenidge asked.

Scattering crumbs, I walked clumsily into the garden. It is difficult to play by oneself in a formal garden, watched by two adults. I walked over gravel to the pond. Liesel trotted after me and dropped a tennis ball at my feet. I threw it, low to avoid pink roses and a grey bird-bath. And again, and again, and desperately again, with cries of 'good dog' and 'well caught', 'good dog, Liesel' and attempts at girlish laughter until I thought I would cry, trapped in that garden, wondering when it would be possible to go inside but not wanting to, wishing I could go home. At last the ball bounced into the pond making goldfish disappear, floating in the centre among the water-lilies. Liesel ran inside to tell. I was mortified to see Mr Greenidge squatting down with a brush and a dustpan, sweeping up my crumbs.

'I'm ever so sorry. The ball's gone in the pond.'

'Never mind,' said Mrs Greenidge. 'Poor Liesel's quite exhausted. You've worn her out with your game. She's not used to such violent exercise.'

'I think I'd better go home now. Thank you for having me.'

'Come again soon,' Mrs Greenidge said. 'Next Sunday.'

'Mrs Greenidge? Could I take Liesel for a walk sometimes?'

'Oh, we'll have to think about that, April. We'll see you on Sunday.'

Before he opened the front door, the two of us standing on the bristly mat, Mr Greenidge kissed me again.

'You won't tell?' he whispered.

I ran along the road in the late Sunday afternoon straight to the Rising Sun, and sneaked round the side, giving the low hoot of an owl that was our secret call. The kitchen window was flung open by Mrs Richards.

'What do you think you're playing at, hooting like an owl in broad daylight on other people's property? Ruby's not coming out, she's got work to do.' She slammed the window.

Five

The tea-room was unusually busy and I was helping in the kitchen, trying to ignore a gang of kids at the back door buzzing around like wasps, pestering me to hand out free ice-cream, when Ruby pushed her way through them, and the whole kitchen lit up. We had not seen each other for days and I was still in fear of Mrs Richards marching up our path dragging Ruby by the arm.

'Get us a ginger nut,' came from the doorway. 'Oi, Ginger Nut, get us a lolly!'

'Are you all right?'

'Yes. I couldn't come out before. They made me clean the whole pub.'

'Your mum's really cruel, isn't she? Like a horrible old witch,' I said sympathetically.

'No, she isn't!' Ruby flared up.

'But, you said . . .'

'Anyway, your mum's fat.'

'No, she isn't!'

Outraged and hurt by the insult to my mother I pulled a red pigtail hard and saw tears come into Ruby's eyes, before she pulled my hair and I leapt on her.

'Mrs Harlency, Ruby and April are fighting,' came a voice from the back door as my mother came into the kitchen.

32

'Stop it at once, the pair of you. I'm ashamed of you, April. And you lot can buzz off,' she told our audience. 'Telling tales won't get you any favours round here.'

'She started it,' we both said at once.

'I don't care who started it. I'm finishing it right now. What's it all about?'

Neither of us could say, of course. My heart ached for Betty, who unaware of Ruby's dreadful words, told her to wash her hands and gave her an apron and a knife and set her to buttering, and eating, bread. I smouldered, until Ruby whispered, 'Your mum's not really fat.'

'Well then your mum's not really a horrible old witch.'

Although she was. When Percy heard about our fight later, he said 'I warned you about that one's temper, didn't I? Proper little firecracker.'

He sounded almost admiring, making me feel a damp squib in comparison.

'I started it.'

But the Archers music came on the radio and Percy was doing a dance round the kitchen with a tablecloth on his head.

'Fancy going out for a drink later?' he asked Betty.

'Well, I do. But let's try the George tonight. I don't really like that crowd at the Rising Sun much, even though they have got a piano.'

'Don't you like Lex and Gloria?' I said.

'Oh, it's not that.' She looked uncomfortable. Good. 'It's Mr and Mrs Richards to you,' she said.

'Supposing that person with the torch comes back?'

'Now, you know that was only a dream. Besides, we won't be gone long. You can stay up and listen to the wireless if you like.'

There was a story in one of my fairy-tale books, outgrown now, about a mother goat and her seven kids. The mother has to go out, leaving the kids at home, and she warns them not to open the door to anybody but her. If someone should knock, the kids must say 'show me your hoof', so that they can tell if it really is their mother before letting anyone in. Needless to say, the wolf comes and thrusts out a hairy foot disguised as a

33

goat's hoof. 'Show me your hoof' had become a code for Betty and me, meaning don't open the door to a stranger. As Percy and Betty left for the pub she called out, 'Remember, show me your hoof', and closed the door.

At once the quiet, familiar house on a light summer evening became a place of shadow and terror. A wolf's foot twitched the lace curtain on the tea-room door. A madman was hiding in the toilet or the garden shed with an axe, waiting to creep towards the back door. I tried to read. *Valley of Doom* by C. B. Rutley, Ruby's and my favourite book, was not a wise choice for a person alone in the house. We had found this terrifying tale of espionage in the Balkans at a jumble sale and the adventures of the plucky English twins, Bob and Dick, who saved the world from domination by the arch-villain, HE, were scary enough reading in a sunny orchard under the plum tree. At night though, the forest petrified by HE's nerve gas, where no bird sang, and the Schwartz Schloss bulking against the sky, became horribly real, and HE reared huge and invincible, 'Evil personified', in his crimson robe and mask. I closed the book, too frozen with fear to find another or to switch on the radio and flood the silence with music and voices.

Then I heard it. A noise I recognized at once as 'the scrape of stealthy footfalls'. Any second now, the treacherous Carruthers would be tapping on the window with a long stick.

'Hoo hoo.'

I jumped in the air and sank back into the chair with relief. Ruby.

'Hoo hoo hoo.'

But was it Ruby, or Carruthers, a wolf or the madman with the axe? Or an owl?

'Hoo hoo hoo.'

The back door rattled. I picked up the poker.

'Hoo hoo – open up, fathead! It's me. Didn't you hear me doing the low hoot of an owl?' she accused when I unlocked the door and let her in.

'Yes, but I didn't know it was you. What have you done to your eye?'

A stain like ink was spreading down her cheek under swollen lids.

'My dad did it. By accident. What's the point of having a secret call if you don't reckernize it? I bet you thought I was an owl, didn't you?'

I could tell she was lying about her eye. It was shocking, ugly and painful-looking, nothing like the neat black eyes that people in comics got.

'He's evil personified,' I said, adding quickly to forestall another quarrel about our parents, 'what are you doing here? Won't you get into trouble?'

'They won't know. I often come out at night and they never notice. I'm as stealthy as a cat.'

'It was you the other night, wasn't it? With the torch! Why didn't you say? I was scared stiff. I thought it was a murderer, or your mum.'

Ruby shrugged. 'I thought we could have a midnight feast. Anyway, my mum wouldn't really come round, she's all mouth. Her bark's worse than her bite.'

I imagined a snarling Gloria sinking her teeth into Ruby's arm, and shivered.

'Are you coming out? Your mum and dad won't be back for ages. I saw them going into the George.'

'I can't. I'm not allowed.'

'Coward. Cowardy cowardy custard, dip your nose in mustard. You're scared.'

'No I'm not.'

'Yes you are. You're even scared of an owl. And of your mum and dad.'

'I am not. They'll be back soon, they said so. You better go. You can have an ice-cream if you want.'

'All right, but you're still scared. I'm not scared of anything, even ghosts. I bet I wouldn't be scared to spend the night in the railway carriage all by myself.'

'Bet you would.'

The very thought frightened me, and I was unaccountably nervous about Percy and Betty finding Ruby here, but more afraid of her parents' anger.

'Here you are. Hurry up. Your mum and dad will kill you if they find you've gone out. Anyway, you were terrified when they shut you in the cellar, you told me.'

'No I wasn't and they won't. Anyway, it's only early yet.'

I locked the door behind Ruby, upset by her wounded eye, and feeling that I had let her down, and taking in the knowledge that a father could injure his child.

I woke the next day to unfocused dread, a wildly beating heart and disseminated anxiety, and wondered what I was afraid of. There was a trip to Hastings soon – Ruby and I had joined the Sunday school for that reason – but it couldn't be that. School was far away over the horizon. Then I remembered. Ruby's eye and her visit. Mr Greenidge's kiss. Tea at the Greenidges' on Sunday.

'Come on lazybones,' my father was calling.

'We've got to help your mother all we can now,' he said when I went down to the breakfast I couldn't eat. It was raining. A day began of dreary responsibility with fear gnawing like the fox under the spartan boy's cloak, and my parents unusually snappy, when washing-up water splashed onto my legs and made them itch and a gang of cyclists burst through the door and took off their dripping capes, flinging raindrops everywhere and making puddles on the floor. A day of sour milk and burned toast and broken-winged butterfly cakes. In the afternoon Mr Greenidge came in with Liesel in a little waterproof coat.

'I can't come on Sunday,' I blurted out. 'I've got to help in the tea-room. It's our busiest day.'

'What's that?' Percy bustled with his note-pad.

'I was just saying that I can't go to tea on Sunday because I've got to work here.'

'Never mind, perhaps another day,' said Mr Greenidge, looking hurt. 'I'm sure Mrs Greenidge will understand, eh Liesel? You were looking forward to a game, weren't you old lady?'

Now Liesel was gazing up with reproachful moist eyes, and laid her head on disappointed paws.

36

'Don't be daft,' Percy said. 'We'll manage without you. Just have to dock your wages.'

He winked at Mr Greenidge, who laughed.

'That's the ticket.'

In the kitchen Percy hissed at me, 'What did you want to say that for? Making me out to be some sort of slave-driver. What are people going to think, eh? You'll get me shot.'

It seemed that everybody was put out by my friendship with the Greenidges. Ruby was in a sulk at spending Sunday afternoon on her own, my parents run off their feet with ramblers wanting sandwiches, and flasks filled, when I set out, grey and leaden-legged for Kirriemuir. Passing Albie Fatman and Titchy Vinnegar going towards the river with home-made fishing rods, I envied them and felt self-conscious. They never had to go out to tea and they, and the girls playing five stones on the pavement, seemed so fortunate and carefree. Somebody shouted out after me, 'There she goes, there she goes, all dressed up in her Sunday clothes.'

Mr Greenidge was in a faded green Aertex shirt. Again, he embraced me in a hard, silent squeeze at the door as Liesel leaped up scratching my leg with her claws. Mrs Greenidge was reclining in the conservatory as if she hadn't moved since my previous visit. Our conversation was as strained as before and I didn't know why she had invited me. I looked anxiously at the tea tray, and saw that the sugar basin was there.

'Teaspoons, Clement,' said Mrs Greenidge languidly.

'I beg your pardon, dear?'

'Teaspoons. You've forgotten them.' In the silence that followed I had to offer to fetch them, like a polite child. The spoons were lying on the kitchen table and I had them in my hand when he came in.

'Ah, good. You've found them I see.' He pulled me towards him and kissed me when I stood trapped in his arms, as unresponsive as a spoon. My leg itched where Liesel had scratched it and my heard was thudding in fear.

'That was nice, wasn't it?' he whispered.

Liesel's ball had been fished out of the pond and again we performed a game for our audience, tiring Liesel out. The only

37

thing different from last time was that I discovered frogs hiding under the dank mats of plants near the pond, and I remembered my mother's injunction to offer to wash up.

'Just carry the tray through, thank you, April. Clement will do it later. I'm sure you must have quite enough of washing dishes at home.'

'No, not really. I mean, I don't mind. I like it – it's sort of my hobby.' Trying to correct Mr Greenidge's impression of my father as slave-driver, I stumbled over my words.

'What a strange girl. When I was your age I'd much rather have been out playing with my friends. Well, if it would really give you pleasure, we mustn't stand in your way.'

So I found myself at the Greenidges' sink washing up through a blur of humiliated tears, a girl with no friends whose hobby was washing dishes, and Mr Greenidge pressing his body into mine from behind.

I still loved Liesel but now I wished I had never set eyes on her. The Liesel I had wanted would walk perkily on her red lead with Ruby and me, run with us along the path to the orchard and sit up sweetly in a doll's dress and bonnet. Now, on my way home, I thought of her as sharp-muzzled, like Red Riding Hood's wolf in her grandmother's nightdress and lace cap.

It was about this time that my parents joined the local Labour party and the Copper Kettle became the venue for committee meetings. Normally, these were held once a month but there was some sort of election impending, to do with the Rural District Council, and evenings were taken over by party members, pamphlets and leaflets. As in our pub days, I was left to my own devices but now I was able to take advantage of the long summer evenings.

The big boys and girls used to sit on the bridge smoking and laughing, swinging their legs over the river, and sometimes calling out rude things to people who passed. Ruby and I had crossed over onto the other side of the road, nervous of what they might say but I thought the girls were like Shirley poppies in their summer skirts. Night-scented flowers in the gardens along the High Street were sweet on the heavy, mothy air, windows and back doors stood open, releasing a bray of laughter, a burst of music from radio or television, voices, as we drifted along.

'Let's spy on somebody,' said Ruby.

'Who?'

'I know! Major Morton.'

Fear stopped us on the pavement. Then we knew we had to do it.

The playground gate was locked of course. We climbed over the railings and dropped down onto the asphalt and tiptoed across to the school house, and keeping close to the wall, crouching down, crept round to the back of the house. The kitchen light was on. We peeped over the windowsill and saw a table with piles of dirty dishes and empty bottles. There was nobody there, but we could hear faint music coming from somewhere. We inched our way to the side of the house, then, standing on an overgrown flowerbed in the smell of bad drains, we stared into a lamplit room. A man and a woman in a pink petticoat were dancing, holding each other tightly, hardly moving. Her hair was uncoiled over bare shoulders. Major Morton's eyes were closed. As they shuffled in a half-turn to face us we saw him, shockingly, grope blindly to clutch and nuzzle a breast with his mouth, and that the woman was Miss Fay. Her eyes were shut too and there was a dreamy look on her face. Ruby clutched my arm, pinching so hard I almost screamed, and then we turned and fled across the playground expecting at any second furious shouts and a slashing cane, as we scrambled over the railings and ran down the street.

In the safety of my back garden, lying panting on the grass I said, 'I can't believe it. Major Morton and Miss Fay dancing. Slow, slow, quick sharp, slow.'

'I know. Why do you think she took her dress off?'

'Search me. Hot, I suppose. You don't think they're in love, do you?'

'They must be. Only who could be in love with either of them? I wonder if they're going to get married.'

'We can be bridesmaids.'

The idea was so comic and yet so terrifying that we burst into slightly hysterical laughter.

'Supposing his wig falls off?'

Our laughter was forced and shrill and I could not get the picture of Miss Fay in her pink petticoat out of my mind, with her hair released from its tight class-room fig and crinkling on her shoulders, Major Morton's lips on her bosom.

A few days later the news spread through the village that Major Morton had been taken away in an ambulance. Their dancing was inexplicably connected with Major Morton's departure and I was left with a queasy feeling at having spied on something secret and sad.

Six

I was changing the tablecloths with Percy, singing along to 'How Much is that Doggie in the Window?' on the radio when, 'Stone the bleeding crows!'

A tractor had stopped in the street outside the tea-room. A woman dressed in black, with a black hat, clutching a suitcase, an umbrella and a handbag was perched like a crow on top of bales of shining straw.

'Granny Fitz!'

I rushed out as the tractor driver, John Cheeseman, caught the suitcase which a tiny black foot kicked towards him.

'You'll have to lift me down.' Granny Fitz was set on the pavement, where I threw my arms round her, breathing in the familiar smell of lilies of the valley and gin.

'Mind my costume! I'm all over straw as it is and I hope I haven't been bitten.'

She slapped at the seat of her neat skirt and a spray of glass violets trembled on her lapel.

'Thank you very much, young man. You saved my bacon there. Don't forget, if ever you're passing the Drovers Tavern, Herne Hill, it's on the house.'

John Cheeseman looking completely bewildered, jumped back onto his tractor and sputtered away leaving a cone of blue exhaust.

'April, let's have a look at you then.'

She held me at arms' length, scarcely taller than I was, and clucked.

'How do, mother-in-law.'

'Percival. Are you going to take my bag in or are we going to stand out here on the pavement all day like a music-hall turn for the entertainment of all and sundry?'

A little crowd of kids, with their sixth sense for any diversion, had appeared from nowhere. Percy picked up the suitcase.

'Oi, Ape, is that your nan?'

'April's the name, and I'll thank you not to shorten it,' retorted Granny Fitz.

'Blimey. I wouldn't want her for a nan,' we heard as we went inside.

'So this is the famous Copper Kettle.' Granny Fitz looked round the room. 'Where's your customers? It's gone eleven and the place is empty. Where's my daughter? Haven't done away with her, have you, Percival?'

'Mum!'

Betty came running downstairs and hugged Granny Fitz.

'You shouldn't be charging around like that in your condition. You ought to be taking it easy – not that that's much of a problem round here from what I see. Where's all your customers, Bet?'

We were saved by the entrance of Mr Greenidge and Liesel. He raised his panama and took his usual seat. 'That's a bit more like it,' said Granny Fitz loudly as Betty led her into the back. 'One of the old school, you can always tell.'

'April, love, can you attend to Mr Greenidge?' Betty said.

He made me sit down while he drank his coffee and tried to persuade me to have a cake. He rubbed his knee against my leg under the table. I was nervous, and wanted to see Granny Fitz.

'Granny Fitz arrived on a tractor,' I told him, as he thumbed tobacco into the bowl of his pipe.

'I'm not surprised.' Suck suck suck.

When he got up to go he pressed half a crown into my hand.

'I can't. I'm not allowed to take money. For a present, I mean.'

'Call it a tip then, for the prettiest waitress in town. I won't tell if you don't.'

He winked, and left me with the big silver coin burning my palm.

Although Granny Fitz's visit came out of the blue, she was no stranger to Kent and had memories of going down 'opping as a girl. 'Farthing a bushel they paid us in them days. Big barrels of cider we had. Dancing under the stars to the old squeeze box. Laugh! We had some high old times. Fighting the gippos – there was one young feller, gipsy he was – oh, well this won't get the baby a new frock, will it? Let's have a look at your books then, Bet. You have been keeping your accounts properly, haven't you?'

'Of course we have, if it's any of your business,' said Percy angrily. There was a blue Challenge duplicate book with a sheet of carbon paper in the drawer. Its pages were quite blank.

'It is my business, if I remember rightly.'

Percy went into the garden slamming the back door.

'Never mind him,' said Granny Fitz. 'You show me where I'm to sleep and put my things and I'll give you a hand to get the dinner on when I've unpacked.'

'You'll have to go in with April, Mum. There is the baby's room but we haven't got it sorted yet and it's full of all sorts. We don't really have dinner, as such, at lunchtime,' she added apologetically, 'what with the café and all to think of.'

'What nonsense. I always made sure you had a cooked dinner no matter how busy we were, didn't I? No wonder that child's looking so peaky. And you should be eating for two.'

'Peaky? April's as brown as a berry.'

'Brown as a berry she may be, but underneath, she's peaky.'

Granny Fitz handed me her black purse.

'Here. Run down the butchers and get us a nice piece of frying steak.'

'I – I can't.'

'What do you mean, you can't?'

43

'I can't go into Mr Boddy's shop. There's all dead things in there. He kills things.'

'Well of course he does. That's what butchers are for.'

Charmaine Vinnegar would be there in her bloody cap and apron.

'But I promised my friend Ruby that I'd never go in there. He killed all her piglets and made them into sausages.'

Granny Fitz was groping in her bag for something. She pulled out a little green bottle of gin saying, 'Well get a pound of pork chipolatas then, if that's what you want. In my day children ate what was put in front of them.'

'You don't understand . . .'

'I understand someone's asking for a smack. Now, get along with you.' I dragged furiously along the road with one foot in the gutter. Outside the Co-op I had a brilliant idea. It was a small brown-painted outpost of the South Suburban Co-operative Society that smelled of locust beans. Mr Barrett, neat as a Dutch doll with painted black hair, came through from the back to serve me, and gave me a free halfpenny chew.

'Boddy's was shut,' I said when I got home, 'so I got these instead' producing with a mixture of triumph and trepidation, instead of a bloody newspaper parcel of sausages, a tin of peaches and a tin of condensed milk and putting them on the kitchen table.

'Well, I must say!' Granny Fitz exclaimed. 'I can see I didn't get here a moment too soon.'

'I'm going down the pub!' said Percy, making for the back door.

'But Perce, you never go . . .' Betty started.

'Hang on, son,' Granny Fitz called out grabbing her purse and jamming down her hat, 'I'll come with you. That Rising Sun looked a nice little place,' and they were gone.

'Fancy some peaches?' said Betty.

With Granny Fitz in my room I felt trapped. I had offered to sleep in a hammock in the garden but, 'Where are you going to get a hammock from, eh? Make it out of a cat's cradle?'

Percy had gone, crossly, on the bus into Elmford, the nearest

44

town, to buy a camp bed, which was wedged between my own bed, containing Granny Fitz, and the window. To get out, I had to climb over Granny Fitz who was a late and noisy sleeper. I never seemed to be able to get away from Mr Greenidge now. If he wasn't taking tea or afternoon coffee, he happened to be in the shop, Crosby's or Beasley's, or the Co-op, whenever I was sent on an errand, or to be going up the church path when we came out of Sunday school.

One afternoon though, I was free, on my way to call for Ruby. Granny Fitz had gate-crashed a Darby and Joan Beetle Drive in the village hall, Betty was reading in the garden and Percy in charge of the tea-room. I was wearing shorts, I had Mr Greenidge's half-crown in my pocket to spend with Ruby, and we would go to our secret headquarters for the first time for ages. I was whistling, my other self was turning cartwheels along the pavement.

'Hoo, hoo, hoooo.'

I whirled round. There was Mr Greenidge behind me.

'How did you know that? Our secret call?'

'Hoo hoo,' he laughed.

I was outraged.

'You've been spying on us. That's our secret call.'

'Don't look so angry. Can't I be in your secret society? I know lots of tricks.'

'No you can't. It's private.'

'Oh, go on . . .'

I began to be embarrassed for him.

'I've got to go.'

'Where are you off to?'

'To call for Ruby.'

He gripped my arm, saying, 'You're sure you're not going to meet any other boyfriend?'

'Of course I'm not.'

It sounded wrong, as if he thought he was my boyfriend. He looked old and sad, staring at me with his blue eyes under frowning white eyebrows, and I felt sorry for him.

'April, can you meet me this evening? About six, by the telephone box in Lovers Lane. Please say yes.'

'I don't know if I'll be able to.'

My heart started to flutter anxiously.

'Please, April, Just for five minutes.'

'OK. I'll try. I've got to go. Really and truly.'

'Thank you. Thank you.' He pressed my hand.

I walked on, deflated now, with six o'clock to dread all afternoon. Ruby's father was washing at the kitchen sink when I got to the Rising Sun, bare-chested, running the tap and honking his nose with a horrible sound. He scowled at me as I went past.

When we reached the orchard we found that the plums had been picked. Broken leafy twigs withered on the grass under the trees with the spoiled fruit. It was dreadful to think that people, strangers, had been in our kingdom. We raced to the railway carriage fearing the worst, but it was as we had left it. Our things were untouched.

'You know what this means?' I said. 'Now nobody will come here for ages.'

'I wish we could live here for ever. Just us. Never go home, or back to school. Just stay here always, even when we're grown up.'

'We've got to change our secret call,' I told her. 'What shall we have?'

Ruby thought. 'How about the lone cry of the peewit?'

I could think of no good reason for disappearing, especially with Granny Fitz imposing her order on our household, so at five to six I just went out to the back door into the garden and then ran as fast I could to the telephone box at the top of Lovers Lane. He was waiting, and pulled me behind the box and kissed me.

'What did you want to see me for?'

'Just that. Just to see you.'

'Oh. Well, I'd better go now. I didn't say I was going out.'

'April, you know I love you, don't you?'

I didn't know what to say. I was shocked and yet I wasn't surprised.

46

'Do you love me?'

'Yes.'

I had to say it because he looked so pleading. Then a herd of cows came round the corner on their way home to be milked, and we were trapped against the wall as they passed, huge, jostling each other, agonizingly slow. As haunch after haunch, great staring eyes and hoofs and udders and stubby horns and dewlaps undulated along in a seemingly endless procession, Mr Greenidge held my hand tightly out of sight.

'This is a piece of luck,' he said.

I knew they would have missed me at home. As soon as the last tail flicked past, and the herdsman with his long stick, I raced home. If only I had a bike or roller skates.

'Whatever became of manners?' Granny Fitz demanded. 'Dashing off like that with never a by-your-leave. You'll have to pull your socks up when you come to stay with me, young lady. Is that cows' muck on your shoes?'

'What?'

'Don't say what, say pardon. You're coming to stay with your grandpa and me while your mum has the baby.'

'But – but, it'll be Christmas . . .'

'The Drovers Tavern is famed far and wide for its festive cheer,' said Granny Fitz.

That baby chalked up another crime. Christmas away from home, away from Ruby. While it celebrated here, with Mum and Dad. 'I thought the baby was supposed to be a special Christmas present for me,' I whined.

'Be your age,' said Granny Fitz. Percy and Betty looked too guilty to say anything.

The vicar of St Michael and All Angels was Mr Oswald, remote, tall, thin and grey like a heron in his black cassock with a melancholy long-beaked face. Mr Seabrook was the verger, an irascible character who shouted at the Sunday-school children if they set foot on the grass or dared to play leapfrog over the gravestones, and he would rush out cursing any wedding guests who disobeyed his injunction against confetti. Most sets of wedding photographs had one or two pictures spoiled by his demonic bristling face and witch's broom.

The Sunday-school teacher was Mr Drew, a smooth plum of a man in suede shoes. His repertoire, like his class, was small and usually on Sundays we sang 'Loving Shepherd of thy sheep' and listened to the story of Blind Bartemeus or the Raising of Jaïrus's Daughter. The collection was taken in a soft purple velvet pouched bag and some put money, or whatever they might have in their pocket, in and some took money out. Titchy Vinnegar was usually to be found at Beasley's sweet shop and tobacconist after Sunday school.

One morning I plucked up courage to say to Mr Drew, remembering the beautiful Bible picture stamps I had collected in London, 'Please, Mr Drew, at my last Sunday school we used to get coloured stamps and stick them in our stamp albums. When your album was full you got an Attendance Prize.'

'We do things differently here,' he said. 'If we want stamps we purchase them at the Post Office or order them from Stanley Gibbons's catalogue.'

Nevertheless, Hastings shimmered on the horizon, blue and seagull white.

The morning of the Sunday-school treat dawned bright and fair, as in the best story books. The sun was shining through the pink and yellow roses on my curtains. I had a white dress patterned with red cherries, white socks with a red stripe, plimsolls stiff with whitener and cherry-red ribbons in my hair. Granny Fitz had risen early to make my packed lunch and wave me off; as the church clock struck a quarter to eight we rounded the corner to see two ice-cream and seaside blue Bluebird coaches sitting outside the church. Our small Sunday school had suddenly spawned two coach-loads of supporters who were climbing in already to get the best seats. I looked anxiously for Ruby in the crowd. Everybody was dressed in their best clothes, some of the girls were wearing party frocks, hair ribbons fluttered like butterflies and the boys' hair was Brylcreemed to their scalps; there were painted buckets and a tin spade had drawn the first blood. We realized that a sort of fracas was taking place. An adherent of a rival church had been caught trying to board the coach.

'Sir! Please, sir! Mr Oswald. He can't come, Mr Oswald, he's a Baptist!'

'Just a minute, you, boy.' Mr Oswald pulled him off the steps by the back of his shirt.

'Is it true that you are a Baptist?'

'It is! He is!' shouted our Sunday school.

The boy, clutching a brown paper bag, hung his head.

'Well, are you or aren't you a Baptist? Speak up. What's your name?'

'John.'

Mr Oswald wavered visibly.

'Go on then. But if I find out that that paper bag contains anything except locusts and wild honey, you're in serious trouble, my lad.'

The Vinnegars were piling into one of the coaches. Old Ma Vinnegar, her enormous husband Tiny and all the young Vinnegars. But where was Ruby? I was getting desperate.

'Move along, all aboard,' Mr Oswald was saying. 'Why do we call these coaches Time and Tide? Because they wait for no man.'

'Don't worry,' said Granny. 'She'll be here.'

'But the coaches leave at eight sharp! Mr Drew said anybody not here at eight sharp would be left behind like foolish virgins and it's five to eight now!'

'Run up the road and see if she's coming then; I won't let them go without you.'

I tore along the street expecting to meet Ruby running towards me. I ran all the way to the Rising Sun where panic gave me the courage to bang on the back door. Gloria opened it in nightdress and curlers.

'She's not coming.'

Too out of breath to speak, my side pierced by a stitch, I could only gasp and stare, holding onto the lintel for support. She tried to close the door but I grabbed the handle.

'Please, Mrs Richards, please let Ruby come. I promise we'll be good, please!'

'Get your hands off that doorknob. She's not going and that's final. She's a wicked little thief who can't be trusted.'

'She is not a thief!' I yelled 'Ruby!'and then a nasty smile broke out on Mrs Richards' face, and I heard it, and turning, saw a blue-and-cream coach rumbling past with the sound of 'One man went to mow, went to mow a meadow' droning out of its windows. I threw down my packed lunch and sank onto the step with my head in the lap of my cherry dress. The door slammed behind me. Through black, bitter despair I heard the engine of the second coach. I would not look up to see it pass.

'Beep Beep Beeeep.'

Three loud blasts on the horn. 'Beep Beeeep Beeeeep.' I lifted my head and saw, through the blur of tears, the coach pull to a stop outside the Rising Sun. And Granny Fitz was jumping down from beside the driver and bustling towards the yard in her high heels calling 'Ru-bee, Ru-bee, come on sleepyhead, you're keeping everybody waiting!'

I scrambled up and the back door burst open, thrusting out Ruby in her old green dress and black plimsolls, shoved from behind, and we were running towards the coach with five shillings pressed into my hand by Granny Fitz and everybody singing, 'Why are we waiting?'

As the coach passed Kirriemuir Mr Greenidge was standing at the gate looking sad and waving, and lots of people waved back. I did too, knowing his wave was just for me, but I couldn't feel very sorry for him because my heart was too full of love for my granny and joy that Ruby was beside me.

'Why did your mum call you a thief?'

'She said I stole some money, but I never. I think it was my dad. Anyway, I don't want to think about them.'

The seats were blue prickly velvet and we sang 'There were ten in the bed and the little one said, roll over' and 'Ten green bottles' and 'Put another nickel in, in the nickelodeon', on board the Bluebird of happiness in the smell of boiled eggs and bananas on our way to the sea.

Seven

On the first day of the autumn term the whole school was assembled in the canteen, which was a wood and asbestos 'hut' on the far side of the playground. Usually each class had morning prayers in its own room as there was no hall. A tall thin man in a gingery tweed suit with leather elbow patches and a green bow-tie addressed us. You couldn't help seeing the cane, broken in two, on the table in front of him. Whom had he broken it on?

'Good morning boys and girls. I am your new headmaster, Mr Reeves. I'm afraid I have some sad news for you. Your old headmaster, Major Morton, died two weeks ago and I know how sorry you will all be to lose him.'

A muffled cheer came from the back and gasps, whispering and nudging broke out. I thought, how terrible to have somebody cheer at the news that you were dead and Ruby and I looked at Miss Fay but she was pushing her way through the children who parted in fear, to get to the boy who had cheered. She dragged out Eric Endell by his ear, which had gone bright red, and smacked him hard again and again and stood him on a dinner-table.

'Thank you, Miss Fay,' said Mr Reeves. 'Now, if I may continue. We will remember Major Morton in our prayers and then we shall all join together in singing the school song,

"Come boys and girls of Stonebridge School, Lift up your hearts and sing".'

Nobody knew that we had a school song, so Mr Reeves and Miss Fay sang it, with Miss Elsey who taught the infants' class pretending to join in, although it was obvious she didn't know the words, and everybody trying not to laugh. You could see the red marks on the backs of Eric's legs.

'All right, you can get down now,' said Mr Reeves to Eric.

He picked up the two pieces of the broken cane and we thought he was going to use them on Eric, but he dropped them into a waste-paper basket and dusted off his hands as though they were dirty.

'Fall in, everybody,' said Miss Fay. She looked furious, with her ears as red as Eric's.

'Fall in what, a bucket of water?' Ruby whispered loudly. Miss Fay only glared at her, and you could feel that things were going to be different.

New shiny yellow rulers and wooden pencils had come, and ink pens and the inkwells on our desks were cleaned out and filled. The class-room smelled of fresh ink and wood and the infants' class smelled of the Plasticine like strips of coloured ploughed fields that replaced the ancient cannonballs of camouflage green and brown, and the sharp scent of raffia and new reading books. We were given hymn books with cloth covers the colour of the square of viridian in my paintbox at home and Mr Reeves's bow-tie and Mr Reeves's name was that viridian green. 'Daisies are our silver, buttercups our gold,' we sang, 'these shall be our emeralds, leaves so new and green, roses make the reddest rubies ev-er-er seen.' Mr Reeves was married with three children, one in his class, one in the infants, and a baby.

Ruby and I asked our mothers if we could stay to school dinners instead of coming home. My mother said it seemed silly when home was so near and Mrs Richards said it was a waste of money when there was always food in the bar. Stale crisps, Scotch eggs, pork pies, pickled eggs. Ruby used to pick off the crumby meaty shells of the scotch eggs and throw them, and the pork pies, into the weeds at the end of the yard. I had one pressing reason for wanting to stay to dinner, which was that Mr Greenidge was always waiting just along the road to walk me back as far as the Rising Sun. I began to feel embarrassed by people seeing us together so often. He would look up and down the road, and kiss me quickly if nobody was coming. I started to feel sick with guilt every dinner time. 'Will you walk back to school with me?' I asked Betty one afternoon when anxiety fizzed in my stomach like sherbet lemons. The inside of my cheek was always sore now, where I chewed it, as though I had sucked too many sharp boiled sweets.

'Whatever for? A big girl like you!'

'Someone bullying you?' Percy asked.

'No.'

'Are you quite sure?'

'Yes.'

'What's up then?'

'I'm scared.'

'Scared? What on earth are you scared of?'

'I'm scared that man with a knife and a sack might jump out on me like he did on Charmaine Vinnegar.'

'That's just a silly story, village gossip. Anyway, it's broad daylight and you're not going anywhere near Station Hill, are you?' Percy said.

'Oh come on then,' Betty said, 'just this once.'

She was wearing a flowered smock over her skirt, like the smocks the teachers wore at school, but bigger.

'Afternoon, Mr Greenidge,' she called out cheerfully as we passed him, with Liesel on the lead.

'Good afternoon, Mrs Harlency. A lovely one, and you are looking blooming if I may be permitted to say so.'

'Thank you, kind sir,' said Betty, blushing. I scowled, embarrassed for both of them, and patted Liesel.

'How about tea on Sunday, April?' he said, twinkling his blue eyes. 'Mrs Greenidge was saying only the other day that you've quite deserted your old friends.'

'That would be lovely,' Betty said.

As soon as we were out of earshot I said, 'Do I *have* to go?'

'It would be very rude not to once you've accepted. Why,

don't you want to? I thought you always had a lovely time, playing with Liesel? It's very kind of them to ask you.'

I hate Liesel, I thought. It's all her fault. I hate her stupid ball and I hate the stupid frogs under the plants by the pond and the stupid goldfish.

'What's a dicky ticker?'

'Oh.' Betty looked solemn. 'It means somebody's got a weak heart.'

'You mean—it could break? Or stop?'

'Look, there's Ruby waiting for you. Can I go back now?' She gave me a kiss and a little push.

'Off you go.'

It was true that I had not been to the Greenidges' for some time. The summer holidays had been full; Ruby and I had gone to the orchard whenever we could, and now blackberries were ripe in the hedges and on Donkey Hill where we went out with other children to fill bowls and seaside buckets, and to pick rose-hips which we split and rubbed the hairy seeds down the backs of each other's necks. We called it itching powder. Betty made our blackberries, Ruby's and mine, because Mrs Richards didn't want any, into pies and jam for the tea-room.

Two ladies, Miss Codrington and Miss Rix, artists, who lived at Beaulah House, a few minutes' walk away, where they held painting and craft classes, started coming in sometimes for morning coffee and once or twice they brought people from London in for afternoon tea, but apart from them and Mr Greenidge it was still all passing trade and we had one bad experience with some hop pickers who ran out without paying, rough, stained people. I had seen Mrs Greenidge a couple of times in Crosby's with a shopping basket, leaning on a stick and wearing a straw hat, and tried to avoid her. Granny Fitz had stayed another week. We bought her a set of false teeth made out of rock at Hastings. She unwrapped the cellophane and clacked them like castanets. 'Now there's a dilemma,' she said. 'If I eat these, I'm going to need false teeth − but I'll have already eaten them.' She wrapped the white teeth in their sugar-pink gums up again.

Granny had disapproved of Betty's and Percy's new Labour party friends, adding her opinions to a particularly acrimonious meeting, out of order, 'I'm a true-blue, red-hot Conservative and I don't care who knows it.'

On Sunday I dawdled along to Kirriemuir with a biscuit bone for Liesel in my pocket. The virginia creeper on the Rising Sun was turning scarlet and Ruby was sitting by the hedge making ballet dancers out of fuchsia flowers by removing all the stamens except two delicate red legs in black velvet ballet shoes.

'Why can't I ever come? It's not fair.'

'It's not my fault is it? I never wanted to go in the first place. I can't help it if they don't ask you. It's not up to me, is it?'

'Lucky beggar.'

I had to leave her sitting there with a row of red and purple ballerinas in the dust.

Something seemed different as soon as Mr Greenidge closed the door behind us. He held me for longer than usual so that I felt correspondingly nervous and uneasy, expecting Mrs Greenidge's voice or the tap of her stick.

'Where's Liesel?' I said when he let me go.

'Ah. Liesel's gone for a little holiday. I quite forgot, when I asked you to come today, that Mrs Greenidge was going to stay with her sister for a few days. Wasn't that silly of me?'

'You don't mind, do you?' he said when I didn't answer.

'No,' I had to say, but I felt odd, just the two of us there in the quiet hall with the knights in armour.

'I brought Liesel a present.'

I took the bone out of my pocket.

'How kind. She'll love that. Let's put it in the kitchen for her, shall we?'

Liesel's clean dish and empty water bowl were standing on their sheet of newspaper.

The biscuit bone clanged hollowly into Liesel's enamel dish. There was a bar of chocolate on the table. I hoped it wasn't for me. I didn't want it.

'I see you've spotted your little treat, Miss Sharp-Eyes.'

My sweet-tooth shrank and disappeared and I could taste the

big brown squares blocking my mouth and throat as I mumbled, 'Thank you,' leaving the chocolate where it lay.

'Shall we go and look for frogs?' I said. I wanted to cry but there was nothing to cry about in the kitchen that smelled of the scrubbed wooden draining board with hard bleached tea towels hanging and quiet underwear dangling from the pulley.

'In a minute, I've got something to show you upstairs. Something you'll like . . .'

I trailed after him, up the stairs for the first time, my heart beating too fast, onto the landing fenced in by the minstrels' gallery. Squares of ruby and emerald light fell from a stained-glass window onto the thick carpet and dark brown doors stood closed.

'In here.'

Mr Greenidge opened one of the doors and led the way into a room. I saw a wide pink quilt, shiny and scalloped, on a high wooden double bed, a dressing-table with a fluted rose-pink skirt and a glass top where a triple glass reflected objects of coloured glass and silver and a turquoise scent spray with a silk tassel. The window divided the garden into little squares. I caught sight of myself in the mirror, a sunburned face, untidy brown sunstreaked pigtails, startled eyes, and that foolish feeling that had swept over me the first time in the conservatory came back and everything was suddenly distant, as in a dream. I had that sense of remoteness that can occur in a noisy class-room, when you are there and yet not there, with voices roaring all around you.

'Where is it?' I heard myself saying, far away.

'Where's what?'

'The thing you wanted to show me.'

'Over here.'

It was a lacquered cabinet standing on the crocheted runner along the top of the chest of drawers, an edifice of glowing wood inlaid with birds and leaves and flowers and mother-of-pearl, the most beautiful thing I had ever seen, and I wanted passionately to own it and for a second the hope flared that he might give it to me.

'Open the doors,' he said.

The two sides swung outwards releasing a strange old perfume faint and musty, to reveal little shelves, opening onto drawers with tiny mother-of-pearl knobs. A green Chinese scent bottle painted with flowers stood on one of the shelves in the doors and each shelf and drawer showed something magical and miniature; black elephants with tusks of ivory, a carved walnut that unscrewed and held a blue scarab, pins with heads of coloured glass, tiny Chinese or Japanese figures, a doll-sized fan, pencils no bigger than matchsticks, shoes that fitted on a fingernail, pink and gold rimmed cups that a raindrop would fill, more and more treasures that I gazed at with reverence and covetousness as they lay in the palm of my hand. How I wished Ruby were there to share them.

'Come over here a minute.' Mr Greenidge was sitting on the bed patting the pink eiderdown.

I stood awkwardly in front of him, holding a string of yellow beads like corn on the cob. He took the necklace from my hand and slipped it over my head and pulled me to him.

'Lie down for a moment,' he said.

'Why?'

'Please. Just for a little cuddle.'

I was as wooden as a puppet as I lay on the high bed feeling silly.

'Put your arms round me. There, that's nice isn't it?'

Mr Greenidge started kissing me.

'Kiss me back.'

I kissed his cheek, above his beard, where his skin felt soft.

'You don't mind if I touch you, do you?'

He was out of breath.

'Can I touch you – there?'

'Where?'

He put his hand in the leg of my shorts. I was rigid with embarrassment. He touched the elastic of my knickers. I sat up, my face on fire. Mr Greenidge groaned.

'You know what I'd like to do if you were older?' he said.

'But – you're already married . . .'

'Come on, you'd better be getting home.'

His hair was sticking up in white tufts and he looked upset.

I slid off the bed, not liking to mention tea. I didn't want any, anyway.

'April,' he said in the hall when we were downstairs, 'I don't think it would be a good idea to tell them at home that I forgot that Mrs Greenidge wouldn't be here. They'd think me such a silly-billy, wouldn't they?'

I nodded.

'Will you come to see me tomorrow? Please.'

I nodded again, wanting only to be outside.

'Promise?'

He looked so sorrowful and clutched my hands.

'I promise.'

'And you won't say anything to Mrs Greenidge, will you?'

I shook my head.

'We understand each other, don't we?'

But I didn't really understand. As I walked along the road I heard him shout. 'April! You forgot your chocolate!'

I pretended not to hear. I had this knowledge that Mr Greenidge wanted us to get married and I didn't know what to do with it. Then I began to feel so guilty for leaving behind the chocolate that he had bought me that I sat on the allotments gate, not knowing whether to go back for it, half-way between Kirriemuir and home, with tomorrow already a grey looming cloud.

I let myself in furtively through the back door and went upstairs to lie on my own bed with my rabbit Bobbity. Mr Greenidge loved me. I believed that, but I was tainted with the terrible shame I had felt when Titchy Vinnegar tried to pull down someone's knickers in the playground or when the boys jumped up to look over the door of the girls' lavatories. After a while I got up and found my paintbox and painted red spots all over my face and went downstairs.

'Mum, I don't feel well.'

'Oh, hello, love. I didn't hear you come in. What have you been up to, did you have a nice time?'

'I think I've got chickenpox. I feel really ill.'

'You'll feel better when you've washed that paint off your face,' said Betty. 'What's that?'

She poked my chest and a hard bead was impressed on my skin. I had forgotten to take off the yellow necklace. All the painted spots on my face ran together in a blaze of guilt.

'Mrs Greenidge said I could borrow it. I've got to take it back tomorrow.'

Betty was looking at me sharply.

'Are you sure she said you could? Let's have a look.'

She pulled the necklace out of my T-shirt.

'These are gorgeous. They look like real amber. Oh I do like pretty things! Still, diamond bracelets Woolworth's doesn't sell, as the song goes.'

'I'll buy you a diamond bracelet one day,' I said. 'When I grow rich.'

'Say the bells of Shoreditch,' said Betty.

Later, when she came up to say good-night, I caught hold of her skirt and pulled her back.

'Don't go.'

'I must. I've got a huge pile of ironing waiting.'

'Just stay for a minute.'

I remembered Mr Greenidge wheedling at me to lie on the bed and shivered. Betty put her hand on my forehead to check if I really was ill.

'Mum?'

'What?'

'Oh, nothing.'

Betty sat down on the bed.

'Look, love, I know you don't want to go to Granny's when the baby's born but . . .'

'I do,' I interrupted. 'I wish I could go now!'

A hurt look shadowed her face, then she bent down and kissed me lightly on the forehead, saying, 'Well, then, you haven't got that long to wait,' with a 'Good-night' that made me burst into tears as the door clicked behind her. I took Bobbity under the covers and tried to pretend that we were cosy in a burrow with turnips hanging from the ceiling as I had when I was little, but it didn't work any more. Bobbity was named after a wild rabbit in a Ladybird Book, *The Runaway*, who took Sandy, a pet rabbit, under his wing, or paw when he escaped from his hutch. In times of trouble I retreated underground:

> Bobbity had lit the lantern,
> Sandy caught his breath again:
> So they finished tea in comfort,
> Snug and safe, down Rabbit Lane!

Bobbity poured milk from a striped earthenware jug into the bowl which Sandy, sitting on his three-legged blue stool, held out trustingly; there were three fat red carrots on the floor and lettuce leaves for supper, but it was no good. I couldn't be a rabbit any more. Foxey was waiting at Kirriemuir and a string of yellow beads lay on my dressing-table.

In the morning as we walked to school, the hedges were covered with glittering spiders' webs, exquisite nets and shimmering tents draped over leaves and twigs. We bent pliant privet twigs into loops called cobwebbers to capture them, but the webs never looked as beautiful once we had scraped them off the hedge. The diamonds fell from them, they became greyer and might hold a shoal of tiny dead flies and the cobwebber become a horrid gummy trap. I thought of the diamond bracelet I would buy for Betty one day.

'Had a good day at school?' Betty asked when I got home.
'No.' I pulled a face.
It had been a grey unpleasant day. With the hands of the clock dragging inexorably towards the time when I must take back the necklace to Mr Greenidge, who probably thought I had stolen it.
'Daddy, in Scripture, Miss Fay said that she had a friend who was a prison chaplain and he said that he would rather see a man hanged than flogged because when a man is flogged he loses his self-respect.'
'Ho, yes,' said Percy, 'I can just see some bloke walking to the gallows shitting himself with self-respect.'

'Percy!'

Betty came into the kitchen.

'Sorry, love. Sorry, April, but sit down, I want to tell you a story. There was a chap who used to drink in a pub called the Fox and Hounds where your mother and I were working. Jack Cornfield was his name and he was the mildest, gentlest fellow you could wish to meet. Well, to cut a long story short, this Jack Cornfield's wife and daughters were murdered and Jack Cornfield was arrested and sent for trial at the Old Bailey. Now everybody at the Fox and Hounds knew that Jack Cornfield couldn't have done it, he was a family man who wouldn't hurt a fly, but they found him guilty and they hanged him. Six months later, the lodger, who had been living in Cornfield's house, topped himself. They found him hanging in the cellar where the murders had taken place. So, you can tell your Miss Fay from me that capital punishment is a crime committed by the state, that no self-respecting country can justify. They put him in the Chamber of Horrors at Madame Tussaud's, Jack Cornfield.'

I said nothing. I saw again the flypaper, studded with winged corpses, that had hung in the tea-room when first we saw it, turning gently in the warm air and I saw a man dangling by the rope around his neck, twirling slowly from a beam in a blood-splashed cellar, and a convict in a suit of broad arrows stumbling towards the gallows.

'And that goes for flogging too,' Percy said. 'It's barbaric and obscene.'

The blood had all drained out of me as from the murdered woman and girls, leaving me waxen and weak. The very name, Chamber of Horrors, made my flesh creep.

'Whatever was Miss Fay thinking of? In a scripture lesson too,' said Betty.

I could not speak of the terrible cat-o'-nine-tails Miss Fay had swished verbally before our horrified eyes. The lone cry of a peewit cut through my blood-stained thoughts.

'Come in, Ruby.' Betty looked relieved at her arrival.

'Is April coming out?'

'She hasn't had her tea yet. Have you had yours?'

Ruby shook her head.

'Well you can have something to eat with April and then you can both pop round to Mrs Greenidge's. April's got something to give back to her, haven't you love?'

We had our tea, listening to *Children's Hour*.

The smile fell from Mr Greenidge's face when he saw the two of us standing there.

'Yes?' he barked, as if we were strangers or Bob-a-Job cubs.

'I brought these back. I took them by accident.'

I held out the necklace. He stared at it as if he'd never seen it before and I remembered that Ruby thought Mrs Greenidge had lent it to me.

'I mean Mrs Greenidge said I could borrow it.'

'I'll see she gets it.'

He almost snatched the beads and slammed the door.

'Blimey,' Ruby said, 'what's up with him? I thought you said he was nice. I think he's really bad-tempered and rude.'

Before I could stop her, she had grabbed a handful of gravel and flung it at the galleon on the front door and we were both running down the street. At the allotments I doubled over with a stitch and guilt at how hurt Mr Greenidge would be feeling.

'You shouldn't have done that,' I said.

Ruby turned a cartwheel, her legs flashing, her pigtails sweeping the road. We walked on, with Ruby hopping on and off the edge of the pavement, until we came to a group of girls playing with a ball. Ruby dashed into their circle, snatching the ball from the air, and threw it to me amid shrieks of indignation. I caught the ball and flung it hard, an outburst against the horrible day. It hit an older girl, Myrna Pratt, on the chest and she crumpled, crossing her arms protectively over her school blouse.

'Couldn't've hurt that much,' Ruby jeered, while I stood paralysed by what I had done.

Doreen put her arm around Myrna, who lifted her face and accused, 'Anyway, I'm developing, April Harlency, and now I won't ever be able to have any babies and it's all your fault!'

'Come on, Myrna, let's go and tell your mum,' said Doreen,

enjoying the drama. 'Come on, Juney, we're going up Myrna's house to report April to Myrna's mum! April Fool!'

She yanked Juney by the arm and off they all trailed, leaving Ruby and me alone in the street.

'April Fool,' Juney shouted over her shoulder.

'Dad, what's developing mean?' I asked that evening.

'It's when you take a photograph and it's just a negative so you have to put it in some developing fluid to make the photograph appear, or develop the picture.'

We hadn't got a camera and I was none the wiser. I just knew that I had ruined Myrna Pratt's life, somehow, by hitting her with a rainbow-coloured rubber ball. My only hope was that, as Gloria Richards had not carried out her threat to come round and seize my mother's skirt, Mrs Pratt would not arrive on our doorstep to tell my parents what I had done. I went up to my room.

'April, can you come down here a minute?' Percy called up the stairs. I thought of running away, of hiding for ever in the railway carriage in the orchard.

'April?'

Mrs Pratt and Myrna were in our kitchen.

'I never meant the ball to hit her, it was an accident!'

'Accidentally on purpose,' said Myrna.

'Sheer spitefulness, I call it,' said Mrs Pratt.

'There you are,' said Betty, 'it was an accident. April would never throw anything at anybody deliberately. That's not the way she's been brought up.'

'I'm sure she's sorry, aren't you, love?' Percy said. 'You never meant to hurt Myrna, did you?'

'Yes, I mean no. I'm sorry.'

'She did it on purpose,' said Myrna. She simpered, 'Now I won't be able to have any babies.'

'Don't be daft,' said Percy, 'what's that got to do with it? Tell you what, how about an ice lolly? Go on, April, get a lolly for Myrna to show you want to make friends again, and one for Mrs Pratt too.'

The Pratts were beaten. They went off sucking their lollies, tossing their heads and sniffing as they passed the small audience that had gathered.

'I do think those mother-and-daughter outfits are a mistake,' Betty said. 'Makes them look like a cruet set.'

I laughed with relief, but there were problems which could not be melted like ice.

Eight

Beulah House, where Miss Rix and Miss Codrington lived, had once been an orphanage. The two-storeyed white clapboard building, with its hollyhocks flaunting bells over the white picket fence, had a campanile housing the great bell that used to regulate the orphans' lives, and a white dovecote occupied by descendants of the original brood. Now, in the Beulah School of Arts and Crafts, the soft fondant hues of the hollyhocks were compressed into pastels and chalks. Roses, violets, lemons, viridians, they were like the cocktail cigarettes Miss Rix smoked, and subtle apricots and the crimson that splashed the inside of the hollyhocks' bells around the pollen-laden clappers.

Miss Rix was tall, with a pale, oval face and black hair drawn into a loose knot from a white centre parting and she wore fabrics with zigzags, dots and squiggles.

'Matisse is my God,' she told me. 'Who is yours?'

'God.'

Miss Codrington, fair and slender, reminded Ruby and me of the Willow Fairy in *Fairies of the Trees* by Cicely Mary Barker. You could just see her in a green dress, with her golden hair loose, holding onto the long green leaves while she dipped her toes in the green river, and it was easy to imagine wings like a dragonfly's growing from her shoulders. The two artists had a Bedlington terrier, Boy, who looked like a little grey lamb, and a hive of bees, and white ducks who lived in a wooden house on the river bank at the end of the orphans' vegetable garden.

'I'm surprised that two such attractive girls haven't managed to find themselves a husband,' Betty said.

'They're artists,' said Percy. 'They live for their art. Even so . . .'

Miss Rix and Miss Codrington were expecting twenty week-end guests and on Sunday a professor from London, Professor Linus Scoley, was coming to give a lecture: 'Samuel Palmer, Ancient or Modern?' They were in a flap about having to cater for so many and had come to ask if their visitors could have their meals at the Copper Kettle, and if we would provide afternoon tea on the Sunday at Beulah House.

'We've bitten off more than we can chew,' they confessed, 'and we're up the creek without a paddle.'

'We're really more of an eggs, sausage, beans and fried slice establishment,' Betty told them, looking worried. 'I know it says FUNCTIONS CATERED FOR on that notice on the door, but truthfully we had tea parties more in mind. There's been no call, up till now, and we haven't got the facilities for anything too sophisticated like your London people would expect.'

'Oh, please, Mrs Harlency! We simply won't have time to be in the kitchen as well as running the classes. Some composite dish is all that's called for – a simple goulash perhaps or ratatouille . . .?'

Betty stared at her speechless, slowly shaking her head.

Miss Codrington bowed her own head in her hands, her fair hair falling over her fingers, a broken fairy mumbling,

'It was a stupid idea. We've overreached ourselves. We'll be the laughing stock of the art world. We'll just have to cancel the whole thing.'

She lifted wild, despairing eyes to Miss Rix, who said, 'Too late for that. I suppose – I suppose I *could* get Mrs Vinnegar in . . .'

That clinched it.

'No need for that,' Percy stepped into the conversation, 'we can't have you ladies being the laughing stock of the art world. We'll cope somehow, and the Copper Kettle will do you proud.'

Miss Rix threw her long arms round him and kissed him on the cheek.

'You darling man! Oh, bless you, bless you both! Any time you want some free tuition, painting, sketching, papier mâché or burnt poker work – just say the word!'

'Beadwork and barbola,' put in Miss Codrington.

'That won't be necessary,' said Betty a trifle sharply.

Percy was still looking surprised and pleased by the kiss.

'I do hope it won't be too much work for you, Mrs Harlency,' they kept saying, now that it was settled.

'Oh, do call me Betty, and I may look like a barrage balloon on legs but I'm fit as a flea.'

'Betty, you're an angel! You've saved our lives. And you must call us Dittany and Bobs, now that we're such friends.'

'I hardly like to,' said Betty after they had gone, 'but if those are their names . . .'

Dittany Codrington and Bobs Rix: I loved saying those names. Bobs was short for Roberta.

Betty told Ruby to ask her mother if it would be all right for Ruby to help out as a waitress for a small payment.

'She couldn't care less what I do,' said Ruby.

'I'll ask her then, if you like,' Betty decided.

The visitors were allowed to make their own tea and coffee as they wished in the big kitchen of Beulah House, and cocoa and buns would be provided last thing at night.

Friday night meant supper for twenty-two, including Dittany Codrington and Bobs Rix. The café had never looked so beautiful, with all the lamps glowing in their pink shades and fairy lights looped round the picture rail. Bobs Rix had put a bottle of wine on each of the tables that were in use; she and Dittany ate at a table for two, which meant they had a bottle of wine between them, while the others shared among four. The glasses were on hire from the Rising Sun.

A grinning slice of melon with its teeth sprinkled with ginger was set at each place. The guests themselves, in their artistic colours, were brightly coloured candles wavering and flickering round the tables.

'Too too quaint,' I heard one say.

'Absolutely priceless,' a pallid man asserted, forking a square tooth of melon into his pale mouth set in a long white-and-yellow beard.

The main course was a curry which went down very well with the artists.

'My compliments to the chef,' a stout man in a wine-coloured jacket told me, 'I'm an old India hand, and I can safely say this is as good as anything I tasted in Bombay.'

'Oh, better,' his wife, in a cardigan embroidered with tufts of wool, corrected him. 'I could never impress on Chutney the importance of getting the right proportion of curry powder to the fried sultanas and apple and mince.'

She choked.

'Do you think we could have some water?' her husband twinkled.

'What a pretty glass,' embroidered cardy gasped, gulping her water.

'It had St Ivel cheese spread in it,' I explained, 'that's why its got those blue flowers on it.'

'Perfect,' said wine-coloured jacket. 'Of course his name wasn't really Chutney, it was something unpronounceable. Chutney was just an affectionate nickname. He loved it, didn't he darling? He was our cook,' he explained.

The meal, finished off with ice-cream and fancy wafers, was a triumph. One of the artists even licked his glass dish in a jokey way, going 'yum, yum, yum'. Percy, though, was conferring worriedly with Bobs Rix, whose hair was slipping from its knot and falling in curtains on either side of her rosy face.

'When you've been in the licensed trade as long as I have . . .' he was saying.

'We'll just have to adjourn to the pub,' Bobs decided, 'and they can pay for their own.'

People were trooping through the kitchen and out the back to the toilets. Betty reluctantly directed the more impatient upstairs to our bathroom. At last they were all gone, leaving us with precarious mountains and hills of washing up. The geyser was going fit to blow a gasket and we boiled kettles and saucepans to keep the hot water coming.

Half-way through, Percy made Betty go to bed. She looked exhausted and we all had to be up early for the breakfasts. I was spreading a clean cloth on a table when something made me look up. Mr Greenidge's face was staring at me through the window, and disappeared.

Fewer than a dozen of the guests turned up for breakfast, looking ill and bad-tempered.

'I've paid for this so-called weekend and if that involves eating a fried breakfast, so be it, but I draw the line at prunes,' said a women grimly. Her long black hair was beaded with yellow where it had trailed into the yolk of her egg. 'I don't know what they put in that curry last night but whatever it was, it was lethal.'

Betty, who overheard this, bristled.

'I have it on good authority that the Rising Sun was drunk dry last night and eaten out of pickled eggs.'

The woman shuddered and her teacup rattled in its saucer. She pushed away her plate and lit a cigarette.

At eleven o'clock the tea-room was empty when Mr Greenidge stomped in with Liesel. Mrs Greenidge must have come back then.

'Why are you doing this to me?' he hissed, frightening me, when I brought him coffee.

'Doing what?'

'You know exactly what you're doing. Playing hard to get. Bringing your friend round when you knew it was our last chance to be alone. Avoiding me. How can you be so cruel? Don't you love me any more?'

'Everything all right, Mr G?'

Percy came through from the kitchen where he, Betty and Ruby were making sandwiches for the artists' picnic lunch.

'Right as a trivet, Percy, right as rain. Lot of queer types about this morning though.'

'Bohemians,' said Percy. 'From the art school. We're doing the catering.'

'Art school, my eye,' Mr Greenidge spluttered into his coffee. 'I'd keep an eye on Missy here if I were you. Hardly the sort of company I'd care for my daughter to keep. If I had been blessed in that way.'

'Oh, they're all right. Takes all sorts, eh?'

He took a salt cellar from a table and went back to his work.

'When can I see you?'

Mr Greenidge's eyes were glittery, as if he were going to cry.

'Monday. After school.' Anything to make him go away. 'Did Liesel like her bone?'

'What? Madam's back in residence so it's no good you coming to the house. Meet me by the phone box, we'll have to go for a walk.'

'I'll try. It's difficult. Ruby expects me to play with her.'

'Get rid of her. Make some excuse. *Please*, April. Do it for me.'

'Get rid of her' sounded as if Ruby were rubbish, or a stray dog that followed me around.

I had to break my promise not to enter Boddy's the Butcher when I was sent round to collect pork chops for the evening supper. Ruby understood, because she had been forced to go there herself on occasion. Charmaine Vinnegar handed me the pieces of dead pigs in a large paper bag. Little Juney was playing quietly with a bucket and spade in the sawdust chewing something, and Sorrel Marlowe was there with her mother, who was being served by Mr Boddy in his straw boater. I hadn't seen Sorrel since the Lady Marlene incident and she stuck her nose in the air.

'Stop eating the meat, Juney, I've told you,' said Charmaine. 'It'll give you worms.'

'Well really!' said Mrs Marlowe, going pale as the slab of lard.

I ran out of the shop, my stomach heaving as if with raw meat and white fat.

Brown windsor soup, pork chops with roast potatoes and

cabbage, blackberry and apple crumble was the menu for tonight. Betty cooked the cabbage with bay leaves to take away the smell and sprinkled it with caraway seeds. From time to time the baby kicked hard and you could almost see its foot through her white apron.

'He wants to come out and help with the washing up,' said Percy.

'Percy!'

Ruby and I stared as if the baby might burst through my mother's stomach clutching a washing-up mop.

Professor Linus Scoley was due to arrive on the 2 o'clock train from London.

'Somebody should meet him,' Dittany worried.

'We'll meet him, won't we, April?' Ruby volunteered.

'Bless you, that would be wonderful. You'll recognize him at once – he's exactly like the Henry Lamb portrait of Lytton Strachey.'

'Who's he when he's at home?' I thought, and Ruby said.

'Oh, silly of me. Professor Scoley is tall, with a beard and long tubular legs. Make sure you bring him straight to Beulah House, won't you, so that he can have some refreshment before his lecture at 3 o'clock.'

'We could take Boy,' said Ruby.

'Off you go then, girls,' Percy said at half-past one. 'And remember, this bloke's a dead ringer for Lytton Strachey.' He winked.

'If we were in a William book we'd come back with the wrong professor,' I said.

'Or an escaped lunatic,' said Ruby, clipping on Boy's lead.

A smell of Sunday dinners drifted over the High Street as we walked along with Boy capering like a little lamb beside us. I picked a dahlia from somebody's allotment and tucked it in his collar. Doreen Vinnegar passed us, on the handlebars of her brother Sack's bicycle and called out, 'Why wasn't you two in Sunday School this morning?'

'We had better things to do,' Ruby replied cheerily. 'So there, Vinegar Bottle.'

Two lady artists, guests at Beulah House, came flying down the church path in a whirl of skirts and smocks and folding easels, spilling tubes of paint, with Mr Seabrook the verger chasing after them, waving a spade and shouting, 'Go on. 'op it! Get them pointy-legged things out of my graveyard, making holes in my lawn! Call yourselves artists! You couldn't creosote a fence, none of you!'

We were laughing with our left arms linked behind our backs and Boy's lead in my right hand, when I realized we were approaching Kirriemuir.

'Cross over the road,' I said.

But Boy started yapping and we heard Liesel going frantic running up and down the hedge barking and Mr and Mrs Greenidge appeared at the gate. She held the scrabbling Liesel in her arms.

'Poor Liesel,' Mrs Greenidge soothed her. 'Poor old girl. Never mind, then.'

Mr Greenidge just looked down at Boy's drooping dahlia and back at me. I dropped my eyes.

'Who's your smart new little friend with the gay flower in his collar?' Mrs Greenidge asked.

I remembered that she did not like dahlias.

'He's not really my friend. We've got to take him to the station to meet a professor. I still like Liesel best,' I tried to explain.

'His name's called Boy. He's a Bedlington terrier,' said Ruby.

'*He* is called Boy. His name is Boy.' Mrs Greenidge smiled sadly. 'Don't forget your old friends entirely, April.'

I shook my head.

'Come on or we'll be late,' said Ruby. 'What did she ask what his name was for, if she already knew?' she complained as we walked on.

'Don't ask me. I expect she's a loony.'

I saw myself in their bedroom again, playing with the magical cabinet, squeezing her turquoise scent spray; her silver brushes and combs, her yellow beads, the corner of the high bed with the rose-pink quilt reflected in the mirror.

'What's up with you?'

'Nothing.'

Station Hill smelled of leaf mould and the unripe conkers, brought down by a night of rain, that studded the broken tarmac at the sides of the road in drifts of twiggy debris. The sky was blue between gold-tinged leaves.

'You know that man with a sack and a knife who jumped out on Charmaine Vinnegar?' I said. 'Well, why did he have a sack?'

'To hide her ugly face. To stop her screaming.'

'They never caught him though, did they? He could be here now, behind a tree. In broad daylight.'

Suddenly broad daylight was a terrifying place.

The three of us tore uphill through the autumnal tunnel of trees, three harsh breaths panting across the station yard, through the booking hall and onto the platform where Ruby and I collapsed on the seat. Behind us, on the fence, was an enamel advertisement that said, 'Virol. Anaemic Girls Need It'.

'Oi, you kids! Platform tickets, if you please,' came the voice of the station-master.

'Pretend we're deaf and dumb,' said Ruby.

The train's face was visible down the track, growing bigger as it came towards us. It pulled into the platform and we stood up nervously. The guard's van opened and men in shorts handed out bicycles to each other. Mr and Mrs Smith from the post office stepped out of a compartment, slamming the door loudly in the warm air.

'He's not here. What shall we do?'

The guard was waving his green flag to the driver, and in the blast of a whistle a carriage door flew open spilling a long, reddish-bearded man, with hat, stick, briefcase and glasses onto the platform. He stood, like a bewildered daddy-long-legs in green tweed. As we approached him a winged sycamore seed spiralled slowly down from the sky and settled on his hat.

'Go on, then, say hello.'

'No, you.'

We nudged each other along giggling. Then I stopped dead. Behind the other cyclists, apart from them, wheeling his bike towards us, was Rodney Pegg. We stared in silent mutual horror.

'Come *on*.' Ruby tugged my arm. Boy pulled on his lead.

'Excuse me, are you Professor Linus Scoley?'

'Why?' His voice was reedy and suspicious. 'Who wants to know?'

'He's drunk!' Ruby whispered.

'How do you know?'

She looked at me pityingly.

'How do you think?'

Now I could smell his metallic breath. His eyes glittering behind his thick spectacles added to his insect-like aspect.

'We've come to meet you, to take you to Beulah House. Miss Codrington and Miss Rix sent us. For your lecture . . .'

Whether it was the word lecture or the names of his hostesses that did it, Professor Scoley crumpled.

'Oh, God. Is that what I'm doing here? I can't, I simply can't. All those, those bacchantes with sketchbooks, tearing me to pieces.'

But what was Rodney Pegg doing here? I felt faint.

'Come on, you've got to. Everybody's waiting. My mum's making a special afternoon tea.'

'That,' said Professor Scoley, 'puts the tin lid on it.'

I took hold of one of his arms and Ruby grabbed the other, retrieving his briefcase which had fallen to the platform, and we pulled him along towards the booking hall where the station-master was waiting.

'Have you got your ticket?' I asked.

He tried to flap ineffectually at his pockets, which was difficult as he was holding his stick and we were holding him up.

'Never mind. Just pretend to be deaf and dumb if he asks for it.'

Professor Scoley shrugged us off and straightened up.

'Good evening, officer,' he said to the station-master. 'These young ladies and I are all deaf and dumb.'

The man let us pass, saying,

'You're that red-headed kid from the Rising Sun, aren't you? I'll be having a word with your dad later on.'

'No, I'm not her. She hasn't got a dog.'

'Where is the car?' asked Professor Scoley.

74

'What car?'

'The car to take me to my doom. The hearse. Why aren't those two harpies Bobs and Dittany here to look after me? Dobs and Bitterly.'

'They haven't got a car. We've got to walk, but it's not far. Come on, we'll be late.'

'This is monstrous. A monumental discourtesy. Gimme my briefcase, you girl.'

He took a long swig from a silver flask.

'My dad'll kill me,' said Ruby. 'Shall we just leave him here and run away? Go and live in the railway carriage? Please?'

'We can't. Anyway he might not tell.'

Professor Scoley lurched to the side of the road and fumbled with his trouser buttons.

'Walk on, quick. Don't look.'

We heard it gushing onto fallen leaves, a watering can full, a hosepipe full. When it stopped at last, we turned round to see Professor Scoley slumped against a tree trunk, apparently asleep.

'This is hopeless. Go and get my dad. I'll stay here with Boy to guard him. Go on, Ruby. Run!'

She ran off down the road leaving me with the Professor and Boy. After a while he opened one eye, looked at Boy, and said, 'Why is that sheep here?'

The church clock struck half-past two. A middle-aged man and woman hand-in-hand came down the hill. They stared at us as they passed, walked on a few paces, stopped and turned back.

'Is your father ill, dear?' the woman asked.

'He's not my father.'

'Best not get involved dearest,' the man murmured. 'You never know . . . can't afford to get caught up in any situation.'

'He's an escaped lunatic. I'm just guarding him till the police get here.'

'Jolly good,' said the man. 'That's the ticket.'

Off they went. Professor Scoley was snoring and a blood-sucker was walking up his beard towards his open mouth. I flicked it off with a twig. I thought of all the scones and sandwiches and cakes in our kitchen waiting to be carried round to Beulah House. Dittany and Bobs going mad with anxiety. Professor Scoley's teeth were yellow, his shirt gaped open under the bow-tie half-hidden in the rivulets of his beard, his flies were buttoned wrong. Boy sniffed at a tallow shin above a fallen woollen sock. The church clock was striking the quarter when Percy came round the corner with our wheelbarrow, Ruby running at his side.

We pushed the Professor through the village with his long green herring-boned legs doubled up and his arms draped over the sides of the wheelbarrow. Needless to say there was a bunch of boys hanging about on the steps of the rec.

'Penny for the Guy!' they shouted. Then somebody, probably Titchy, exclaimed. 'Stone the crows! He's dead!'

'Stupid boy,' said Percy, pushing on, sweat pouring down his face. 'I've told your mother to get some black coffee on the go. I'm not having this geezer letting those girls down.'

We hurried on with the boys at our heels round to the back door of the Copper Kettle.

'You run round and tell the girls there'll be a slight delay. Say the train was late, but the Prof's on his way.'

Percy rested the barrow on our grass saying, 'Right, Professor, time to sober up, old chap.'

But all the black coffee in the world couldn't wake him. Titchy, if it had been he, was right for once. Professor Linus Scoley was dead.

Dittany came panting through the gate pushing the boys aside, with flapping sleeves. 'What on earth's . . .'

Percy, white-faced, barred her way.

'You must prepare yourself for a shock. I'm sorry. That lecture – Samuel Palmer: Ancient or Modern? – well, I'm afraid its going to be more a case of Hymns, Ancient and Modern now. With particular reference to the funeral service, if you take my meaning.'

Betty had her arms round me and Ruby, shielding us from the dead man.

'Go on, all you kids. Go home,' she said. 'No, go and get Dr Barker. Tell him it's urgent.'

Percy sat down on the grass with his head on his knees. 'I've just pushed a corpse through the village in a wheelbarrow.'

Dittany was on her knees sobbing onto the Professor. She looked up, her face all red and bleared.

'April, be a love and go and fetch Bobs. And tell her to bring my sketchbook and a pencil.'

Nine

The Copper Kettle was closed on Monday as a mark of respect. Our kitchen and garden had been full of people suddenly on Sunday afternoon: Dr Barker, Constable Cox, Bobs and Dittany, assorted children. Eventually Mr Oswald arrived and said a prayer. And an ambulance came and Professor Scoley was lifted onto a stretcher and driven away. Ruby and I watched from the kitchen door. We had been sent inside, rather pointlessly, as the afternoon was already impressed on our memories for ever. Dittany had whizzed through her drawing book, making sketch after lightning sketch.

'Morbid,' said Betty. 'Still, that's one model who'd keep still for you, I suppose.'

Dr Barker ordered Betty to rest. He was worried about the effect of the shock on her and the baby.

'There was nothing you could have done,' he tried to reassure Percy, who was walking around stunned, like a man who had been hit on the head. 'There will have to be a post-mortem, or course, but my immediate diagnosis is heart. The little girls may be called at the inquest, I can't say yet but that will be up to the coroner. Try not to distress yourself.'

'But a wheelbarrow,' Percy said. 'Poor old bugger. Pardon my French, Doctor.'

'To him, "the reed is as the oak",' said Dr Barker snapping shut his bag.

Professor Scoley's long green legs had been folded like bent reeds in the barrow. I had told those people he was an escaped lunatic and I would never know if he had heard. Somebody had shouted 'Penny for the Guy'.

I felt drained, set apart and yet oddly, shamefully, excited. I did not want to go to school to face curious questions and accusations in the playground.

'Don't let's go,' I said to Ruby, when I called for her.

'Where would we hide?'

The orchard was the obvious place. We stared at each other and turned and ran in the opposite direction to the school.

'How will we know when it's time to go home for dinner?' she said, when we were safely on the path beside the river. Neither of us had a watch.

'By the sky. The sun will be directly overhead at noon.'

It was a grey morning and besides it would take at least half an hour to get home from the railway carriage.

'When we get hungry, we'll know it's getting on for dinner time, and we'll start for home,' I said.

'I'm hungry now.'

We stopped at the spring under the elder tree and scooped up handfuls of ice-cold water to drink and ate bunches of elderberries.

The orchard grass was cold and wet and our socks and shoes were soaked through. We lit a fire to dry them inside the railway carriage, and the air smelled smoky and damp and of scorched socks. Rooks' ragged caws sounded desolate in the sky outside; we heard the distant thud of gunshots, the farmer with his gun.

'Wonder what they're doing now?'

'Milk time, probably.'

I heard the clatter of the milk crates, the sound of bubbling milk and air gurgled through straws, smelled the sour smell of the creamy silver bottle tops, and with a sick lurch of the stomach, I remembered that I was Milk Bottle Monitor that week.

'What's that?' Ruby said, 'over there in the corner?'

'What?'

'That white thing.'

She walked barefoot to pick something up, and held a man's white handkerchief between finger and thumb, at arm's length.

'Somebody's been here!'

The dangling handkerchief, dusty from the floor, with a blue border, had a blue initial *C* in one corner. I snatched it and threw it on the fire. A brown burn appeared and then flames pierced the cotton and charred it. *C* for Clement.

Suddenly fear possessed Ruby. 'Let's get out of here!' She started dragging a damp stained sock over her foot, pulling on her saturated plimsolls. We stamped out the fire and Ruby opened the door slowly, half expecting a murderer to be standing there. The orchard stretched before us, lonely, full of tree trunks where somebody could hide.

'Run for it!'

I closed the railway carriage door and we fled, stumbling through the rough grass. I felt terror too. Although I knew who had been in our secret house, that did not mean a madman with a pitchfork or gun, or sack and knife might not leap out to bar our way.

May Chacksfield was down the meadows, poking damp sticks into her shopping bags. No point in asking her the time, but at least she wouldn't tell anybody she had seen us. Half-way up Lovers Lane John Cheeseman overtook us on a tractor, reminding me of Granny Fitz's arrival in state atop a wad of hay.

'Got the time please?' Ruby called out to him.

'If you've got the inclination.'

'Pardon, Mrs Arden?'

'Quarter to eleven.'

Only quarter to eleven and a vast morning stretching behind us. We took a long short cut round the edges of fields to the church, where we hid in the belfry among plush red and blue bell-pulls which we dared not touch lest they peal out the betrayal to the whole village that two pupils were playing truant from school. Hopping the wag, as Granny Fitz would have said.

Dittany was in the tea-room, when at last I went home for dinner, drinking coffee.

'April, I'm sorry to have to ask you this, but did Professor Scoley say anything before he . . . any last words, I mean . . .?'

'He said something about Baccanites or something like that.'

'Baccanites? Bacchantes?'

'Bacchantes, that's right. What are they?'

I didn't tell her that he had said they were waiting to tear him to pieces.

'Bless him, his mind was on classical sculpture to the last. That's a comfort. Did he say anything else?'

'He said he was really looking forward to the lecture and the afternoon tea.'

'Which turned, alas, to funeral baked meats. Strange how grief can sharpen the appetite. Was that all?'

'Well, his actual last words were "why is that sheep here?".'

Something made me say the truth.

'Sheep? Was there a sheep?'

'No, he meant . . .'

'The Lamb of God,' Dittany exclaimed.

Her face was radiant. She pushed away her cup and saucer and stood up.

'I must tell Bobs.'

She walked out like a sleepwalker without paying for her coffee. I took her cup and saucer through, finishing a half-eaten Welsh cheese cake on the way, glad that I hadn't told her the Professor had called them Dobs and Bitterly.

I remembered something else Professor Scoley had said, 'Mum, what's harpies?'

'Toilet cleaner,' Betty said, 'which reminds me, but look at the state of you! Whatever have you been doing at school this morning?'

'Nature study, Miss Fay took us on a nature walk.'

'Well, it was very inconsiderate on a Monday morning when

some people had clean frocks on and look at your socks! I've a good mind to go up the school.'

I knew she wouldn't, and ate my egg and chips and half an individual fruit pie with increasing nervousness for afternoon school. Then, feeling like a criminal, I went up to my room. I could not do my mother's writing so I took my John Bull Printing Outfit and inked the little rubber letters that spelled out:

Dear Miss Fay, I am sorry April was not at school this morning because she was sick. Yours sincerely, Mrs Harlency.

Miss Fay read my note in silence and then she read Ruby's while we hovered in front of her desk. I had been told to change my dress and socks, while Ruby was still in her elderberry-stained blouse and jumble-sale gymslip, and her soaked plimsolls with grass seeds in the eyelets.

'What a coincidence that you should both be unwell at the same time, and how nice that you should both make such a speedy recovery, but your mother's handwriting, Ruby, leaves much to be desired, I'm afraid. What is our golden rule?'

'A finger space between each word, Miss Fay,' Ruby mumbled.

'Quite so. Perhaps next time you are taken ill your mother might like to borrow Mrs Harlency's John Bull Printing Set. It's at times like these I miss Major Morton most,' she sighed.

'And his cane,' one of the boys called out. Miss Fay ignored him.

'You can both stay in after school and write sincerely two hundred times on the blackboard.'

'I can't,' I said at once, and gasped at my own daring.

'There is no such word as can't,' said Miss Fay.

She was wrong. I can't meet Mr Greenidge now, I thought, and didn't know if I were more frightened or relieved. A grey misery built up in my chest all afternoon until, by the time the others had put their chairs on the desks and left, I could hardly breathe. Miss Fay wrote 'sincerely' on the top of the blackboard, the new green double blackboard, and went through to Mr Reeves's classroom.

I didn't mean to, I didn't know I was going to do it but suddenly I was sitting with my head on my desk crying and I could not stop. The handkerchief in our secret camp, Mr Greenidge, Professor Scoley, all the lies I was enmeshed in shook my shoulders, under Ruby's arm, and gushed out of my eyes.

'What's up, ducks? Kept you in has she?'

Mrs Carter who cleaned the school had come into the classroom. Her flowered overall and silver bucket dazzled and wavered in front of my eyes but I could not stop crying.

'It can't be that bad,' she said, 'here, wipe your eyes.'

She put her arm around me and mopped at my face with a handkerchief. Her kindness made me cry again, gulping against her soft bouncy flowers that smelled of disinfectant.

'You don't want to take no notice of old Troutface.'

'Look, April,' Ruby was giggling. 'This'll make you laugh.'

She had chalked 'sincerely 200 times' on the board. It made Mrs Carter laugh.

'Go on,' she said, 'go and tell her you've done it and you're going home.'

All three teachers were sitting on desks, Mr Reeves on his own desk, smoking cigarettes.

'Please, Miss Fay, we've written sincerely two hundred times so can we go home now please?' Ruby asked.

'Just a moment, young lady. You don't leave these premises until I'm satisfied that you've carried out your task.'

Mrs Carter was standing with her back to us, her arms wobbling as she cleaned the blackboard.

'Oh, afternoon, Miss Fay. Just doing the blackboard for you. Wiping the slate clean, so to speak.'

She beat a little cloud of chalk dust from the striped board rubber.

'Do I detect insubordination?' Miss Fay demanded. 'Are you trying to undermine my authority, Coralie Carter?'

83

'Can't keep me in after school now, Miss Fay. Only doing my job.'

Mrs Carter looked like a big cheeky schoolgirl and Miss Fay looked old and tired and sad. She turned on Ruby and me.

'Get out of my classroom. Out of my sight. You make me sick, the pair of you.'

'Good old Mrs Carter!' said Ruby, when we were safely in the street. 'Why were you crying?'

'I don't know.'

My eyes felt sore and gritty, with thick, swollen lids.

'What will you tell your mum when she asks why you've been crying?'

'I know,' I said. 'I'll pretend we've fallen out and then I can say we've made up again. I'll call for you later.'

'OK.'

As soon as Ruby had gone in, instead of going home, I set off for Lovers Lane. Even if he had given up and gone home, I could say I had gone there, and he wouldn't be able to tell me off.

He was waiting behind the telephone box with Liesel sitting beside him, off the lead.

'Darling. I'd almost given you up.'

He hugged me, in broad daylight. I wriggled free.

'But you've been crying! What is it? Has somebody hurt you?'

I shook my head.

'If anybody hurts you, I'll kill them. I mean it, April. Have you any idea how much I love you?'

I shook my head again. Then that seemed ungrateful, so I nodded.

'But what about – what about Mrs Greenidge?'

'Damn Mrs Greenidge! Damn and blast her to hell!'

He slashed at nettles and goosegrass with Liesel's lead, sending green heads flying.

'Why doesn't she just get on with it and die and get out of our way? Mrs Greenidge, Mrs Greenidge, Mrs Greenidge.'

He was lashing and whipping the plants in a frenzy. Liesel

yelped and ran a few feet up the road where she sat quivering and whining. I started to back away.

'Wait,' he called as I turned to run. 'I've got something for you.'

I was too scared not to walk slowly towards him. He pulled a paper bag of sweets from his pocket.

'Thank you very much.'

It was a quarter of dolly mixture. I looked at the tiny jellies and coloured sweet sandwiches.

'I've got to go home now. I'm late home from school,' I said.

Mr Greenidge's blue eyes were hard as glass and still angry.

'Oh, yes, you go, now you've got what you came for.'

It wasn't fair. I didn't know what to say. I walked up to Liesel, who was still shivering, and gave her a sweet.

'Goodbye, then,' I said.

'April, wait. Let me walk with you. I'm sorry I got cross. It was only because I love you, you do understand, don't you?'

'Yes. Would you like a dolly mixture.'

I held out the bag to him.

'You give me one. Pop it in my mouth.'

He stooped down and I had to feed a jelly into his soft wet lips. His teeth clamped on my finger.

'Grr, grr,' he went, like a dog with a bone.

I pretended to laugh. There were teeth marks on my finger.

A stone hit me hard in the back, the shock knocking the breath out of me. I whirled round.

'You rotten liar, April! I hate you. I'll never be your friend again.'

Ruby was scarlet with rage. She turned and ran up the lane.

'Ruby, wait!'

I ran after her.

'April' came Mr Greenidge's voice, Liesel dashed along beside me, jumping up, trying to bite my skirt as I ran uphill, barking as if it were a game.

'Ruby, please wait.'

'April, come back.'

I tripped and fell heavily on my hands and knees, and lay helpless as Ruby disappeared.

Mr Greenidge picked me up. He tied his handkerchief round one of my knees. The other knee was bleeding too, and my hands. He carried me home.

'Put me down. Put me down. Somebody will see.'

I writhed, trying to escape but he strode on, carrying me like a big baby up the path to the Copper Kettle.

'Got a poor wounded soldier for you, Mrs Harlency,' he told the horrified Betty. 'Not to worry though, no bones broken. Lucky I happened along when I did, eh?'

Betty fetched Dettol and cotton wool and tweezers to get the grit out of my hands and knees.

'What a kind man, to bring you home. We'll have to wash and iron his hanky for him, won't we?'

She swabbed and tweezed. I screamed.

'He's a nasty horrible old man. I hate him.'

'Now, now, I know you've hurt yourself but there's no need to take it out on Mr Greenidge.'

I lay on the sofa with big bandages on my stiffening knees and plasters on the palms of my hands. Ruby would have to be sorry now. But she didn't know I was hurt. She hated me.

There was a Labour Party meeting that evening, where the main item on the agenda was the forthcoming Grand Guy Fawkes Dance. Every time somebody knocked on our door my heart jumped in the hope that it was Ruby, but it never was. I lay awake late into the night, with my wounds throbbing, listening for the lone cry of the peewit.

Ten

In the morning the bandages had stuck to my pyjama trousers and my legs were so stiff I could hardly walk. I was lying on the sofa listening to *Housewives' Choice*, wondering miserably what Ruby would have thought when I didn't call for her. Would she worry about me at playtime? Who would she play with? Who would be Milk Monitor? Betty came in and sat in the armchair with her feet up on a stool.

'My back's killing me. I wish this baby would get a move on. The thought of two more months of this . . .'

She hummed along with a request for 'The Humming Chorus'.

'I wish it would get a move on too. I wish it could be born tomorrow.'

'Do you, sweetheart? That's nice, well it's not really that long now.'

If I had a baby in a pram with me, I need never be alone with Mr Greenidge again; I would push it in front of me like a shield.

The baby's room was ready, smelling of pale-yellow and white paint. A new cot stood waiting and in the baby's white chest of drawers was a pile of thick soft nappies and tiny vests and long nighties embroidered with rabbits and lambs and matinée jackets. The bottom drawer held bonnets, bootees and mittens and a pea-green woollen buster suit knitted by one of Granny Fitz's regulars at the Drovers. The baby had flannelette sheets and cellular blankets edged with silk from the tally man, and a shawl of snow-white spiders' webs. Mrs Vinnegar had tried to make Betty buy her old pram, which had survived several little Vinnegars including the twins and had been used latterly to carry firewood, shopping, and potatoes and strawberries home from the fields where Mrs Vinnegar helped out from time to time.

'It's all coach-built. A scrub out with Vim and a touch of elbow grease and it'll come up lovely, good as new. Bit of sandpaper on the chrome.'

The thought of Doreen crowing 'that's our old pram' was hideous. Percy had come to the rescue by saying that he had one on order from Swadlincote's in Elmford.

'On the never-never,' Mrs Vinnegar sneered. 'If some people are determined to bankrupt theirselves.'

Percy, who had been in the tea-room, came through carrying a big box of Black Magic.

'Present for the invalid.'

'Dad!'

I had never had a box of chocolates to myself.

'Don't thank me. They're from your knight in shining armour, Sir Greenidge, the Green Knight, not Sir Percival I'm afraid.'

'Oh.'

I saw the pewter knights who stood in the hall at Kirriemuir.

'Isn't that kind,' Betty was exclaiming. 'But a pound box!'

'The Green Knight was bad,' I said.

'Just a joke. Anyway, April, I reckon you should write him a little letter to thank him, don't you?'

I held out elastoplasted palms.

'Use your printing set,' Betty suggested. 'You could manage that and it'll give you something to do. I can't sit here all day. And I suppose we'd better soak those bandages off.'

Percy was singing to the wireless:

'Just Molly and me
And baby makes three –
We're happy in my blue Heaven . . .'

I couldn't even be ill, injured, without Mr Greenidge poking
his nose in. And it was all his fault in the first place.

'You must be feeling poorly. You haven't opened your chocs,'
Percy said.

I tried a feeble smile but my chin wobbled. I suspected that
Mr Greenidge would have said nothing to Mrs Greenidge about
my fall or the chocolates and a letter from me would get him
into trouble.

'Daddy?'

I wanted to tell him everything then, about Mr Greenidge
being in love with me and making me meet him but trying to
speak was like pulling lint and bandages from a bloody knee.

'What's that, sweetheart?'

'Nothing. It doesn't matter.'

'I'll get you a comic later and I expect Ruby'll be round to
check up on you. Now d'you want me to open these for you?
What's your favourite, liquid cherry?'

Dinner time came and went, but Ruby did not. I didn't want
my spaghetti on toast or mug of milk.

'I'm supposed to be Milk Monitor this week.'

'Never mind. You can go back tomorrow.'

Where was she? Why hadn't she come? She really must hate
me. Well, I hate her too then. Perhaps she had told about
seeing me in Lovers Lane with Mr Greenidge. But whom could
she tell? Everybody at school. I imagined their taunts – I know
you now, April – April loves Mr Greenidge. It was chalked on
the playground and scratched on the lavatory wall. *Listen with
Mother* came on the radio with its sad signature tune: Nin a
non, nin a non.

'There's something wrong, isn't there? Besides the Professor,
and falling over, you've been very moody lately,' Betty said the
next morning. It reminded me of the advertisement for California Syrup of Figs: Mother, when a merry child seems

moody . . . I'd never tasted California Syrup of Figs but it sounded delicious.

'Have you fallen out with Ruby, is that it?'

The tears that came to my eyes told her she had got it right.

'Never mind, love, I'm sure you can make up again at school, it can't be that serious.'

I didn't answer.

A wire-netting run had appeared in Ruby's backyard and some long-legged chickens were scratching in the dirt.

'You've got some new chickens,' I said when Gloria opened the door.

'Pullets, They're nothing to do with me. *He* bought them off some bloke in the bar. Ruby's gone, if that's what you've come about.'

'Gone?'

'You *have* been in the wars, haven't you?' She made it sound as though I'd done something stupid. I limped into the playground feeling sorry for myself. In my pocket was the note explaining my absence and asking if I could be excused PT. Miss Fay was always scornful of such requests and found the bearer of them some horrible job to do.

'All in, all in, captain's calling!' Doreen shouted, and six or seven girls, Ruby among them, rushed over to her and got into a huddle. It was much worse than being a new girl. A football hit me on the head and one of the boys pushed me aside. 'Out of my way, stupid.'

Thick, shameful tears rolled down my face. My head was buzzing where the ball had hit it. I wished we had never come to Stonebridge. Homesickness swept over me and I felt completely desolate on the edge of that teeming playground.

'Cry-baby. Duz oo want oo's mummy, den?' came a jeering voice.

More than anything in the world.

Then I felt an arm go round me and heard Ruby's voice. 'You leave my best friend alone, come on, April.'

Miss Elsey was blowing the whistle for us all to get into line.

Everybody was staring at my tear-stained face and bandaged knees.

'Had your eyeful, or d'you want the ha'penny change?' Ruby snapped. 'What happened?' she asked me as we queued up.

'I fell over. After you ran way, I was trying to catch you up to explain.'

'I followed you, why didn't you tell me you were going to meet Mr Greenidge? You said you were going home; what did you go to meet him for?'

'Why did you follow me?'

'Dunno, didn't want to go home, I suppose.'

'I didn't either. I just felt like going for a walk. I didn't know I was going to meet anybody. I couldn't help it if he gave me some sweets, could I? I never wanted them in the first place and he made me put one in his mouth. I was going to save the rest, honest.'

Miss Elsey's whistle chirruped feebly. 'Silence,' she pleaded.

'Don't let's ever quarrel again,' I said.

Half-way through the morning terror gripped me, that Betty would be dead when I got home, but she wasn't.

'Promise me you won't die in childbirth.'

'As if I would.'

After school that afternoon Ruby came round carrying carefully a paper bag containing a dozen pullet's eggs.

'Mum said to give you these.' She handed the bag to Betty.

'Oh, how kind, aren't they little!'

'They're from our pullets.'

The eggs were snowy white, brown and speckled, half the size of hen's eggs, like marbles compared to Bobs's and Dittany's blue-green duck eggs.

'Don't forget to say thank you very much, will you, Ruby?'

I could see that Betty had changed her opinion of Gloria and wanted to be friends, and I was pleased. Then Ruby had to say, 'They're ninepence.'

Gloria had had her hair done for the inquest, at Belinda-Jayne's, and she was wearing a navy blue costume with a gold brooch on the lapel, a white blouse and navy-and-white shoes. With her blonde hair, stretching her mouth to apply fresh lipstick, snapping shut her gold powder compact, she did look like a film star, and she moved in a cloud of scent and cosmetics. You could not have imagined her banging about with a brush and dustpan in a fried-egg, cigarette-ash dressing-gown. Ruby had new black shoes with silver buckles and new white socks, her hair was in loose, crinkly waves, held off her face by two round tortoiseshell slides and she wore a kilt and a red jumper. I was wearing my kilt too, Black Watch, whereas hers was red and yellow, and a blouse with a navy-blue cardigan in blackberry stitch and my hair was in one neat plait tied with a matching tartan ribbon. I held tightly to Percy's hand with my own, whose fingers felt fuzzy because my nails had been cut for the occasion. Percy had brilliantined his curls and he was handsome as a film star too in his charcoal-grey suit with a narrow chalk stripe and black tie, except that he had cut himself shaving and stuck a fleck of cigarette paper on his chin to staunch the blood. He held his hat, which Betty had steamed into shape above the kettle, in his free hand as we went up the steps to the Coroner's Court, the four of us who had travelled into town by bus, in a haze of anxiety and cigarette smoke.

Percy, Ruby and I stopped dead in our tracks in the entrance hall. Professor Scoley was standing there in a black suit, smoking a pipe, talking to Dittany and Bobs. I gripped Percy's hand. Ruby grasped mine. Was he a ghost, or had he never really been dead, or had he come back to life.

'Professor Scoley, this is Mr Harlency and the two little girls, and Ruby's mother, Mrs, er . . .'

'Richards,' said Gloria, 'pleased to meet you I'm sure, but aren't you supposed to be . . . I mean, that's why we're here, isn't it?'

She was the only one of us who hadn't met Professor Scoley, but she was puzzled. Ruby looked as if she were about to be sick, with the freckles seeming to swirl on her white face.

'Supposed to be dead?' said Professor Scoley in his reedy voice, with a bleak smile.

'Professor Scoley is Professor Scoley's brother,' Dittany explained.

'Lionel Scoley.' said the Professor. 'How do you do?'

Percy pumped his hand vigorously clapping him on the arm, as if now that little misunderstanding had been cleared up, we could all get on with enjoying ourselves. Then he put on a solemn face, saying, as the cigarette paper wagged on his chin. 'Allow me to offer my condolences, Professor, tragic business.'

'I take it you're the chap with the wheelbarrow.'

Percy looked embarrassed.

'It was brand new, that was the first time we used it . . .' I said.

A policeman told us all to go in. The panelled room smelled of polish. It was cold and I felt clumpy in my cardigan which had been knitted by a woman in the village who had a brass plaque on her gate which read Miss L. D. Pollard, Machine Knitter – Registered Blind. If it had been me, I'd rather have had a guide dog. The edge of my kilt was scraping my bandages and I wanted to suck my fingers to stop them irritating. I whispered to Percy to take the paper off his chin.

The station-master testified that Professor Scoley had been behaving in an eccentric manner and had travelled without a ticket.

'Would you say, from your experience, that this suggested a deliberate attempt on the late Professor's part to defraud the railway, or might it have been attributable to the absent-mind-edness associated with a man of his calling?'

'I wouldn't know, Sir. All I can say is, he told me he was deaf and dumb and so were those two young girls who came to meet him, and they had failed to purchase platform tickets.' My heart lurched. I felt shamed. There was a policeman and a policewoman there, as well as Constable Cox.

'Should I offer to pay?' I whispered. Percy shook his head. The coroner turned to Professor Lionel Scoley. 'Professor Scoley, would you say that your brother's behaviour as described by Mr Mullard was typical of him or that it suggests that he was feeling unwell? I take it that he was not deaf and dumb, in view of the fact that the purpose of his visit was to deliver a lecture? Professor Scoley?'

'I beg your pardon? Sorry, miles away.'

Our legs were trembling as the policewoman led Ruby and me up to where the coroner leaned over to take in our version of events. Then Percy was called.

'If I'd realized the Professor was ill, I'd have called an ambulance,' he said.

'As it was, you assumed that Professor Scoley was just drunk and you loaded him into the wheelbarrow with the intention of sobering him up before his lecture.'

'Yes sir. When you've been in the licensed trade as long as I have . . .'

'You mustn't blame yourself, Mr Harlency; you did all that could be expected of you in the circumstances.'

The verdict was that Professor Scoley had died of natural causes. Heart failure. Bobs or Dittany was sobbing quietly with an occasional loud sniff.

Outside, it seemed as if nobody knew quite what to do. Professor Scoley was polishing his spectacles with a khaki handkerchief. Percy offered round his cigarette case. Gloria looked cross, somehow disappointed, as if she had her hair done for nothing and she needn't have bothered to buy Ruby those shoes. 'Why don't we all go back to the Rising Sun, for a bit of a . . . pick-me-up?' she suggested, flicking a thread of tobacco from her lip.

'She nearly said "a bit of a knees-up",' Ruby whispered to me, not quietly enough. Gloria cuffed the side of her head. Everybody looked embarrassed, except Professor Scoley, who said 'Jolly good idea,' and we all, except Constable Cox and Mr Mullard, had to pile into his dark-green Alvis.

'Mind your great feet on my nylons. You girls could've gone on the bus,' Gloria grumbled. Then, pretending to be nice, she said, 'That's a pretty cardy, April, did your mum make it?'

'No, it was Miss L. D. Pollard, Blind Machine Knitter.'

'She's not totally blind,' snapped Gloria, making Miss Pollard sound like a cheat who faked all that Fair Isle and blackberry stitches.

Poor Professor Lionel Scoley, I thought and wondered if sometimes he might think he saw his brother Linus when he looked in the mirror. Dittany, who was squashed between him and Bobs in the front seats, was trying to comfort him by repeating that Linus's last words had been of the Lamb.

'My brother was Jewish. We both are.'

'Oh but I am sure God wouldn't hold that against him, in the circumstances.'

Ruby and I started singing quietly, simultaneously, a skipping rhyme we often used:

> 'Nebuchadnezzar the King of the Jews
> Bought his wife a pair of shoes
> when the shoes began to wear
> Nebuchadnezzar began to swear
> When the swears began to . . .'

'Oh, do stop it,' Bobs cried in an agonized voice.

'That's enough,' said Percy sharply. I sulked, fidgeting itchily on his bony knees.

'What do you mean, they've gone to the Rising Sun?' Betty demanded when Ruby and I got back. I explained about Professor Scoley's twin brother. 'Twins, eh? It doesn't seem possible that there should be two of him. Perhaps you'd better get the wheelbarrow ready,' she added nastily.

'Have you been busy, Mum?'

'Rushed off my feet, I don't think. Only your Mr Greenidge and a travelling salesman in ladies underwear.'

We stared at her.

'How did you *know*?' I asked.

At school in the afternoon Miss Fay was casting the Christmas play. Although it was only October, the parts of Father Christmas, the fairy queen, children, reindeer, elves and fairies were handed out. Ruby's and my names were not called. We looked at each other in growing hope and anxiety: either Miss Fay was saving us for something special, or we were not going to be allowed in the play.

Mr Reeves popped his head round the class-room door.

'How's it going, Miss Fay?'

'All done, Mr Reeves.'

She shot a baleful glance at me and Ruby.

'If the mince pies can be trusted not to go gallivanting off to inquests during rehearsals.'

Mince pies. I felt like a mince pie, hot, the edges of my pastry crumbling, as I sank down in my chair.

One of the infants, a tiny, bossy girl called Trina with two big pink bows in her hair, squeezed past Mr Reeves and came into our class-room, saying 'please Miss Fay, Miss Elsey says can she borrow Albie please because somebody's been sick *all* over the floor.'

Albie heaved himself up, gripping the sides of his desk, as if he might throw it over. His face was bright red.

'Just because I'm fat everybody thinks I have to like clearing up sick. Well, I'm sick of it.'

'You've got to,' said tiny Trina, 'Miss Elsey said so.'

We all laughed at this infant bossing Albie around, but Albie looked close to tears.

'It's not fair.'

'Life isn't fair, Albert, as you'll find out soon enough. Now do as you're told and run along and help Miss Elsey at once, quick sharp,' Miss Fay said.

Albie glared at her, without moving.

'It's got nothing to do with your being fat, Albert. Now if you continue to defy me, perhaps we can find somebody else to play Father Christmas, with the aid of a couple of cushions in his costume.'

'Sir, do I have to?' Albie appealed to Mr Reeves.

'You heard what Miss Fay said, now off you go.'

Mr Reeves looked a bit sick himself and you could see that he was just backing Miss Fay up. She didn't seem grateful. Albie lumbered out, muttering under his breath, 'Supposing *I* was sick, who'd clean it up then?' and we heard Trina's piercing voice: 'AND it's gone in the waste-paper basket as well!'

The next time Pat Booker had one of her nosebleeds, Miss Fay dealt with it herself, at arm's length, and when two boys in the top class, Mr Reeves's, were ill after eating all their own Harvest Festival gifts, Albie was not summoned.

I put Michaelmas-daisies and golden rod on the tables in the tea-room. The church at Harvest time was so beautiful it made you catch your breath at the reds, yellows, magentas, of beet-roots, apples, tomatoes, dahlias and chrysanthemums, striped gold and green marrows, wreaths of hops and fluted pumpkins, polished potatoes, blazing sunflowers and an enormous glazed loaf in the shape of a sheaf of corn leaning against the pulpit, and the rustling gold ears of real sheaves. Hundreds of scarlet hands clasped the Rising Sun as the Virginia creeper turned, fluttering and trembling but holding it firm. Rose-hips' red lanterns against the blue sky and the hawthorn's red beads jolted my heart. Ruby and I made necklaces of conkers. I would have been so happy if Kirriemuir's red brick had not bulked at the end of every lane of thought.

'I've got something to show you,' Mr Greenidge said when I brought him his coffee. I stood up from patting Liesel. He took, from his inside pocket, my letter, on toytown stationery with a golliwog stamp, the remains of a babyish post office set.

'I carry it next to my heart,' he said, kissing the envelope and putting it back in his pocket. ' "Love from April." ' I hadn't known what else to put. Percy had given him the letter.

'I hope those pretty knees are not going to be scarred.'

I was hoping they would be. The bandages had been replaced with small plasters now and my hands were quite healed.

'I'm not going to press you,' Mr Greenidge said.

I started nervously although we were alone, imagining myself pressed to his chest.

'I won't nag you into meeting me, I know it isn't fair. I'll just wait until you feel like coming to see me, how's that? Can't say fairer than that, can I? Just don't leave it too long, will you? That's all I ask.'

'Everything all right, Mr Greenidge?' Betty came through as Bobs, wearing a russet-coloured dress, walked in with a basket of mushrooms. Her hair was tied back, in a spotted scarf.

'Tickety-boo, Mrs Harlency.'

Although it wasn't. In some ways it seemed worse, because I would never want to go to Kirriemuir again.

'Dittany and I have been helping ourselves to nature's bounty,' Bobs said, 'and we thought you might like some.'

'Mushrooms on toast, yum, yum.' Mr Greenidge snapped his beak like Wise Owl in Wise Owl's story. 'Where did you find those splendid specimens?'

'Just in the meadow by the river, but there are masses all over the place, this seems to be a bumper year for them. Dittany and I are going to make a study of the local fungi, we might even make a book together, illustrated with woodcuts perhaps, or water-colours.'

'I could do you some on toast, Mr Greenidge,' Betty offered.

'Thank you kindly my dear, but no.' Mr Greenidge stood up, and put some money on the table.

'Methinks I might go a-hunting nature's bounty, myself. A little treat for Mrs Greenidge. My lady wife, alas, cannot get about as much as she would like,' he said to Bobs.

'I know, rotten isn't it? Early mornings and evenings are the best times for picking. Actually there are many more edible fungi than we realize, but one has to be careful, of course.'

'Come, Liesel, my little truffle-hunter.'

Mr Greenidge ruffled my hair on his way out. We heard Liesel snap at Boy who was sitting outside.

'Actually,' Bobs said, 'I believe they use dachshunds for hunting badgers in Germany.'

'Trust them,' said Betty.

'It's not Liesel's fault,' I said, remembering Miss Fay telling us that Londoners had thrown stones at dachshunds in the street in the First World War. Truffle and Nougat was the name of one of the Black Magic chocolates Mr Greenidge had given me.

' "Samuel Palmer: Ancient or Modern?" We'll never know now,' Bobs sighed.

'Well, I suppose there's a bit of the ancient and modern in all of us,' Betty attempted to console. Her mouth twitched as though she were trying not to laugh.

She fried the mushrooms for our tea in bubbling black butter that soaked through the toast.

Eleven

Winter arrived on the fifth of November. The blazing bonfire on the recreation ground roasted our faces while our feet froze in our wellingtons on the muddy grass. A cold, damp pall of gunpowder hung over the village the next day as children collected the dead volcanoes, burnt-out fireworks and twisted sparklers encrusted with cold black lava. Then thick white crunchy frost sparkled everything and made lace curtains on the inside of the windows, and the afternoon sun was a low red lantern lighting the fields. Each morning we hoped that the river would be frozen overnight but although puddles crackled underfoot, the river ran on bitterly brown. Workmen were up on the slippery roof of the village hall repairing the damage done by a volley of rockets on the night of the Labour Party Grand Guy Fawkes Dance. Young Conservatives from the town were under suspicion, although the Vinnegar twins had been questioned as a matter of routine.

Betty had been sitting watching the waltzers gliding over the talcum-powdered floor to the music of Jack Frost and the Frigid-aires when it seemed that a bomb had been dropped. The lemonade leaped out of her glass as the dancers scattered. Nobody was hurt, Jack Frost's baton pointed and the Frigid-aires blitzed into 'Begin the Beguine' and the dance went on. Betty was quite shaken though. Percy and Mrs Morse, the membership secretary of the party, won a spot prize, a bottle of sherry which he had let Mrs Morse have. Nothing to do with her complexion as you might have thought, Betty explained to me, a spot prize was awarded to the couple caught in the spotlight when all the lights were turned off.

It got dark so early that Ruby and I couldn't go far after school, and the long walk to an icy railway carriage was uninviting compared with eating cinnamon toast and hot buttered crumpets in the Copper Kettle. Rehearsals for the school play were underway, and I discovered the role of a mince pie was more taxing than one might have thought. We glued blobs of cotton-wool snow onto the class-room windows and made paperchains and shiny red and green lanterns and cut out holly leaves and berries to stick on Christmas cards to take home for our parents, and when you looked up from your work you thought it really was snowing because the windows looked so pretty and it felt safe and happy inside the class-room with its glowing coke stove where Miss Fay warmed the back of her skirt and dried wet gloves and socks.

On clear frosty nights the pavements sparkled with rime and rang beneath our feet, frozen plants creaked in the gardens and the sky was full of cold flashing stars that seemed as bright as the star of Bethlehem. A magical, glittering transformation had taken place in the Co-op. Ruby and I stood outside, window shopping in clouds of frozen breath, planning what we would buy. You could almost smell the French Fern soap and talc, the Cusson's Apple Blossom, the Bronnley Lemons, the baskets of fruit soaps nestling in tinsel, through the glass; you longed to feel them heavy in your hand and sniff the soft yellow soapy bloom of the lemons, and the green pine cones and the tang of the tangerines. And there were round and rectangular tins of toffees with Father Christmas or kittens or puppies on the lid, and hexagonal boxes of rose-scented Turkish delight dredged in powdery icing sugar, dried figs and glistening dates on their bony stem in an open box whose lid, lying alongside, showed three camels black against an orange desert sky, like the camels of the three kings; and the precious gifts, in the Co-op window, the lipstick in a foil lantern that Ruby wanted for her mother, the crystallized fruits, the scent I was saving up to buy for Betty, glittered like gold and frankincense and myrrh.

Tangerine peel and walnut shells burned with green and blue flames on the red coals of the fire. Flames that flared up like dragon's breath to lick the grains of salt we had sprinkled on the nuts, and sputtered, sometimes a coal spat and split to show its volcanic heart and soft grey ash sifted beneath the grate. Percy was reading, Betty was reading and knitting and I was making Christmas cards. A concert was playing on the radio. My growing disappointment with my crayoned holly and Christmas trees and nativities was compounded when Percy, leaning over the table, said, 'I like this one, of the nun doing her ironing.'

'It's Mary with baby Jesus in the manger!'

'Percy, don't tease – oooh.'

Betty pressed her fist into her back.

'What's up, love?'

'Ow, nothing! Just my back playing up.'

'Are you sure?'

'I think so.'

Percy went to make a cup of tea. When he came back Betty said, 'That's how it started with April. I had chronic backache for two days.'

'But it's not due for another couple of weeks.'

'I know. Still, you never know . . .'

Nothing happened that night, but the next morning I was woken by a sweet spicy smell, and when I went down Betty had already made two dozen mince pies which were cooling on wire racks.

'We've decided it would be best if I took you up to your gran's today, pet,' Percy said, 'to be on the safe side. It looks as though the baby might come early.'

'But it's the school play the day after tomorrow! What about Ruby, she can't do the mince-pie dance on her own!'

A baby cocooned in a white shawl, my brown crêpe-paper

mince-pie costume, flashed through my brain as I flung myself on Betty, clinging to her, the baby bulking between us.

An hour later I was half dragged, half-propelled through the door of the Copper Kettle. My last sight of my mother was blurred by the cotton-wool snow I had stuck to our windows as I tried, finally, to behave like a big, sensible girl. The closed sign was on the door. We hadn't had time to buy the Christmas tree.

Mr Greenidge was coming along the road with Liesel; I knew he would have been watching out for me on my way to school – where Ruby was now, wondering what happened to me and Miss Fay, furious at my missing the dress rehearsal, would have marked me absent on the register. Percy put down my suitcase to speak to Mr Greenidge. I bathed Liesel's neck with tears.

'So we think the stork is on his way?' he twinkled. 'And little missy's off to London town.'

'I don't want to go. I want to stay here and look after Mummy.'

Mr Greenidge slapped his forehead. 'Stupid of me – I wish I'd thought sooner – April could come to us. I'm sure Mrs Greenidge would be delighted.'

I looked at Percy, not knowing what to think.

'It's a kind thought, but her granny's expecting her and it's all arranged. Wouldn't like to disappoint her. Come on, April, or we'll miss our train.'

'Cheer up,' said Mr Greenidge. 'Look on the bright side. This way you'll be home for Christmas.'

He took two shillings from his pocket and gave them to me, looking so kind that for a moment I wished I could go with them.

As we passed the Co-op with its window heaped with treasures, I said, 'I don't see why I have to go at all. It's not as if *I'm* a baby. I can look after myself and you, and the tea-room.'

'We don't know how long your mother will be in hospital and if you're at your granny's I can come and go without having to worry about you. It won't be long and when you come back your baby brother or sister will be waiting for you.'

I saw a stork flapping its big wings over the village holding a baby suspended in a white nappy in its long beak, like the stork from my christening cake, which still tasted faintly of marzipan if you licked its hollow inside. Not that I believed now that the stork brought babies, but I had no knowledge with which to replace the image. Hospital was a grey frightening word; a sign saying HOSPITAL, PLEASE DRIVE QUIETLY hinted at patients lying in high white beds, whose dying must not be disturbed.

I darted round the side of the Rising Sun and stuck a letter to Ruby through the door. Lex was crumbling scotch eggs into the pullets' run. He glared at me, but seeing Percy waiting, called out, 'Cold enough for you?' to him instead of saying something nasty to me.

Mr Mullard, whom we had last seen at Professor Scoley's inquest, gave us our tickets as the train pulled up. I was worried that he would ask for the money for the platform tickets Ruby and I never bought, but he seemed to have forgotten about them. 'Sad business, that, about the Professor. Still, what can you expect?' Percy had gone out to telephone Granny Fitz early and she was meeting us at Herne Hill. He was getting the next train back to Stonebridge. He had bought me some jelly babies and sat opposite me in the train, smoking and watching me.

'Why do you bite off their heads like that?'

'It's kinder than eating their feet first, so they don't feel it.'

'Well it looks horrible.'

Hurt, I stuffed the bag of green, black, red and yellow babies in my pocket. I never asked for them in the first place.

Christmas decorations were up at the Drovers, shiny gold and silver garlands that twisted restlessly to reveal their blue and green undersides, meeting at the huge gold-foil bell hanging from the centre of the high ceiling. The bar was picked out in pointed coloured lights that flashed off and on. Half a dozen silent drinkers were scattered round the vast saloon as we went through. A couple sat at the bar behind which, his back reflected in the mirror among the lights and bottles and glasses, stood Grandpa Fitz polishing a glass. 'Like fairyland, isn't it?' he said, gesturing round the room with his glass cloth.

'Yes, Grandpa.'

Grandpa Fitz was a tall, melancholy-looking man with white hair which had a wide yellow streak, and a yellow moustache flecked with Guinness froth, and a thin cigarette, burning, or gone out, stuck to his lip and another in readiness behind his ear. He had very large ears, flat to the sides of his head but huge and intricate, and he had been deaf in one of them since the First World War. Gerald Fitzgerald had been born in County Antrim, which made me a quarter Irish. He sold me a raffle ticket for the Drovers Grand Christmas Draw.

'I suppose your mum's made all her pies and pudding and the Christmas cake?' Granny Fitz said as we went up to my room.

'Yes, but we haven't iced the cake yet.'

The room was cold and my teeth chattered. Soot pattered into the empty grate.

'Should've been done weeks ago. Have you got your marzipan on at least?'

There was an empty stone hot water bottle on the bed, hard and icy to the touch. I took Bobbity out of my bag and sat him on the shiny yellow quilt.

'I don't care about any stupid Christmas cake.'

'In that case I don't suppose you care about the iced fancies we've got for tea.'

I didn't, but I had to pretend to.

Later that afternoon I overheard Granny talking to a woman in the snug.

'I think it's worse when your daughter's having a baby than having one yourself, don't you? You wish you could go through the pain for them.'

Pain? Although I knew women died in childbirth in books, nobody had told me it hurt to have a baby. I closed my eyes and prayed.

The sheets were freezing and the stone hot water bottle scalding when I lay in bed that night with waves of noise from the pub coming through the floor and a ragged rendering of

'Rudolph the Red-Nosed Reindeer', followed by a female voice breaking like a glass on 'I Saw Mummy Kissing Santa Claus, Underneath the Mistletoe Last Night.'

'Your dad is keeping the books up to date now, I hope?' Granny Fitz said at breakfast. 'Has business picked up at all?'

'Yes.'

'So you've built up a clientele of regulars, have you? Can't rely on passing trade in the winter. Or riff-raff for that matter.'

I saw them sitting in the tea room, the men we made at school from coloured raffia that tasted bitter and could cut your tongue.

'Local ladies coming in for their morning coffee? Afternoon tea?' Grandpa Fitz's eyes were like china marbles with a swirl of grey and red flecks. His hand trembled as he wiped egg from his moustache and his teacup rattled in its saucer. He took the cigarette from behind his ear and tried to light it but the match kept going out. I took the matchbox and struck a match and held it until the cigarette glowed.

'Can I see your Crystal Palace after breakfast, Grandpa? Is it finished yet?' Granny Fitz gave a bitter laugh. Grandpa had been engaged in building the Crystal Palace out of matchsticks. There were to be trees made from twigs and bits of sponge dipped in green paint and the great fountains would be cascades of silver twisted from the paper in cigarette boxes set in lakes of mirror glass, to the amazement of the crowds of pipe-cleaner people.

'Can I, Grandpa?'

'I'd better get on through to give George a hand,' said Grandpa, and went into the public bar where George the barman was clattering glasses.

'It went up in flames, like the original. What they call poetic justice, as somebody in the bar said,' Granny Fitz told me when he was out of earshot. 'Better not mention it again. Broke his silly old heart.'

'Oh poor Grandpa!'

It was a raw, grey morning smelling of ashtrays and carpet dust.

'I wish the baby would hurry up and come. Granny, does it hurt very much to have a baby?'

'No worse than going to the dentist.'

'Gas or Cocaine?' You were given the choice. A needle or smelly rubber mask over your face; children spitting blood into a row of white basins.

'You clear the table while I wash up, and tell your grandpa we're going shopping and we'll be back presently.'

'I've got to buy my Christmas presents but I haven't got much money.'

'Don't let's worry about that.'

I went into the bar. Grandpa wasn't there. 'George, can you tell Grandpa we've gone shopping?'

'Pardon Mrs Arden?' said George, a friendly Geordie with a Hitler moustache that wouldn't grow properly over the scar on his lip.

> 'Pardon Mrs Arden
> Me chicken's in your garden.
> If it wasn't for his liver,
> I'd drown him in the river,'

I said, reminded of the school playground and Ruby.

'Please can you tell Grandpa we're going shopping.'

'OK, Toots,' said George. 'Don't do anything I wouldn't do. Buy me something nice for Christmas, won't you?'

With sinking heart I added George's name to my Christmas list. Even with the two shillings from Mr Greenidge I hadn't got nearly enough money. A ten-shilling note was sticking out of the open till; a flock of butterflies beat their wings inside me. George had gone down to the end of the bar and was stacking crisp packets. I could hear Mrs Lynch the cleaner's carpet sweeper in the saloon.

'April!'

Granny Fitz saved me from becoming a thief but I sat miserably beside her in the bus, sure that she could tell that I was the sort of girl who would rob her own grandparents. I felt guilty, although better at the same time when she took a ten-shilling note from her purse and told me to put it in mine. We went to Bon Marché in Brixton, a grand emporium of delights, and we were sitting with a pot of tea and éclairs after we had finished our shopping when I suddenly remembered Ruby's black eye, when Gloria and Lex had accused her of taking money from the till, and I went hot and cold.

'Granny, if you think of doing something wicked but somebody stops you from doing it, does it still count?'

'Oh I expect so. Depends. Look at the way your jumper's sticking out of the sleeves of that coat. How long have you had it now?' I had unbuttoned my coat, which had once been a shade called Old Rose, with wine-coloured piping. When I stood up my skirt hem hung below it.

'Committing adultery in your heart,' said Granny Fitz.

'I've missed the school play.'

'Never mind. Perhaps you can do it at home for Grandpa and George and me.'

'I don't think so.'

I thought of Ruby doing the Mince-Pie Dance by herself. They would have to change the words of the song, and I knew I would never have dared to sing by myself in front of an audience.

> We are the Mince Pies
> Sugar and Spice.
> Warm us up
> And we taste nice.
> A sprig of holly
> in our tum.
> We are the Mince Pies
> Yum yum yum.

Then we had to lead the plum pudding, the turkey and the yule log into:

> Down the chimney
> Who will come?
> Jolly Old Santa Claus!
> Filling stockings

One by one!
Jolly old Santa Claus!

Miss Fay had written the play herself, about a greedy boy, played by Titchy Vinnegar, who wakes up to find his stocking filled with ashes and soot.

'Betty's been taken in,' Grandpa Fitz informed us on our return. 'Five o'clock this morning. No news yet.'

'Give us a brandy, Gerald, and a bottle of pop for April.'

'I'd love a Babycham,' I said.

'A chip off the old block,' said Grandpa, winking.

'That's enough of that, here's to our little girl,' Granny knocked back her brandy.

A blue haze of smoke hung over the tables, dominoes clacked and a sad-faced woman with wispy hair sitting at the bar raised her frothy glass of milk stout saying, 'To our little girl, God bless her.'

'Take your pop upstairs, April,' Granny said.

It was not until I put on the new coat Granny had bought me, navy blue with a velvet collar, that I realized how cold I had been. I twirled around in front of the long mirror in my grandparents' bedroom admiring myself in the coat, and its matching hat which I knew I would never wear at home. The very thought of the comments it would attract made me cringe and think of Miss Fay's haunting account of a knight running the gauntlet. Her lessons were so full of things I wished I didn't know.

Something woke me in the night, a dream perhaps, that left me feeling frightened. I put my feet onto the cold linoleum and then padded along the corridor, still half asleep, to Granny and Grandpa's room. Their bed was empty, the bed-clothes pushed back. I groped my way down to the public bar. Granny was there in her dressing-gown and Grandpa with a cardigan over his pyjamas, and George wearing a purple silk dressing-gown and Arabian Nights slippers. The fairy-lights were twinkling round the bar.

'Here she is!' said Grandpa. 'Come and wet the baby's head.'

'You've got a lovely little baby brother,' Granny hugged me, her face wet with tears.

'Is Mummy all right?'

'Both doing fine. She and Daddy send their love.'

I had a fleeting sense of miles between us, the distance to a blurred nativity scene.

Grandpa was singing, ' "It's a boy, it's a boy, it's a something, something boy." '

He poured cherry brandy into a liqueur glass and handed it to me. I sipped liquid fire. George went over to the piano and struck up, singing along,

> 'Sweetest little fellow anybody knows.
> Don't know what to call him
> But he's mighty like a rose – '

He broke off. 'Why don't they just call him Rose?

> 'Smilin' at his mummy
> With eyes so shining blue
> Makes you feel that heaven
> Is comin' close to you.'

Granny joined in and Grandpa said, 'Weighed in at 7lbs 12oz. What a little champ, eh?'

Bittersweet melting cherries slid down my throat and happiness unfolded in the petals of a crimson rose and the sun blazed out in my head.

'Hey, everybody, I've got a brother!'

'No more lonely only,' said George.

A red jewel flashed in my chest and fairy-lights flicked off and on, dappling our faces with soft puffs of colour and the shining foil garlands swayed and twisted gently and I felt pure diamond-faceted joy.

Twelve

Peter was a little marzipan boy; he was like the eskimo on the Christmas cake, with his face peeping out of his white shawl; he was a vanilla ice-cream, Peter Nicholas Harlency. From the beginning he was in danger of being cannibalized.

'Look at those little legs!' cried Granny Fitz. 'Couldn't you just eat them?' And Betty took playful bites from his talcum-powdered bottom as if it were a doughnut smothered in icing sugar. We were all head-over-heels in love. Peter's dark fuzz of hair was like thistledown when you kissed his head.

Granny and I arrived at the Copper Kettle on the morning of Christmas Eve. She had to get the train back in the afternoon, and Percy had arranged for the taxi, from the Three Brewers.

I stood in my new coat and hat and gasped at the beauty of our room, the Christmas tree and paper garlands, before falling into my mother's arms. Percy had met us at the station and as we walked past the Rising Sun I begged to stop to say hello to Ruby.

'Plenty of time for that later,' Percy said.

I gave the lone cry of the peewit but Ruby did not appear.

'I'll see her at the crib service anyway,' I said. 'We can still go, can't we?'

'Don't see why not, just you and me though. I don't think your baby brother's up to singing carols yet.'

'Bless his little cotton socks,' added Granny. There were just two clouds in my frosty, sparkling sky. One was in the shape of the turkey which I had unfortunately won in the Drovers Tavern Christmas raffle, a huge pink thing that Granny had insisted on bringing with us. It had been beheaded and you could see dark pockmarks in its goose-fleshed skin where the feathers had been plucked out, and its claws had been cut off leaving yellow stumps filled with dried blood. The other cloud was a red-brick house called Kirriemuir. I had a hard red rubber bone in my bag, Liesel's Christmas present, which squeaked when you rubbed it on your front teeth, and smelled of the dentist's. But when to deliver it? Perhaps I would push it through the letterbox and run away.

Percy and I stood at the back door of the Rising Sun. Lex opened it, in a white shirt with sleeves rolled high and tight over his tattooed biceps and his belly bulging.

'What d'you want?'

I held Percy's hand tightly.

'We wondered if Ruby was coming to the crib service,' he said.

'What? No, she isn't, it's Christmas Eve, in case you hadn't noticed, and I've got a pub to run.'

He started to shut the door.

'Hang on a minute,' Percy put his foot in the door. 'That's why we're here, because it's Christmas Eve. There's a special service for the kiddies at the church and I'm sure Ruby would like to be there.'

'Oh are you? Well, you can mind your own bloody business. You've got a nerve coming here, trying to turn my kid against her family, giving her ideas. I know your game, mate. Bleeding commie!' He was squeezing Percy's shoe in the door.

'Just a minute, *mate*. Who are you calling a commie? If you paid your own kid a bit of attention instead of . . .'

Percy was forced to withdraw his foot. He was as thin as a curly-haired elf compared with Lex, who was giving off gusts of angry, stale sweat.

'Merry Christmas to you, too, pal! Come on, pet, I'm sorry

you had to witness that. Effing B, pardon my French. Not fit to have a child on the premises – some people shouldn't be allowed to have children.'

I had to run to keep up with him, on the sparkling pavement, past white hedges, under bright holy stars, past the Co-op's enchanted cave. The bells of St Michael and All Angels were ringing, and people walking to church called out greetings to each other.

'Put your hat on, April,' said Percy, taking his off at the church door.

'I can't, somebody might see.'

Hundreds of night lights placed all around the church, on the rood screen and under the stained-glass windows and round the font, dipped and doubled through my tears, the candles and the brass chandeliers dazzled and fused the aisle into an avenue of rainbows. It was the most special night of the year and Ruby wasn't there. When Mr Oswald led the choir through the church singing 'Once in Royal David's City' a grey salty sob racked my chest. Boys became angels walking in clouds of incense through the cold air that smelled of wax and mysteries, processing to the choir stalls past the thatched stable on the steps where Mary and Joseph knelt with the shepherds and ox and ass, and I understood that Jesus in the manger had been a baby just like Peter.

I could not speak when we stood outside after the service. Mr Oswald was in the church porch shaking people's hands and wishing them a happy Christmas. I smiled shyly at children I knew, embarrassed at having been crying.

'Very touching, wasn't it?'

The Greenidges, Mrs Greenidge tapping the frosty paving stones with a silver-headed stick, walked right behind us.

'I saw that our little April was quite moved,' Mr Greenidge went on. 'Had to pipe m'own eye, I don't mind telling you.'

'I hear congratulations are in order,' said Mrs Greenidge. 'A little boy just in time for Christmas.'

'Yes indeed. Well done old chap. Got your pigeon pair now!' Mr Greenidge clapped Percy on the back.

'You might take my arm, Clement, this path is like an ice

rink. I think you'll find that "a pigeon pair", strictly speaking, refers to twins.'

Like Professor Scoley and Professor Scoley.

'Merry Christmas, Merry Christmas,' people were saying. Mrs Vinnegar's voice came through the darkness. 'Get off that grave or I'll brain you. Right, I'm telling Santa Claus not to come. I've warned you!! I'll give you "While Shepherds Washed Their Socks by Night"!'

'Pop in sometime over Christmas April, Liesel's got a little present for you,' said Mr Greenidge.

'Has she?' said Mrs Greenidge. 'She didn't tell *me.*'

Bobs and Dittany caught up with us.

> 'Torches, torches,
> Run with torches
> All the way to Bethlehem'

Dittany sang, swooping the light of her torch in circles. They were wearing knitted hats and scarves and Bobs had stuck a sprig of holly in her lapel.

'Oh, it's all such a wonderful mixture of the pagan and medieval! One feels just like a druid cutting the sacred mistletoe and yet one falls on one's knees before the crib in the simple unquestioning faith of one's rude forefathers! "Welcome Yule, Thou Merry Man",' she sang.

'Are you going to hang up your stocking, April?' Dittany asked. 'We are.'

Worried for them, I looked up at the sky, but the stars were so bright it was easy to believe in Father Christmas and his sleigh shimmering and jingling over the rooftops.

The Rising Sun looked as pretty and inviting as an iced gingerbread house and sounds of mirth and jollity, 'Good King Wenceslas' on the old joanna, came through windowpanes shiny as sweets. Ruby's bedroom window was dark.

A thin cry, that expanded like a concertina, woke me in the middle of the night. There was something heavy at the end of the bed and glimpsing a reindeer's antlers by the door, which was ajar, I shut my eyes tight. I couldn't believe it and yet my heart was pumping wildly in restored credulity. In the morning while it was still dark I jumped out of bed and switched on the light. Where the reindeer had stood was a pale-green bicycle. I cycled, with difficulty, the short and narrow road to my parents' room with my bulging stocking draped over the handlebars. Their light was on and Betty was propped up on pillows feeding Peter. We all had breakfast in the big bed with Christmas carols on the radio. Everything in my stocking was magical, from the tiny gold candlesticks, the china horse, the glass tube of little silver balls that you used to decorate cakes, coloured pencils, a diary, a seagull brooch, pale-green angora gloves that matched my new bicycle, to the glass snowstorm ball that made a blizzard when you shook it, that drifted over the tiny house inside, and a pearly handled penknife. Betty was thrilled with her bottle of lavender water and the stockings Granny Fitz had helped me choose and Percy was delighted with his socks. I had also cajoled a bottle of cherry brandy from Grandpa for them to share.

'Go on, Dad, open it, it's the most delicious drink you've ever tasted. It makes you really happy.'

'Bit early in the day for me.' He gave me a peculiar look. 'Well I'd better get that turkey in the oven.'

'I'm not having any,' I said at once.

'To tell you the truth, I don't really fancy it either,' Betty said.

'Oh well, in that case – but what can we do with it? Seems wrong just to throw it away.'

'Give it to a poor man gathering winter fuel.'

'Put it out for the birds,' Betty said. 'No, I take that back – what a horrible thought. Why couldn't you have won something nice like a cake or crackers?'

'I tried to give it to George,' I said, 'but he wouldn't take it. He said: "God knows how long those giblets have been inside it." '

I had given him a miniature bottle of whisky for Christmas, knowing he would be pleased. 'Coals to Newcastle,' he had said.

'I'll throw it in the river,' I said. 'When I go out on my new bike.'

'OK. Don't tell anybody though, April, you do know your bike's second-hand, don't you? But it's got a new saddle and a new bell and brake blocks and Daddy spent ages painting it for you.'

'It's the best bike in the world.'

To my amazement Ruby was standing outside the Rising Sun looking miserable and holding the handlebars of a gleaming brand-new red bicycle with flashing chrome and a saddlebag.

'Go on, ride it up and down the street. Get out there and show the bloody thing off!' Lex came out after her. 'Get up on that flaming saddle when I tell you.'

He saw me and smiled, showing yellow wolf's teeth. It was the first time I had seen him smile, and it was scary.

'Morning, young April! Merry Christmas. See Ruby's lovely new bike that she got for Christmas? Supersonic, eh?'

'Merry Christmas, Mr Richards.' I dismounted from my bicycle which, to my shame, had shrunk and seemed a sickly green beside Ruby's crimson steed. I gave its saddle a reassuring pat.

'Why don't you girls go for a nice ride, seeing as April's got her old bike. Dad paint it up for you, did he? This one cost me a packet, I'll tell you, but only the best for my little girl, eh Ruby?'

'I'm just going to get your present.' Ruby leaned her bicycle against the frosty hedge. Her mouth was all rough and frayed round the edges, as if she had smeared on a pink clown's mouth.

'Mind the paint with those bleeding twigs,' said Lex.

Ruby returned with a brown paper bag.

'Come one, let's get out of here,' she said, putting it in her saddlebag.

'Ruby! don't be late for dinner now.' Gloria called from the kitchen. 'Oh, April, tell your mum I'll be round to see the new baby soon.'

Why were Lex and Gloria pretending to be nice to me? I couldn't believe they'd bought that brand-new bicycle for Ruby.

My own bicycle, unbalanced by the bag on the handlebars containing the turkey and Ruby's Christmas present, wobbled all over the place as we rode alongside each other.

'I like your bike.'

'I like yours. Where shall we go?'

'I've got loads of things to tell you.'

'I've got to go down the river to throw this turkey in.' I explained about the bird.

'I know,' Ruby said, 'why don't we dump it on old Boddy's doorstep?' Her fingers were going dead from the cold.

We tipped the turkey, tied up in greaseproof paper, onto the step of the shop and pedalled away laughing into a keen, cutting wind that tore our breath away, shouting, 'Merry Christmas, Mr Boddy!'

'Let's go back to my house,' I yelled. 'You can see our baby.'

It was still difficult to realize that Peter was really there, and would always be here now, with his crying like an orange-coloured paper concertina.

Peter closed his hand round Ruby's finger when she held his.

'He loves me, look!' she said in a tone of wonder. After a minute I wanted him and jiggled around impatiently beside her. Peter opened one eye and then the other. 'Oh, his little blue eyes, they're as blue as sapphires. Look at him looking up at me, Mrs Harlency. Oh, I wish he was mine.'

'You can come and play with him whenever you like,' Betty said. 'Your mouth looks sore, you should put a bit of Germoline on it. Don't lick it, you'll make it worse.'

'Let's go up to my room,' I said.

'Happy Christmas, April.' Ruby took a parcel from her brown paper bag. It was wrapped up in a comic and tied with string. Inside was the box of April Violets soap and talc from the Co-op window.

'Oh Ruby, it's lovely. Thank you.'

'You can read the comic and the string might be useful.'

I folded the comic carefully and looped the string into a neat figure of eight, feeling sad, and buried my face in the cold sweet fragrance of spring.

'Here's yours. Happy Christmas.'

'Pretty paper. I would've got some only I didn't have time.'

My absence and Peter's arrival had made us shy with each other. We both knew that Ruby hadn't been able to afford any wrapping paper and I couldn't say that it couldn't matter less.

'Go on, open it. Shall I tell you what it is?' I urged, knowing she would love it.

It was a jewellery set with glass beads, in separate compartments, that you could make into necklaces and bracelets.

'They look like real jewels,' Ruby said. 'Diamonds and rubies and sapphires and emeralds.' She touched each shimmering tray with awe.

I showed her my penknife. We had both hoped for a knife.

'Did you get one?'

She shook her head.

Downstairs again, Ruby pulled something from her pocket.

'I forgot. I've got a present for Peter.' It was a woollen pom-pom, grey, brown and green, in which I recognized threads of an unravelled kettle holder.

'It's beautiful, Ruby. He'll love looking at that. Let's hang it up in his pram for him. Peter's got something for you, too!'

Peter gave Ruby a box of Payne's Poppets.

When Ruby had gone Betty said to me, 'What's up with you?'

'Just because you like Ruby and Peter better than me!'

I gave the little lamb, hanging on blue ribbon from a pale blue ring, which I had bought in Bon Marché with Granny's money, a vicious flick.

'Ruby's present was special, because she made it herself. I'm surprised at you, April. I thought you'd understand.' She stroked the hair back from my forehead. I did understand, and I wished I'd made a stupid pom-pom.

The kitchen was full of steam and the smell of roasting potatoes and brussels sprouts and chestnut stuffing. The Christmas pudding was jumping about in a saucepan, rattling the saucer Percy had put on top of its basin. The table was set with a cracker at each place, a bowl of walnuts and tangerines at the centre and sprigs of holly stuck behind the calendar, the colander on the shelf, the utensils hanging on the wall.

'Who needs a turkey as long as we're all together?' said Percy.

It was only later, at tea-time, when we were all wearing paper hats and the mince pies came out of the oven, that I realized I had forgotten to ask Ruby about the school play. She had said she had lots of things to tell me, but she hadn't said much at all. I didn't even know what she had got in her stocking.

Boxing Day brought a powdering of snow and Doreen Vinnegar and Pat Booker on new roller skates knocking on the back door to ask, 'Can we take your baby for a walk?'

'He's too little to go out yet and it's too cold,' Betty told them. She was still in her dressing-gown, tired from looking after Peter in the night.

'Over my dead body,' Percy said as Doreen and Pat skittered away, holding on to each other, shrieking and falling in a heap. Doreen had had her ears pierced with gold sleepers. We were opening up because people liked to get out and about on Boxing Day. I had collected up the charms and scraps from the crackers and felt depressed and flat.

'Don't forget to go and see the Greenidges sometime today to get your present. Why don't you go now, before we're busy?' Percy suggested.

'Some hopes of that,' said Betty.

'All right. Get it over with I suppose.'

'Hey, that's not the attitude.'

The handlebars burned like ice even through my gloves.

'Yesterday's capon, cold with caper sauce,' said Mr Greenidge heartily, as we went through to the drawing-room. My lip, cracked by the cold, was bleeding from his kiss when he opened the front door. 'My darling, my darling, how I've missed you.'

'Merry Boxing Day, April. You're bright and early. We were hoping you would come at tea-time. Suppose I can't offer you a festive sip of sherry?' he said in the drawing-room. Mrs

Greenidge was wearing a silky dress patterned with dull red and green diamonds.

'I wouldn't say no to a drop of ruby port,' I said, like Granny Fitz. The Greenidges laughed.

'Speaking of whom,' said Mrs Greenidge, 'how is your little friend? Chin Chin!'

'Cheerio,' said Mr Greenidge.

'She's very well thank you, she got a new bicycle for Christmas too, like me.'

'Did she, egad!'

Mr Greenidge raised an eyebrow at Mrs Greenidge, who said, 'Mrs Cooper who "does" for me mentioned that Mrs Carter had told her there had been some sort of trouble at the school play?'

They were both looking at me greedily. I felt ill.

'How should I know? I wasn't there, was I?'

'Hoity-toity,' said Mr Greenidge.

'Never mind, we'll hear it on the grapevine eventually,' Mrs Greenidge said.

'Bush telegraph,' Mr Greenidge said. I had no idea what they meant. Miserable and aware of having been rude I stared at their cards on the mantelpiece, most of which were very boring, thick and white with engraved writing and little flicks of red or blue ribbon, but I was seeing our school canteen, that smelled of dinners and trying to imagine what trouble there could have been.

'She never said anything to me.'

The ruby port spiralled like a red glass Christmas decoration down my throat and suddenly I wanted to cry so I bent down to hide my face in Liesel.

'I've brought Liesel's Christmas present.'

Even as I pulled it out of my pocket I saw a blue rubber bone on the floor. None of us mentioned it and Liesel trotted off, to chew her new red bone, showing no interest when I unwrapped my present from her. It was a book, *Black Beauty*, with a beautiful coloured frontispiece and I was delighted, so my thanks were genuinely heartfelt. I had been dreading having to pretend to like some crummy present, laughing my girlish laughter.

'Happy reading,' said Mrs Greenidge. 'I don't think I ever got over the death of poor Ginger.'

I could have gazed at Peter's sleeping face, as he lay in my arms, for ages. I wanted to run my finger along his miniature dark eyelashes and trace the coral triangle of his mouth, but the tea-room, looking a bit dusty, had to be opened for business.

'Perhaps we should have kept that turkey for sandwiches,' Percy said.

'What, and poison everybody, like old Ma Vinnegar?' said Betty. 'And get closed down by the authorities. She'd love that. Can't you just see her crowing over us?'

'Anyway, who wants yesterday's capon with cold caper sauce, whatever that might be when it's at home. Dad, did you hear anything about the school play, about any trouble or anything?'

'Hardly – your mother and I were otherwise engaged at the time if you remember. Why?'

'Oh, nothing, I forgot to tell you that Gloria said she'd be round to see the baby soon.'

'Oh dear, I mean, how nice. Mrs Richards, to you.'

Percy was serving the old couple who sat like spotted lizards in walking boots at the table in the window.

'A tasty snack? I can do you beans on toast topped with one of our special fresh pullet's eggs, Welsh rarebit, fried Christmas pudding.'

They decided on the rarebit, being Welsh themselves. A solitary cyclist was wolfing down baked beans. I went through to make a fresh pot of tea for him and came back just as the door crashed shut. I saw a black balaclava and a bucking bicycle through the glass.

'Funny. I could swear that was young Rodney Pegg. Yes, I'd spot that acne'd phizog anywhere. Took one look at me and scarpered. Well, good riddance. Thought we'd seen the last of him,' said Percy.

Gloria arrived with Ruby. 'Brought you a couple of bottles

of stout to keep your strength up. Careful with them. They got a bit shaken in Ruby's saddlebag, on her new bicycle.'

I hated the way Lex and Gloria kept boasting about Ruby's bike, as if we hadn't noticed it was brand new.

Gloria touched Peter's cheek with a red nail.

'Proper little Bobby Buster, isn't he? I always wanted a boy, but it wasn't to be.' She sighed. 'I had to get landed with a tomboy. Just my luck.'

As Ruby and I went up to my room, abandoning Betty to Gloria, I heard Gloria whining, 'I hope you won't take any notice of any wicked rumours, Mrs Harlency. People can be so cruel with gossip. You know me better than to believe everything you hear, don't you?'

I stopped to listen.

'People are spreading all sorts about us and the takings are right down. You know a kiddie was never more doted on than our Ruby. She's the apple of her dad's eye.'

Gloria was wheedling like a gipsy selling clothes pegs at the door.

'You do your best for them and this is the thanks you get.'

'Come on, April.'

I followed Ruby into the bedroom with a feeling of dread.

'Tell me about the school play, you haven't said anything yet. Did you do the dance on your own all right?'

'It was OK,' Ruby mumbled. She had gone pale and her freckles stood out on her skin, puckered by the cold bedroom air. 'Only I missed you. I felt a right lemon doing it on my own. Pat Booker was supposed to take your part but she got stagefright. The hunt stopped in our yard this morning for a stirrup cup. It was horrible. They call it the Boxing Day Meat.'

'Why?'

'Search me.'

'Mrs Greenidge said Mrs Carter said there'd been some trouble with the school play.'

Ruby sat down on the bed, turning my snowstorm ball over and over making blizzards, her pigtails falling on either side.

'Mrs nosey parker Carter should mind her own blooming beeswax.'

'Ruby! Mrs Carter's nice. She's our friend!'

'Oh, all right then. Mrs Carter was helping us get changed into our costumes and she saw all these bruises on my back and arms and she called Mr Reeves and he got Dr Barker to come round the school, and now she's spreading rumours all through the village.'

Ruby stared into the glass ball.

'What bruises? What did Dr Barker say?'

'Where I fell down the cellar steps, fetching some lemonade.' She wouldn't look at me.

'That's why they bought me the bike, so's people would think they were nice.'

'Did you fall down the cellar steps?'

She raised her head at last.

'I wish we lived in the little house in the snow. Just the two of us, and Peter. No grown-ups. Nobody could get us through the glass.'

'Ruby!' came Gloria's voice. 'Come along, and mind those stairs!'

'Have you still got the bruises? Let me see.'

She shook her head. 'I'm not allowed to.'

'Get a move on, Ruby, I can't stand here all day, I've got a pub to run.'

A sudden flash of sunshine turned Gloria's hair to spun gold and her voice was dripping like a golden honeycomb over her teeth as she tightened the elastic band on one of Ruby's plaits saying, 'Thanks ever so, Mrs Harlency. It's good to know who your friends are. Come on, sweetheart, or Dad'll be wondering where we've got to.'

'What a dreadful business,' said Betty when they had gone.

'What?'

'Oh – never you mind. I dare say it'll all blow over soon. Gossip is a terrible thing, April. It can lead to all sorts of unhappiness. You have to feel sorry for Gloria.'

'I don't think Ruby did fall down the stairs. I bet they pushed her and locked her in the cellar.'

'What?' Betty looked upset. 'Of course they didn't. That's

exactly what I've been trying to tell you, talk like that is dangerous and wicked. It can destroy people's lives. Go and give your father a hand in the tea-room.'

'She's had a poison pen letter,' I heard Betty tell Percy later.

Poison pen? It sounded evil and yet more exciting than the invisible ink Ruby and I made from onion juice. I imagined a fountain pen speckled like a snake squirting venom from its nib, and the recipient of a letter falling to the floor, with the poisoned paper crumpled in her hand. It obviously hadn't worked with Gloria though. Who in Stonebridge could possess such a pen?

'Smacks of a witch-hunt to me,' said Percy.

Gloria as a golden-haired witch on a broomstick, hunted up the village street.

I shivered.

'Mind you,' he went on, 'I wouldn't trust that tub of lard Lex further than I could throw him, which isn't very far.'

'It breaks my heart to think of that poor little bruised mince pie doing her little song and dance,' said Betty.

'A real little trouper.'

And what about me? I couldn't even be a mince pie, thanks to some people. A trouper, a witch and a tub of lard. Confused, thoroughly miserable and irritable, I went out to the shed to clean the spokes of my bike. My jumper was itchy and the cold wind hurt my hair. I leaned the bicycle against the wall and sat on the saddle pedalling backwards, until the chain came off. I bruised my knuckles putting it back on and got oil all over my hands.

I went inside and said I was going to see Bobs and Dittany; Betty was changing Peter's nappy.

'Put your coat on then, your old one,' she said with a pin in her mouth. 'And don't be long.'

My pink coat felt thin and silly now, with my checked skirt hanging down in a frill below it. I stomped along in my wellies. Needles from the Christmas tree had sewn themselves into my cuffs and were pricking my wrists.

'That tree's shedding at a rate of knots,' Percy had remarked. 'Roll on twelfth night say I. Get the brush and dustpan, April.'

Dittany was at the kitchen sink, washing dishes, wearing a man's shirt streaked with paint over a black sweater and trousers, men's socks bulging over black ballet slippers.

'You look thoroughly out of sorts,' she said.

'I am'

'Just give this wassail bowl a wipe, will you. You'll find a dry tea towel on the Aga.'

She lifted an enormous painted china bowl dripping bubbles onto the soggy wooden draining board. The sad bright sound of jazz came from the sitting-room.

'Professor Scoley, Lionel, that is, has given Bobs some of Linus's revivalist jazz records, which was very generous of him in the circumstances.'

'He had a dicky ticker. It could have happened any time. He was like a time bomb just waiting to go off, my dad says.'

'Oh yes, that's the party line, I know. But I can't help feeling that if we hadn't invited him to Beulah House . . .' Dittany wrenched the plug from the sink making a bitter gurgling sound as the water ran away.

'Please don't say "dickey ticker" again, April. It sounds so – so knowing and unchildlike.'

Rebuked, my eyes stinging, I went into the sitting-room where Bobs was kneeling among scattered records in brown paper cases.

'Mind your feet,' she said, too late, as a black crack exploded under the toe of my boot. Our horrified eyes met.

'Never mind, put it in the waste-paper basket quickly and we won't even look at it. Don't cry, it doesn't matter.'

I knew it did matter.

'Do you like this music?'

I nodded tearfully.

'My dad likes jazz, Be-bop.'

Bobs shuddered.

'Why does everything have to be so horrible after Christmas?' I said.

A sticky date, fluffy with dust, lay in the bottom of the waste-paper basket.

'What kind of music does Betty like?'

'Lots. Songs. Opera. Concerts. She could've sung in opera.'

'I'm sure she could have,' said Bobs.

A picture she had painted was on the wall, among many others, of an old black barn held up or pulled down by the ivy that covered it and its door sagging open to show a spilt sack of cattle cake and a heap of old car tyres. You could almost taste the brown nugget of cow cake, hard, dry and dusty in your mouth and impossible to bite through.

Pinned up too were delicate water-colours of mushrooms and toadstools, mauve, purple, orange and lemon, pale umbrellas on slender stalks, fans, frills and wafers on lichen, speckled tree stumps, stalks clumped with leaf mould and gills radiating in soft wheels.

> 'Basin Street
> is the street
> Where all the light and dark folks meet.
> Down in New Orleans,
> The land of dreams . . .'

Bobs sang.

'Look at this,' she said, handing me an old black photograph album, with a stippled cover and spider's web paper between its black pages. 'I found it in the attic. It's Beulah House when it was still an orphanage.'

There, on a faded photograph, was the white house with its bell tower and a blur of white wings and fantails round the dovecot.

'Look at this one.'

A group of small children in pinafores, graded by height, were sitting on the grass. The smallest had their legs in knitted stockings and hobnail boots sticking straight out in front of them and all their hair was very short and they stared into the camera with big sad eyes.

'Are they boys or girls?' I asked.

'Both,' said Bobs.

There was a photograph of older boys in knickerbockers and stockings and collars, like the picture on the Fry's Five Boys chocolate, and bigger girls in pinafores with butterfly sleeves over dark dresses, and a bunch of children swinging their black legs over the sides of a wagon in an orchard of white blossom.

'That could be our orchard!' I said without thinking.

'Which orchard?'

'Oh, just a place I saw once.'

'These are the best,' said Bobs taking a postcard from the back of the album. Fairies and elves with tinted wings capered, holding Chinese lanterns among toadstools and glimmering glow-worms, and all the fairy folk had the cropped hair and hurt faces of orphans.

'Elfin Revels,' said Bobs.

'I wonder what became of them all.'

'Oh, some of them in churchyard lie, and some are lost at sea,' said Bobs lightly, closing the album. Seeing my face, she added, 'I expect they all got married and lived happily ever after. Actually, I believe old Miss Brindle in the almshouses was a Beulah girl. The last of the orphans were sent down under not so very long before we bought the place.'

'Down under? Buried?'

'Of course not, sent to Australia.'

'Transported?'

'No, don't be silly. They went to kindly Antipodean folk who wanted children of their own. It was a wonderful opportunity for them, sailing away to a new life.'

'Supposing their parents came back to look for them and they couldn't find them because they'd gone to Australia?'

'They were *orphans*, April. You are in a morbid mood.'

'But if their parents were ghosts'

'I'm sure that ghosts would know where to find them. Anyway, they wouldn't be ghosts, they'd be angels watching over their children.'

Suddenly it seemed a sad house with the wind howling in the chimney. I thought of the orphans on the deck of a liner on the vast grey ocean, and I wanted to be at home, with my own family.

'I don't think Ruby got anything in her stocking. I don't think she even hung it up,' I told Bobs. 'They've got all their decorations up in the pub, and the Christmas tree, and none at all in the house.'

'Oh, dear. Well, at least she's not an orphan.'

Thirteen

It was a mild, damp morning, green and gold like the Christmas decorations at the Drovers, where the sun struck drooping laurel leaves and prickly sparkling holly hedges. I was waiting outside Crosby's with the pram while Betty was shopping. The sunshine had put us both in a good mood, but when she came out she looked flustered. Mrs Vinnegar drew up alongside us with her old pram.

'Morning, Mrs H.'

'Morning, Mrs Vinnegar.'

Mrs Vinnegar leaned over Peter and pinched his little chin in the ravelled thumb and finger of a grey glove.

'I'll eat you up, yes I will! Yes I will!'

It was already clear to me that Peter had done something extraordinarily clever by just having been born a boy, and all he had to do was lie there in a pale-blue knitted helmet and even old Ma Vinnegar worshipped him.

'I've just been talking to Mrs Edenbridge-Dwyer. Have you ever heard of this "churching of women" lark she was on about?'

'You don't want to take no notice of *her*. She tried that one on me after I had little Juney. Churching, I said, I should cocoa, I haven't done nothing to be churched *for*, thank you very much.'

'But she is the president of the Mother's Union,' said Betty.
'So what?'

When Mrs V. had gone into the shop Betty said to me, 'The point is, Mrs Edenbridge-Dwyer is the sort of person who ought to be coming into the Copper Kettle. It's all very well for old Vinegar Bottle, I mean Mrs Vinnegar, to take that attitude. Some of us are trying to make some social headway in this village.'

'Oh, no. There comes Miss Fay, quick let's cross over.'

Too late. Miss Fay was dismounting from her tall bicycle and neatly kicking the pedal onto the kerb to make it stand up straight. She was wearing a blue peaked hat-and-scarf in one tied under her chin, headgear known to Ruby and me as a Fayhat.

'So this is little Master Harlency, who disrupted our Christmas concert.'

Miss Fay stripped off one of her cycling gauntlets to poke Peter's tummy through the blanket, telling him off before he'd even started school.

'Such a pity they have to grow up,' she said, with a bitter look at me. 'Mrs Harlency, I wonder if I might have a word?'

'Oh, certainly, Miss Fay. April, you walk on ahead with the pram and I'll catch you up.'

'What did she say? Was it about me not being a mince pie? Did you tell her it wasn't my fault?'

I was terrified by what tales Miss Fay might tell, or that I had done something dreadful which I had forgotten about. Betty took over the pram.

'Nothing much. Nothing to do with you. Why, got a guilty conscience?'

'No.'

'You don't want to worry about it, she's got nothing better to do with her time than impose archaic ceremonials on the working classes. We can do without her sort,' said Percy when Betty told him about Mrs Edenbridge-Dwyer.

'But can we?'

Percy had been passing his time with a copy of the *Daily*

Worker delivered by Mr Silver, while we were out. Joe Silver ran the local Communist Party; he had tried to save the Rosenbergs too. They had two little boys, and they were sent to the Electric Chair. He was like a kind uncle to all the children and some people called him Uncle Joe after Joseph Stalin who had died the year before, and good riddance, said Percy. Joe and his wife Molly and their three sons lived in the old Paper Mill, a wooden building weathered like Dittany's beehives, which stood on an island in the river overlooking the deep, wide pool made by a stone dam where water roared in a boiling white waterfall in the winter. Joe Silver was a businessman who owned, among other establishments, a button factory in the East End, Harlequin Buttons, and the Silvers were known for many acts of kindness to people whatever their affiliation. Molly regularly drove old folks from the almshouses to the hospital and she had spoken up for the Vinnegar twins at the juvenile court more than once. Nevertheless there were those, such as Mr Oswald, and Mrs Edenbridge-Dwyer and Lex Richards, who despised the Silvers. Ruby and I had once watched, through a gap in the hedge, two beautiful Indian ladies in saris, like butterflies playing tennis, visitors in shimmering wings from another world, and as they fluttered in that glamorous moated garden which we would have liked so much to enter, bracelets of gold and silver and coloured glass rolled up and down their arms with each shot and return of the ball.

The three Silver boys travelled by train to a grammar school, wearing claret and navy blazers and caps. I was always pleased on the rare occasions when Leo, the youngest, accompanied his father on the *Daily Worker* round. Leo was dark and skinny and looked a bit like a monkey with his soft crew cut and straight legs. He wore glasses and was very brainy. Although he was older than I was, twelve or thirteen, he was friendly, unlike most boys of his age. Myrna Pratt had a crush on his brother Alexander and was always hanging about outside their gate. The eldest boy, as tall as a man in his school uniform, was Karl. I loved all their names.

'That's the Mothers' Union gone for a Burton then,' Betty

said to me when we were unpacking the shopping and Peter from his pram.

> 'She may be weary
> Women do get weary
> Wearing the same shabby dress . . .'

she sang softly as she unbuttoned Peter's little blue coat and found that everything was soaked, even his vest and the sheet.

Ruby came in with her sleeve and her hair sparkling in dew where she had brushed against the hedge. She had a pair of her dad's socks folded over the tops of her gumboots, which gave her a piratical look, and a necklace which she had made from the beads I gave her. I told her that I had to polish the tables in the tea-room before I could come out. Ruby pulled a face.

'I've just been doing that at home.'

She sat watching me work, setting fire to the edge of a paper napkin and quickly beating out the blue frill of fire, before taking the Duraglit to our horse brasses.

'You'll never guess who came into the pub this morning, not in a hundred years.'

'Miss Fay.'

'How did *you* know?' Ruby was indignant.

'Call it a woman's intuition if you like,' I said, quoting from a book.

'I had to go out of the bar of course but I was watching from behind the door. You should have seen my dad. 'Oh do have a sweet sherry, Miss Fay, on the house. Wonderful thing, education, Miss Fay, I'm all for it, course I'm a graduate of the University of Life myself, Miss Fay. Kids nowadays don't know how lucky they are.'

Then Ruby turned into Miss Fay.

'Such a pity you couldn't come to our Christmas concert, Mr Richards. Ruby put her heart and soul into that mince-pie song and dance.'

'Did she really say that? Doesn't sound much like Miss Fay to me.'

' "Oh I really shouldn't, Mr Richards. You'll get me squiffy and that would never do." '

'Perhaps she's taken to the bottle to forget Major Morton. She has got a broken heart, don't forget.'

'Probably. Oh flip. Here comes Mr Greenidge with Liesel the Weasel.'

'Glass is falling,' said Mr Greenidge, stamping his feet.

We giggled, Ruby pretended to drop a glass, but I felt uneasy, knowing he was wishing that she wasn't there.

'More snow on the way, I'll be bound,' Mr Greenidge prophesied, hanging his coat and hat on the hat stand and taking off Liesel's coat and touching my face to show how cold it was.

'You ought to get her some boots. Two pairs – she'd look really cute,' Ruby said.

'You could,' I said. 'I saw some dolls' wellingtons in a shop in London. I could ask my gran to get them for you.'

'I don't think so, thank you, Liesel's feet are perfectly well adapted to the weather. She is, after all, a hunting dog, as Herr Brock would confirm.'

'Her claws are certainly sharp enough,' said Ruby, showing the swelling pink weals on her leg where Liesel had leaped up affectionately to greet her.

'Which of you two charming waitresses will be kind enough to convey my order of a pot of coffee and a selection of pastries to the kitchen? How about you, Miss Ruby, in your pretty necklace, if you'd do me the honour?'

When Ruby had gone through he said, 'The dragon's off to her sister's again on Wednesday. While the cat's away, eh?'

'What?'

He wagged his finger playfully at me.

'Now now, don't play the innocent.'

We heard Peter starting to cry.

'I've got to look after my baby brother.'

His voice dropped to a pleading tone. 'Please, dearest, you won't let me down again, will you?'

'OK.'

When Ruby brought the plate I bit into a rock cake, one I had made myself with burned raisins that tasted like coal. His calling Mrs Greenidge the dragon filled me with alarm and I saw two grey mice scampering on the pink quilt of the Greenidges' bed.

'Penny for 'em,' said Mr Greenidge.

'People always say that but they never give you a penny,' Ruby remarked. I could see that she liked Mr Greenidge now he was being nice to her.

'I was just wondering if it is going to snow.'

Snowdrifts blocked the doors of the Copper Kettle and banked up against the windows and all was cosy while a blizzard howled outside.

'Here you are then, a silver sixpence apiece. How's that?' said Mr Greenidge.

'Gosh, thanks,' Ruby said.

'Thank you,' I mumbled.

'I've got sixpence, pretty little sixpence,
I love sixpence better than my life.
I spent a penny of it, I lent a penny of it,
I took nothing home to my wife,'

Mr Greenidge sang and Ruby joined in the second verse,

'I've got nothing, pretty little nothing
I love nothing more than my wife.'

'Sounds very jolly in here.'

Percy came in with Peter held against his shoulder, dancing a slow glide between the tables, whistling 'Pedro the Fisherman'.

'Join me in a cup of coffee, Percy,' said Mr Greenidge.

'Don't mind if I do.'

When I brought a cup and saucer for Percy he was telling Mr Greenidge about his dream of the old men of the village playing chess in the garden of the Copper Kettle under the stars. Mr Greenidge looked doubtful.

'No harm in building castles in the air though, is there?' Percy said dejectedly.

'None at all, old chap. Where would we be without our pipe-dreams, eh?'

Mr Greenidge took out his pipe and his oily green tobacco pouch.

'Come on, Ruby. Let's go.'

'Doreen Vinnegar's ears have gone septic. She might have to have them off,' Ruby told me.

'Good, serves her jolly well right.'

'Don't be so spiteful. She only got those earrings for Christmas. What's up with you today? Why've you got the hump all of a sudden?'

'I haven't.'

We lay on my bed, head to toe, reading. I had *Black Beauty* and Ruby had *Anne of Green Gables*.

'It's not fair,' she said. 'I wish I was an orphan and could go and live with Matthew and Marilla.'

'You've got red hair.'

'That's what I mean. It isn't fair, some people have all the luck.'

'She could grow her hair long.'

'Who?'

'Doreen.'

'She'd have to, but she'll still be deaf, won't she, without any ears? I wonder if she'll have to go to the special school on the bus?'

'I suppose so.'

The clock in the hall whirred and struck three. I could hear Mr Greenidge's heart's loud ticking through his pullover as he held my face squashed against his chest.

'You're all bundled up like an eskimo. Let's get that wet coat and hat off you.'

'I don't want to.'

I was wearing a red knitted pixie-hood sent by Granny Fitz, and my pink coat.

Mr Greenidge fumbled with the buttons while I stood as stiffly as a pewter knight.

'You didn't tell anyone you were coming?' he asked anxiously, breathing loudly.

'No.'

How could I have? At this very moment Ruby might be standing in our kitchen saying, – 'Can April play?' and Betty answering in surprise, 'I thought she'd gone to call for you.' And Mrs Greenidge might leap snarling from behind a door, breathing fire like a dragon.

'How about a nice mug of drinking chocolate to thaw you out?'

The kitchen seemed safer than the bedroom so I said yes, but we sat at the table in the dining-room where I had not been before, with our earthenware mugs of chocolate on mats with hunting scenes, on the lace cloth. It was a cold dark-panelled room with brown-and-white photographs of rows of men in school caps, and a framed map of Stonebridge in the olden days. Tiny brown bubbles burst on the surface of the hot chocolate and the garden shivered outside the window.

'It's nicer than cocoa, isn't it?'

I couldn't think of anything else to say and he was gazing at me through the steam. The clock struck quarter past three.

'Quarter past already,' I said.

' "Had we but world enough and time," ' said Mr Greenidge. 'Sup up lassie, I've got a surprise for you.'

I followed him dumbly from the dining-room thinking, I'm not going upstairs again, I don't want to, why should I?, scared of the silent rooms and the ticking clock, which had been restored to life, but he led me into the sitting-room.

A television set was standing in the corner.

'A television.'

'Yes. My birthday present to Mrs Greenidge, but I really bought it for you.'

'For me? How?'

I felt dreadful, as though I had spoiled Mrs Greenidge's birthday. I hadn't even known it was her birthday. It was horrible that she thought he had bought it for her.

'Now you've got the perfect excuse to come here as often as you like.'

'But it's not fair . . .'

'Don't be silly. Aren't I going to get a kiss to say thank you?'

'Thank you. Can we watch it?'

135

'There's nothing on now. Come on, where's my kiss?'

I reached up to kiss his lowered cheek and was crushed by his beard.

'Do you want to come upstairs to play with the pretty things?'

'No thank you. I've got to go in a minute.'

'Just for a wee while?'

'I don't want to.'

'Why not, my darling? You enjoyed yourself last time didn't you? Tell me you did.'

'Some of the time,' I had to mumble truthfully, because I had liked playing with the beautiful cabinet.

'There you are then,' he said triumphantly, but I had planted my feet firmly on the carpet and he couldn't make me go upstairs without carrying me.

He sighed and sat down in a big chintz armchair. He patted his knees.

'Come and sit down for a minute.'

Reluctantly I crossed the room and sat awkwardly on a bony knee.

'Let's get comfy; that's better isn't it?'

I felt like a big, stupid doll sitting there with a red face and stiff, itchy legs as he jigged me up and down in the way we did with Peter, to 'Ride a cock horse', or 'This is the way the ladies ride'. I would have died if anybody could have seen me being that enormous baby. This is the way the old men ride, hobble-dee, hobble-dee and *down* in a ditch.

Mr Greenidge was quivering like a jelly. I could feel his arms trembling as held me tighter and rocked faster as if he had forgotten about me. Then he stopped.

'That's enough of that,' he said pushing me off his knee and reaching for his pipe from a little table, knocking over a cardboard tube of the coloured spills he used for lighting it sometimes. The thin pink wood flared with a sweet-scented blue flame as he held it to the tobacco with a shaky hand.

'You'd better get your coat and hat and run along.'

I picked up a handful of the spills.

'Can I have these?'

'Yes, yes, whatever you like. Take them all.'

I didn't know what I had done to make him cross. When I was putting on my coat he came into the hall.

'Darling April, you won't tell where those spills came from, will you? You could get us both into trouble. Promise me?'

They were a pink and green and blue and yellow spikey fan in my hand. I could use them to make something.

'I promise.'

'That's my girl. Will I see you tomorrow?'

'All right.'

'Not if I see you first, so you can put that in your pipe and smoke it!' I said defiantly as I cycled away on the slippery road. The wind whipped my ears and I realized that I had left my pixie-hood behind. It made me feel sad. I felt sorry for not liking it when Granny's friend had knitted it from red wool and Granny had wrapped it in tissue paper. I felt sad about Mrs Greenidge's birthday, and foolish and sly because I knew I had done something wrong.

Ruby was doing some washing, scrubbing the collar of one of her dad's shirts with a nailbrush. A two-handled pan of handkerchiefs boiled on the stove like a witch's cauldron.

'Look what I found. Somebody must have dropped them in the road.'

I showed her the spills, saying, 'We could make something with them.'

'No we couldn't.'

My vague idea of a coloured construction like Grandpa's Crystal Palace splintered.

'Keep them though. They'll come in useful when we go back to our camp.'

I never wanted to go back there since we had found the handkerchief, and I had never mentioned it to Mr Greenidge. I saw his bearded face, spying through the window of the railway carriage.

Lex's handkerchiefs were bubbling like some snails I had once tried to keep as pets in an empty beer barrel. I had a sudden thought. 'Hey, where are the pullets?'

'What pullets?' said Ruby.

Our own house smelled of damp and scorched washing when I got home. Peter's things were draped over the fireguard, blocking out the heat.

'Can we get a television?' I asked.

'When pigs fly,' came the reply.

Early the next morning I slipped out without telling anybody. I had been woken by Peter when the sky was still dark and starry and hadn't been able to go back to sleep properly for worrying about my hat. Supposing Mrs Greenidge should have come back and found it? 'You could get us both into trouble.' Mr Greenidge's kind blue eyes grew hard and cruel, terror bulged against the closed doors of the silent rooms. I had dressed quickly, feeling cold and ugly, the brush tangling in my hair.

Mr Greenidge opened the door in his dressing-gown over pyjamas.

'April, my darling, what brings you here so early? What a wonderful surprise.'

'I forgot my pixie-hood.'

His face fell.

'Ah yes, of course. Come in.'

He shut the door behind us.

'It's in the kitchen, come through.'

The house smelled of cold stale pipe smoke but the kitchen was warm. *The Times*, a half-eaten boiled egg and triangles of toast on a toast rack showed that he had been having breakfast.

'Care to join me?' I could pop another egg in, that would be fun, wouldn't it? We could play that we were an old married couple having breakfast.'

'What about Mrs Greenidge?'

'Damn and blast Mrs Greenidge! Why do you drag her into everything? Can't we just be happy together for a few minutes? Damn Mrs Greenidge to hell! I wish she was dead!'

His face was dark red and his eyes bulging. I backed towards the door. He came towards me with outstretched arms.

'April, don't look so frightened, I beg you – you must never be afraid of me. It's only that I love you so very much.'

138

'I've got to go. I didn't say I was going out.'

I was still scared of him and shaking with shock at what he had said.

He sighed heavily.

'There's your hat, on the chair.'

He tied it gently under my chin.

'Off you go then, Little Red Riding Hood.'

Then he bared his teeth and snapped them saying, ' "What big teeth you have, grandmother!" "All the better to eat you with, my dear." '

The milkman was in the café having a cup of tea with Titch Vinnegar who had taken to riding on the milk float and helping to deliver the bottles.

'Wotcher cock,' said Titchy, sitting there as if he owned the place. Which once he had, I remembered, and it did not improve my mood. His father, Tiny, had come to our back door one night in his old army coat, trying to sell us two dead rabbits. There were also two men who had been climbing up the telegraph pole when I went out.

'Where've you been?' Percy grumbled. 'Give us a hand with this fried bread.' Bacon was squirming and spitting in the other frying pan.

Dittany kept an eye on her doves when Tiny was around, for fear that they would end up as someone's pigeon pie, and worried more about Tiny than the fox getting into her ducks' house at night.

At eleven o'clock Mr Greenidge came in for his morning coffee.

'No Liesel today?' Percy asked.

'No, I'm all on my own-io. Deserted by both my good ladies. A bachelor gay am I.'

He winked at Percy. When we were alone, except for Peter who was perched heavily on my hip, as I had been amusing him while Betty was baking, Mr Greenidge sang softly,

'And when he thinks he's past love,
'Tis then he finds his last love,
And he loves her like no other love before.'

'Coochy-coo,' he said to Peter. 'Where's that peck of pickled pepper Peter Piper picked?'

Fourteen

Miss Fay was in an evil temper on the first day of term. 'Did you have a nice holiday, Miss Fay?' a goody-goody asked her.

'That's enough impertinence for one morning,' Miss Fay replied.

Doreen, who had not had to have her ears off, had been sent to school with a bottle of surgical spirit, to dab on her swollen lobes, which Miss Fay confiscated.

'You can have it back at the end of term,' she said.

With two of the girls in tears, Miss Fay turned on Ruby and me, and separated us. I had to sit next to a girl called Veronica Taplady, which seemed a fancy name for someone who smelled of Marmite and had warts on her hands, which bled when she scratched them. Ruby was put next to Angela Thorn who lived on a remote farm and hardly ever spoke. Her clothes were always full of burrs.

In the afternoon Mr Reeves summoned the whole school into the dining-room. Constable Cox was with him. We quaked in fear wondering who was going to be arrested.

'Good afternoon, boys and girls.'

'Good afternoon, Mr Cox.'

'Be seated,' said Mr Reeves.

'Now children,' said Mr Cox. 'I've got something very important to say to you, so pay attention. Now, I haven't come here this afternoon to frighten you, or to take any of you off to prison. Not long ago, a little girl who lives in this village – I won't tell you her name because she doesn't go to this school – had a very nasty experience while she was playing in Tippetts wood. Fortunately, she's all right, but if any of you have seen a strange man hanging around the village or in the rec or down the meadows or anywhere at all, I want you to tell me, or tell your teacher. This is very important, so think hard. Thinking caps on. Has any stranger approached you, or have you noticed anybody behaving oddly or offering sweets to anyone? Somebody with a bicycle perhaps. Don't be afraid to speak up.'

Mr Cox waited. It was grey and solemn with sleet falling past the windows and a few whispers rustling like sweetpapers.

'Take your time,' said Constable Cox.

Then Doreen's hand went up, uncurling slowly in the silence it created.

'Please sir, a man offered me a sweet.'

'When was this, Doreen?'

'Yesterday,' she whispered.

'And did you recognize him, was it somebody you know?' Constable Cox leaned forward taking off his helmet to hear better.

'Yes sir. It was Mr Boddy.'

'Mr Boddy? And where were you when this took place, Doreen?'

'In the butcher's sir. It was a fruit gum.'

Some of the top class burst out laughing and then everybody was laughing and even Miss Fay's face twitched. Doreen was like a beetroot.

'All right. That's enough!'

Mr Reeves clapped his hands.

'It was very brave and sensible of Doreen to come forward like that. Now, I want you to remember what Mr Cox said and if any of you can think of anything at all unusual or suspicious or see any strangers with bicycles hanging around, tell your parents, tell me or Miss Fay or Miss Elsey or Mr Cox.

Don't play in any lonely places by yourselves, don't speak to any strangers. If anybody offers you sweets, except Mr Boddy, of course, you must tell the nearest grown-up at once, and never ever get in a car or go anywhere with somebody you don't know.'

As we filed out I heard Constable Cox saying, 'Mind you, there must be something odd about a butcher who reports finding a turkey on his doorstep at Christmas. They don't come much stranger than that.'

By home time it was all round the school that the girl was Sorrel Marlowe. Quite a few of the mums had come to meet their children. Mr Greenidge had come to meet me. We were nearly at the Copper Kettle when we saw Betty hurrying along the road.

'Thank goodness it's you,' she said to Mr Greenidge. 'I couldn't be sure at a distance. Just thought I'd pop out to see if April was on her way. There are all sorts of rumours going around.'

'I know. Mr Cox came up the school to talk to us,' I said. 'About a stranger on a bicycle.'

Then I went hot and cold and felt icy water draining from me. Rodney Pegg's angry, spotted face, framed in a balaclava, loomed in my mind, leering.

'April? What's the matter?'

They were both looking at me.

'Nothing. I just thought of something, that's all. Nothing to do with what Mr Cox said.'

My voice seemed to come from far away. I imagined Sorrel Marlowe, in her Fair Isle beret, and matching mittens, her camel coat, in a dark wood and Rodney Pegg with a nylon stocking on his head.

Mr Greenidge was scrabbling in his coat pocket and pulled out a toffee.

'Here you are, have a sweetie. "Sharp's the word", eh?'

The toffee melted in my mouth and I realized Mr Greenidge thought I was going to tell of him. He looked old and frightened, with his nose pocked by the cold and turning purple and his eyes watering as if with tears.

143

'What's for tea, Mum?' I said.

'Wait-and-see,' said Betty. 'Care to join us, Mr Greenidge? You're very welcome.'

'Ah, no thank you kindly, Mrs Harlency. Although wait-and-see is my favourite – my own dear mother used to make it for me when I was a boy. I've, ah, I must make a telephone call to my lady wife, I'm on the way to the telephone box in Lovers Lane. Own line out of order I'm afraid. Must report it, eh?'

The blustering old liar raised his hat.

'I've only ever seen cows down there. Lovers Lane, I mean,' said Betty.

'A trysting place of yesteryear,' said Mr Greenidge, 'a twitton of dalliance for our local swains and maidens fair, our village Romeos and Juliets. Well, I'll bid you both a very good day.'

'What a romantic soul,' said Betty. 'You can tell he's missing his wife, bless him. Why did you suddenly stop back there, as if you'd remembered something? There isn't anything you're not telling me, is there?'

'It was Rodney Pegg.'

'Rodney Pegg?' Her voice rose in disbelief. 'What do you mean, it was Rodney Pegg?'

We were indoors now, taking off our coats.

'I know it was Rodney Pegg who attacked Sorrel Marlowe. It must've been him.'

'How do you know it was Sorrel Marlowe? Nobody's supposed to know that. And what do you mean, "attacked"?'

'It's all round the school. Everybody knows.'

'Oh dear, it's all so nasty,' said Betty.

Percy was in the armchair with Peter asleep in his arms.

'What's all so nasty? That bastard, pardon my French, interfering with that little girl?'

Interfering. It sounded so rude, so knickery, so fleshy.

'April's got it into her head that it was Rodney Pegg, but how could it have been? He lives miles away, in Tooting.'

'We saw him, didn't we, Dad? He came to the tea-room and ran away when he saw Dad. And I saw him getting off a train with his bike, the day we met Professor Scoley off the train.'

They were both staring at me.

'I could have sworn it *was* him, but he was gone so quickly. Took one look at me and scarpered. Why would he do that? I mean to say, I know we weren't the best of friends but we never actually came to blows or anything.'

'All the Peggs hated us,' Betty said. 'People like that shouldn't have lodgers, and the state of the place! That cooker. That toilet.'

'Even so, supposing you did see Rodney, what makes you think it was him that – that – you know?'

'Because he kissed me.'

'He what? You mean you let him?'

Percy leaped up, waking Peter, who cried. I was crying too. 'Did he do anything else?'

'Shush, Percy. Here, give him to me. Why didn't you tell us, love?'

'Because he said he'd strangle me if I did, with one of your stockings,' I wept.

Percy put his arm around me.

'There, there. Hush now, it wasn't your fault.' Over my head he said, 'I'll tear him limb from limb.'

Then he said, 'Come on, sit on Daddy's lap and tell me all about it.'

'I can't. I'm too big.'

'You'll never be too big.'

I sat down, feeling dirty, wishing I'd never opened my mouth.

When I told my brief story, about Rodney fencing me against the wall of the hall with his front wheel, Percy said, 'I think I'd better go and have a word with Constable Cox, don't you? Will you be all right on your own?'

'Oh, I'll close up. Nobody's going to come in now. You can do it, April.'

Ruby was scooting down the path on her bike when I turned the sign on the door round.

'Did you cycle through the village on your own?' Betty accused her.

'Yes. Why? I've got lights on my bike.'

'You two keep an eye on Peter while I get the tea. Put the wireless on. Let's have a bit of entertainment,' Betty said.

Later that evening Constable Cox called round.

'Did he say anything to you, this Rodney Pegg?' he asked.

'No. He just sort of – glared.'

'And he threatened you, did he, back in Tooting? Said he'd strangle you, were those his very words?'

'Yes.'

I was squirming with shame. I felt like a criminal, with Constable Cox in our room, his uniform, asking embarrassing questions in front of Betty and Percy.

'You've got the address then, sir?' he asked Percy, who wrote down the Peggs' name and address on a leaf torn from his ledger.

'This will all be kept strictly confidential, madam,' he told Betty, 'with regard to the information. I'll keep you posted. Thank you very much April, you've been most helpful. Don't worry . . . if young Pegg is our man, we'll soon have him behind bars.'

Then he became informal for a few minutes while he drank a cup of tea. 'Be seeing you, Jim,' said Percy when he showed him out.

'I'm going up to my room,' I said.

'All right love. Do you want a bath a bit later?'

So they thought I was dirty too. Now I would rather die than tell them about Mr Greenidge.

'But I had one last night.'

'I know, I just thought it might be – soothing, relaxing. You can use one of my bath cubes.'

I lingered on the stairs long enough to hear Percy say, 'If I get my hands on Pegg he'll wish he *was* behind bars. I've a good mind to go up to London right now.'

'I'd come with you, if I could. That filthy little swine, I'd tear him limb from limb myself. Best leave it to the police though, for now. I expect they'll contact Scotland Yard.'

I was frightened by their voices, full of hate. They didn't sound like my parents any more. I imagined Rodney pulled apart like a pink doll, his arms and legs wrenched off like tearing cloth. Or behind bars, in a suit of broad arrows, shaking them, whimpering and gibbering like a monkey at the zoo.

I lay on my bed reading *Black Beauty*. I knew I would never get over the death of poor Ginger either.

Fifteen

Three uneasy days passed before Jim Cox came back. 'Well, have they arrested him? Betty demanded.

'I'm afraid not, Betty. The local boys made a thorough investigation and it seems that young Pegg's got a cast-iron alibi for the day in question. I'm sorry.'

'I don't effing believe it,' said Percy.

'They ought to call in the Yard,' said Betty.

'I can assure you that won't be necessary,' Constable Cox said stiffly.

'So they're just going to let the bugger cycle round the countryside assaulting little girls, are they? I've a good mind to sort him out myself.'

'It's never a good idea to take the law into your own hands, sir.'

'Don't sir me, Jim. How would you feel if it was one of your kids? What about my little girl, what he did to her?'

'It would be difficult to make a charge stick on that one, Percy. Given the passage of time and the nature of the alleged assault, and it would be April's word against his.'

'Oh, alleged is it now?' Betty said. 'She was terrified of him. She was sleeping with a kitchen knife under her pillow.'

If I could have crawled under the table, I would have.

'If he so much as shows his spotty face round here again, I'll have him. I'll knock his effing block off! What's his flaming alibi then? It'd better be good.'

'Rodney Pegg was in bed all day with the flu. Both his parents can vouch for him, and we have the unbiased corroboration of two lodgers.'

'I bet,' said Percy bitterly.

'Unbiased, my eye,' Betty put in. 'What about that attack on Charmaine Vinnegar last year then? Did they ever catch the bloke who did that?'

'Between you, me and the gatepost the Police are taking the Vinnegar incident with a pinch of salt. I do understand how you feel. As you say, I'm a parent myself, but barking up the wrong tree with this one isn't going to catch the real culprit, is it? And as long as he's at large, well . . .'

'Did they check his tyres, for mud and leaf mould and suchlike? Has he got one of those things, a wotsitsname, that counts the miles?' Percy made a last attempt to get Rodney Pegg behind bars.

'I shouldn't go playing detective if I were you, Percy. Leave it to the professionals.'

'Tell that to Sherlock Holmes.'

When Constable Cox had gone Percy said, 'If anybody else so much as lays a finger on you, April, you come straight to me, OK?'

So my opportunity to have Mr Greenidge torn limb from limb like a doll or a Red Indian tied to two birch trees (an image that came courtesy of Miss Fay) or his block knocked off so that his smiling bearded face, pipe clenched between teeth, blue eyes twinkling, sailed over the hedge soaring into the paler blue sky, was handed to me, as it were, on a plate. I could have asked for the head of John the Baptist, and I turned away. From time to time I caught Percy looking at me over the edge of the book he was reading or from the door as I went out, or across the room when I was serving a customer, and Rodney Pegg's shadow fell between me and my dad.

Our house had a wintry gloom and an edgy atmosphere, as on a Monday morning when the washing line broke and the clean clothes fell into the mud, or the refrigerator died and all the ice-cream melted, when grown-ups' snappiness gave little yappy flashes of a dangerous weir round a bend in the calm river. I tried to be as helpful as possible and Percy tried to be jolly. I was wiping the mock sundaes, the plaster knickerbocker glory and banana split, with a damp cloth when Percy took the tall glass from my hand and held it up saying, 'Even the knicker-bocker in all his glory is not arrayed like one of these.' The fake cherry gleamed, the plaster wafer fanned out from its swirl of cream in the electric light of the January afternoon.

Although bad temper was the norm at the Rising Sun, I spent more time there now, snuggled up under Ruby's lumpy green quilt in her cold bedroom, our hands freezing as we turned the pages of our books or invented secret codes or smoothed the creases from Ruby's collection of gold and silver paper from cigarette packets and coloured sweet wrappers which she kept in a shoe box under her bed. Her walkie-talkie doll watched over us giving an occasional bleat of 'mamaa' and a glass rabbit I had bought her in Hastings stood on her win-dowsill catching the sun, when it shone, in its long amber ears. We took turns with our favourite books, *Valley of Doom, Little Women, Anne of Green Gables* and *Famous Fives* and *Lone Pine Adventures*, and we were presently obsessed with two jumble-sale purchases, *Lucifer and the Child* by Ethel Mannin and *Deathcap Cottage* by V. L. Preedy, about a woman who poisoned her crippled husband. Its once yellow cover was engrained with grey and a smell of mildew came off its rust-pin-pointed pages and a long-dead spider's egg in a gauzy net was found half-way through the book.

Time went on and no arrest was made and the ordeal of Sorrel in the woods ceased to be a topic of conversation, as if nothing very important had happened after all. Miss Fay had taken up Scottish dancing and caught the bus into Elmford once a week in her kilt, carrying her dancing shoes with their criss-cross laces, which she had shown once to the class, in a special bag. She read us Scottish poems and ballads. Pupils twirled their fingers at their heads behind her back to indicate that she had a screw loose but nobody dared snigger as Miss

Fay stalked between the desks declaiming 'Why does your brand sae drap wi' blood' and waving the blackboard pointer so vividly that it became a dripping sword.

'February Fill-Dyke', she wrote on the board while the rain slashed the playground with silver balls and gurgled in the drains and the class-room steamed with wet wool and meaty cabbagy smells and Veronica smelled of marmite. Doreen's ears healed and she had a home perm.

Granny, who came with Grandpa and George for Peter's christening, had had her hair permed into purple sprouting broccoli; Grandpa was delighted with Peter.

'Look at that leg,' he said, pinching it. 'You can just see it on a plate with gravy and roast potatoes.'

'Don't forget the apple sauce,' said Granny.

They had brought a bottle of sherry and whiskey and one of gin, and wisps of blue cigarette were caught in the watery sun. There were ten of us in the tea-room, with the closed sign on the door, the family, Ruby, George and Bobs and Dittany, eating Peter's cake with a white stork and a silver frill, and Boy, wearing a white ribbon, who would have liked to. Mr Oswald had gone to the christening party of the baby girl, who had been baptised at the same time as Peter. George and Dittany, who had won the honour from Bobs on the toss of a coin, were Peter's godparents.

I was envious of this, my own godparents having been lost along the way before I ever knew them. Granny Harlency had insisted that I should be christened, against Percy's wishes, and Betty said that it was only fair that Peter should be too. Also, people kept asking her if Peter had been christened yet.

'I'm a spoiled Catholic myself, Father,' Grandpa had said, shaking Mr Oswald's hand in the church porch, 'but when in Rome, eh? Better safe than sorry.'

George gave him a silver tankard with his name engraved on it, there was a teething ring with a silver teddy from the regulars, an antique silver-and-coral rattle from Bobs and Dittany, a silver spoon and pusher in a box from Granny and a blue wool golliwog with yellow eyes from Ruby. I had got him a board book called *Barnyard Babies*.

'George and Bobs and Dittany are getting on like a house on fire,' Percy said to me in the kitchen.

'Perhaps he'll fall in love with one of them and they'll get married.'

'I don't think so, old George isn't the marrying kind, and I can't see our ladies behind a bar.'

I was pleased because I would have hated either Bobs or Dittany to move away. All three of them, George and Bobs and Dittany, had cried with Peter when Mr Oswald sprinkled the water from the font onto his wrinkling, astonished forehead.

Somebody was trying the tea-room door.

'Be off with you, this is a private party,' Grandpa shouted.

I choked on my ginger beer. It was Mr Greenidge.

'Sorry,' he called. 'Didn't realize you were closed.'

'Come in, come in,' Percy welcomed him, unlocking the door.

'I saw all these good people and assumed you were open. Wouldn't dream of intruding.'

'Come and join us, Mr Greenidge,' Betty called out. 'Come and have a piece of cake. You're not intruding. We're just having a little tea party for Peter's christening. Family, mostly,' she said apologetically, with a glance at those who were not.

Liesel pulled Mr Greenidge into the party and sniffed jealously at Boy's white bow.

'Sorry about that just now,' Grandpa Fitz told him. 'I didn't know you were a friend. Pull up a chair and make yourself at home.'

'April, where are your manners? Fetch another plate and glass or a teacup. We've got whiskey, gin, sherry or tea or ginger beer, Mr Greenidge.'

'Begorrah, I wouldn't say no to a drop o' the cratur,' said Mr Greenidge, rubbing cold, dry hands.

'A gentleman after me own heart,' cried Grandpa.

I thought it was rather rude of Mr Greenidge to try to mimic Grandpa's voice, but he took it in good part.

'No, don't get up anyone, plenty of room. I'll just squeeze

in here with the young ladies. A rose between two thorns, eh April?'

When I had brought Mr Greenidge's plate and glass I went to sit at the table with George and Bobs and Dittany.

'To Master Peter. A long life and a happy one!' Mr Greenidge raised his glass in a toast.

Everybody joined in with clinkings and 'Peters' and 'God-bless-hims' and only I could tell that Mr Greenidge's eyes were glinting with cold fury.

The party went a bit flat after that. Betty had to go upstairs to feed Peter. Liesel snapped at Boy's tail and Dittany said she ought to shut the ducks up for the night. Mr Greenidge was explaining to Grandpa that he and Granny had met before.

'We had the pleasure, briefly, in the summer. At least, the pleasure was all mine.'

George snorted into his drink, spraying the tablecloth.

'Steady on,' said Mr Greenidge coldly. 'That ginger beer can go right up your nose if you're not careful. I'd better toddle along or my good lady will be wondering what's become of me.'

He held out half a crown to me, so that I had to go over to him and take it from him. I looked at Percy, saying 'No thank you, I'm not allowed to take money.'

Mr Greenidge winked at Percy.

'Who said it was for you? I was going to ask you to pop it into Master Peter's money box as a token christening present from me and Liesel.'

'Rose between two thorns, I should cocoa,' said George when they had gone. 'Spend it on yourself, dear, I would.'

'You went bright red,' Ruby told me.

'Well he made me look greedy in front of everybody. Trust him to spoil everything. It was nice until he had to come barging in.'

'Do you think your mum will let me have the frill off the cake?'

'I've already bagsied it.'

Mr Greenidge had left me melancholy and mean. I didn't

even want the cake frill. Boy began to make heaving noises, his sides working like bellows.

'Too much marzipan I'm afraid,' said Bobs scooping him up and making for the door.

'No, Liesel upset him snapping at his tail,' I said.

Dittany followed them, profuse in her thanks for a lovely party.

A silence fell.

'Drinking in the afternoon,' said Percy. 'Always makes you sad, never fails. When you've been in the licensed trade as long as I have . . .' he broke off, remembering that he was speaking to the Fitzs and George, and even Ruby.

Feet thudded along the path and the tea-room door, unlocked now, flew open and Myrna Pratt and Doreen were inside, out of breath, panting 'Mr Harlency, Mr Harlency! Come quick! Mr Greenidge has fallen over and hurt himself. You've got to come, I think he's broke his leg.'

We all ran out, Percy and George getting to him first and trying to sit him up on the pavement. Mr Greenidge shook George off angrily. Liesel licked his face.

'Get me my stick! I'm perfectly capable – ouch – it's my ankle, twisted the blessed thing under me, some damn fool idiot boys ran me down.'

A wooden box on a pair of pram wheels was disappearing round the corner in the dusk.

Mr Greenidge's face twisted with pain as he stood up, leaning heavily on his stick and tried to put his foot to the ground.

'Let me have a look,' Myrna volunteered suddenly. 'I'm a Girl Guide.'

'Over my dead body. Somebody help me to the doctor's.'

'Come on, old chap! Put your arm round my shoulder, that's the ticket. You can put your weight on me. Easy does it. You girls take the dog and explain what's happened. I think it's probably just a sprain.'

'A bad sprain can be worse than a break,' said Myrna.

'My turn to be in the wars, April,' Mr Greenidge put on a brave smile. 'Now you'll have to bring *me* chocolates when I'm laid up,' he said over Percy's shoulder.

Mrs Greenidge opened the door at once, looking agitated.

'Liesel! *Liebchen*, where have you been? Mother's been so worried about you. Is she all right? Why is she with you?'

She bent down and Liesel leaped into her arms. We blurted out the news of Mr Greenidge's accident.

'It's probably only a sprain,' I tried to reassure her.

'A sprain can be more serious than a broken bone. What a nuisance! It really is too bad. First he takes Liesel out without her coat, and now this! Thank you so much for bringing her home safely.'

When we got back to the Copper Kettle Betty was upset. 'First you all run out leaving the doors open, and now this! Lovely christening this turned out to be! Poor little Peter!'

George had discovered two flat tyres on the Morris Minor.

'It's impossible. I can't believe it,' he said.

I could.

Sixteen

My dream of taking Liesel for walks had come true. How long ago it seemed that I had yearned to have her leaping by my side on her red lead. Now every afternoon after school I had to go straight to Kirriemuir to collect her. Usually Ruby came with me and Mr Greenidge could do nothing about it because he was trapped in an easy chair with his bandaged foot resting on a stool while Mrs Greenidge answered the door to us. Sometimes, she gave us a Marie biscuit or a rich tea in the kitchen before we set off. There were no more cakes and chocolate fingers.

'Liesel looks forward all day to her walk,' Mrs Greenidge said.

'When do you think Mr Greenidge's foot will be better?' I asked her when we returned Liesel.

'Oh, it will be a while yet, Dr Barker says.'

It was all a misunderstanding. I had offered to take Liesel for a walk the first time I had called round to see how Mr Greenidge was, and they had thought I meant I would take her out every day.

'April!' Mr Greenidge's voice, feeble and invalidish from the sitting-room. With an embarrassed glance at Ruby and Mrs Greenidge, I went along the hall.

'Why do you never come to see me? It's torture hearing

your voice and then you just stick your head round the door to say hello and goodbye and run away, can't you spare me five minutes of your precious time? Is that too much to ask? I never dreamed you could be so cruel.'

I was in agony in case the others should come in and hear him.

'I bought you this television in the foolish hope that we could sit and watch it together. How wrong I was. You haven't looked at it once.'

I was gawping like a goldfish with resentment and indignation when Mrs Greenidge walked in, followed by Ruby.

'Thanks, my dear,' said Mr Greenidge. 'Blessed *Radio Times* slid off my lap and I couldn't reach it.'

He had been holding it all the time.

'You're not totally crippled, Clement. You just enjoy being waited on hand and foot. I saw you from the window this afternoon hopping about the garden like a two-year-old.'

'And I'm paying for it now. Blooming thing's really giving me gyp. You don't know the half of it. If only I could identify those young hooligans who did this to me, I'd have them up before the magistrates before you could say Jack Robinson!' He looked keenly at Ruby and me. 'I suppose you're none the wiser? Nobody said anything in the playground? Who do you think it might have been?'

'Jack Robinson,' said Ruby.

'Well, we mustn't keep you. I'm sure you've got more interesting things to do than hang round two old crocks,' Mrs Greenidge said. 'We'll see you tomorrow.'

Mr Greenidge groaned and shifted his foot. 'It feels like a hundred red-hot darning needles.'

I had to go home to Betty and Percy and Peter who did not know that Mr Greenidge thought me cruel.

'I don't like taking Liesel out,' I said. 'Everybody calls her a sausage dog.'

'Poor old Liesel,' said Betty. 'Still, you stick up for her, don't you?'

And so we went on. On the Sunday I had to go to Kirriemuir

alone and the three of us and Liesel sat watching a programme about pygmies in the jungle and eating Battenberg cake. ' "Lips of Finest Fat", eh?' chortled Mr Greenidge. 'What do you think of that for a name, April?'

'I don't know.'

The pygmies had hardly any clothes on and I was relieved when the programme finished and I thought that Mrs Greenidge was as well.

She was wearing a purple cardigan and her face was always purplish now, like an overripe peach. She got out of breath easily and seemed exhausted, perhaps from looking after Mr Greenidge.

I had to get out the words that had been buzzing like disturbed wasps inside me all afternoon.

'I can't come tomorrow. It's my mother's birthday. I'm sorry.'

I didn't dare look at Mr Greenidge.

'Run up to the bedroom, April,' Mrs Greenidge said. 'You'll find some birthday cards on the bureau. It's the second door on the left.'

'I know.'

The breath drained out of me like air from a balloon. They were staring at me.

'I mean, I don't know – what a bureau is.'

I had to cling on to the bannister to get up the stairs on wobbling, tingling legs.

There was the pink bed, the turquoise-tasselled scent spray, the silver brush and comb, the cabinet inlaid with mother-of-pearl, a bird singing in the garden. I found the cards and took them downstairs worried that Mrs Greenidge would think that I had been touching her things or had stolen something.

'Which one do you think your mother would like?'

'The one of the daffodils.'

Mrs Greenidge wrote with a mother-of-pearl fountain pen in thin blue letters, 'With best wishes from Elizabeth and Clement Greenidge.'

The lone cry of the peewit woke me in the middle of the night, a desperate call in the darkness ringing in my head. Then with a shock, I knew the cry had been in my dream. Ruby shouting for help trapped in leaping flames as Deathcap Cottage burned and the thatch was blazing and crackling, except that I knew it was really the railway carriage and the scream had been forced through my own strangled throat. The room flooded with light and Betty stood there blinking.

'What's the matter? I heard you call out. Were you having a bad dream?'

She sat on the edge of my bed in her nightie.

'Where's Bobbity?'

We found him at the bottom of the bed under the covers near my feet.

'What's this?'

Betty picked up *Deathcap Cottage* from the floor and opened it.

'You haven't been reading this rubbish have you? No wonder it's been giving you nightmares. It's disgusting and look at it, the cover's filthy. I've a good mind to throw it in the fire.'

'No, you can't!'

'You don't know where it's been,' Betty shuddered, holding *Deathcap Cottage* away from her. 'It's, it's – tainted. I'm taking it. I won't burn it because I don't believe in burning books, too much like Hitler for my taste, but I don't want you to read it any more, understand?'

I nodded. Ruby and I knew it almost off by heart anyway.

'What's the time?' I asked.

'Past two o'clock in the morning. We should both get back to sleep.'

'Happy birthday, Mum.'

After she had gone I lay in the darkness. The French Fern talc I had bought her was safely hidden in a cardigan in my drawer with the card I had made and the Greenidges' card. Bobbity's long ears were on the pillow beside me, his glass eyes watchfully open, but if I closed mine I could see the spitting, burning thatch with sparks flying into the orchard trees and hear Ruby's frantic peewit scream.

★

Percy took Betty to the pictures in Elmford on the evening of her birthday. He had got up early and came back with a bunch of daffodils from the back garden and hazel catkins. Peter gave her a box of chocolates and the postman brought a card with a £5 note inside from Granny and Grandpa, and one from George. I thought she was pleased with the Greenidges' card, although she was a bit put out that I had told them it was her birthday.

She cried, as she always did when we sang happy birthday and held Peter up to see the candle on her cake. A tiny flame was reflected in each of his eyes.

When Stonebridge people went to the cinema they had to watch the end of the film first, because if they stayed until the finish of the second house, they missed the last bus. Dittany came to babysit. Bobs was at home nursing one of the doves who was sick.

'I love it when he stretches out his legs like that,' Dittany said of Peter. 'Look at the tension on that thigh, it runs right down to his toes. I must draw him. Have you got a pencil and paper?'

I remembered her sketching Professor Scoley as he lay dead in the wheelbarrow. Everybody had been shocked.

'It's just a continuation of Life Drawing,' she had said. 'Taking it to its logical conclusion. Well, not quite, but as far as perhaps one can.'

As Dittany drew, zipping through our Basildon Bond, she told me that she had discovered that the village children always used to dance around the maypole on the first of May in the olden days.

'I'm going to have a word with Mr Reeves. It would be lovely to restore some of the old customs. There must be a maypole lurking around somewhere. "Now is the month of May, when merry lads are playing. Fa la la la la la la la la, fa la la la la la la!" '

'There's no maypole at the school,' I said, alarmed. 'I'm sure I would have noticed.'

'Well it must be somewhere, such a potent totem could not

simply disappear. It must be lying sleeping, waiting to be awoken like the Old Gods.'

It was obvious that Dittany was confused, muddling up totem poles with maypoles. She had brought Betty a gossamer shawl that shimmered with soft rainbows, woven by a friend of hers.

'It's beautiful, but it's too good – when would I wear it?'

'When you go dancing,' said Dittany.

'Chance would be a fine thing,' said Betty. 'The last time I went dancing was on bonfire night and then I was too fat to dance and nearly got blown up by a firework into the bargain. I can hardly do this dress up even now. But thank you ever so, Dittany, both of you. It's really lovely, and I can dream, can't I?'

The buttons down Betty's blue dress were dark-blue pansies, a present from Mr Silver, who had also given her a card of spotted toadstool buttons for me and a set of little engines for Peter.

Peter fell asleep on my lap and I sat with his heavy head sending my arm to sleep while a coal split in the fire and blue-green flames shot out from the glowing chasm and Dittany went on drawing. The shawl draped over the back of a chair glimmered like a gift from fairyland and Dittany's yellow willow fairy hair spread out over her shoulders. When Betty came into my bedroom later I was half woken by her salty kiss that smelled of vinegar and chips.

I tried to bribe Ruby into collecting Liesel on her own but she said, 'You got us into it.'

'Here are your little friends, Clement,' called Mrs Greenidge.

'Go and see if you can cheer him up. He's been like a bear with a sore head all day. Men are such babies when they're ill,' she said to us. 'Worse than babies.'

'How's your head today, Mr Greenidge?' Ruby asked cheekily.

'My head? Nothing wrong with my head. It's my blessed foot, not my noodle you should be asking about, you silly girl.'

'Sorree.'

Ruby got the giggles and had to bury her face in Liesel. I was trying not to laugh.

'Glad you find it so amusing.' He dropped his voice. 'This is where it hurts. Here!'

He struck himself on the heart.

I didn't really think it was funny but Ruby set me off, and then a nervous whinny escaped down my nose and Ruby went into hysterics, rolling on the floor with Liesel, and I couldn't stop and collapsed into a chair.

'Do share the joke. I can't remember when I last had a good laugh.'

Mrs Greenidge was standing in the doorway. I tried to speak but laughter burst out of my mouth and I was hugging my aching stomach with tears running down my face. At last Ruby was able to lift her head and gasp, 'It's Liesel, she's so funny,' before dissolving into fits again as Liesel dashed out of the room.

We had brought ourselves more or less under control when Liesel came trotting in with her lead in her mouth.

'Ha ha ha ha,' went Ruby and I fell back in my chair, helpless again, pink, wet-faced, dissolving in laughter and embarrassment.

We got out somehow, hearing Mr Greenidge's voice behind us saying 'Coming in here like a couple of hoydens', and we leaned, writhed, against the hedge of Kirriemuir until it didn't seem funny any more.

'What were we laughing about?' I said.

'I don't know. Search me!'

We walked on, the last dregs of laughter erupting from our lips every now and then.

'What are hoydens?' asked Ruby.

'I think they're a kind of hyena.' That did it again, swamping the guilty awareness of bad behaviour, making it amusing that we had been two grey spotted animals rolling around the Greenidge's floor, sprawling in their chair.

'The laughing Jackass,' said Ruby. 'I'll just die when we have to take Liesel back, won't you?'

'We'll leave her on the doorstep, ring the bell and run away.'

We didn't though. I handed the lead to Mrs Greenidge, feeling ashamed.

'Have you recovered now?' she asked.

'Yes, thank you Mrs Greenidge – ah ha ha.' We made a dash for the gate.

The next day, Saturday, a gipsy came to our back door. She was selling baskets made from bars of hazel saplings and filled with pale yellow primroses growing out of vivid green moss. The baskets, with their handles made from an arched stick, smelled cold and fresh, earthy and each held a clump of spring-time. We bought one for the tea-room and I loved the rough and smooth feel of the wood, the silvery heads of the nails and the bouncy moss and damp, delicate flowers. I carried it through, and gasped. It was like walking down a sunny lane and seeing a dead bird in your path. Mr Greenidge was sitting there with a big checked slipper on his bandaged foot.

Seventeen

We were in the middle of a mental-arithmetic test when Mr Reeves appeared in the doorway with Dittany. Her hair was piled on top of her head and wound round with a purple and yellow scarf and she wore a sort of smock printed with crocuses over a long purple skirt and wellingtons and her beekeeper's veil was dangling from one hand. She waggled the fingers of her other hand in a little wave to me and I felt myself blushing as we all heaved ourselves to our feet.

'Might we disturb you for a moment, Miss Fay?' asked Mr Reeves.

'We're in the middle of an arithmetic test,' said Miss Fay, moving Mr Reeves and Dittany towards the door, which gave me a chance to sneak a look at Veronica's answers. 'Be seated, class. Hands on heads.'

'Miss Codrington thinks that you might know the where-abouts of the old maypole the schoolchildren used to dance round,' Mr Reeves said.

'Maypole?'

'Yes, you know, a tall pole bedecked with ribbons, that people danced around on May Day.'

'I *do* know what a maypole is, thank you, Miss Codrington. But I'm afraid you won't find one here.'

'But there was a maypole?' said Mr Reeves.

'There was a maypole. But I'm afraid Major Morton burned it.'

'Burned it! But how *interesting*,' said Dittany. 'Did he burn it because of its pre-Christian, phallic symbolism as a totem of fertility?'

'No. For firewood,' said Miss Fay.

Dittany's face fell. Then she said, 'Never mind. *Nil desperandum*. I'm sure we can rig up another one. There must be some craftsman in the village who remembers the old skills. Thank you so much for your time, Miss Fay.'

'Hands off heads,' said Miss Fay. 'Twenty-seven divided by four. All those of you who copied your neighbours while my back was turned will stay in at playtime.'

Albie Fatman groaned.

I was upstairs in my bedroom reading; the clatter of teacups and voices, now emphatic, now disgruntled, now droning on, came from downstairs. Some Labour Party people were having a meeting. Because we lived in a tea-room they expected us to provide first-class refreshments, and I had seen one of them, on another occasion, prodding at a plate of biscuits and muttering, 'Well I vote it a pretty poor show.'

As I lay on my bed I heard feet on the stairs. The door burst open and Ruby stood there, panting, in the summer dress she had worn to school and her green woolly hat pulled down almost over her eyes.

'Ruby! What are you doing here? Why have you got your hat on? Are we playing a game?'

She just stood there, her face working. Then it crumpled and she flung herself on the bed, face downwards. Something slithered out of her pocket. A snake.

It slid slowly to the floor as I watched. One of Ruby's pigtails lay on the floor, still bound with a yellow rubber band and fraying out at the end where it had been hacked off.

'Ruby, what have you done?'

She didn't answer. Her back was shaking. I could see the freckled wing of her shoulder where the buttons had come off her dress.

Tentatively I pulled the bunched-up green wool of the top of her hat. Pink saw-toothed scratches criss-crossed her neck. Her right pigtail uncoiled and flipped out. The left side of her hair bushed out in a jagged mass from its parting.

'You won't half get into trouble. Oh why did you do it?'

Ruby sat up, almost spitting the words from her blotched face.

'I didn't do it. *He* did. With the breadknife.'

'Oh, Ruby.' I put my arm round her. 'Why?'

'Because he hates me.'

'No he doesn't,' I said, distressed at the black thought.

'You know he does. He's hated me ever since I was a little baby, and she's as bad.'

'What are you going to do?'

She couldn't go around like that, all lop-sided.

'Go and get the scissors. Don't tell your mum. I couldn't bear anybody to see me like this.'

She picked up the plait from the floor and held it in place in front of the mirror, as if she would glue it on again.

'Just getting something, Mum,' I said, downstairs.

'Is Ruby still here? It's getting late.'

'She's going in a minute.'

The scissors crunched in two bites through Ruby's hair and the pigtail was in my hand.

' "Oh, Jo, your hair. Your one beauty," ' I said.

Ruby whirled round, snatching the pigtail from my hand.

'I'm glad you think it's so funny!'

'I don't, honestly. I didn't mean it.'

'Look at me! I look completely – hideosic!'

'You don't, cross my heart. It looks really nice, now. It really suits you short. In fact I wish I could have mine cut too.'

'No you don't.'

'Yes I do.'

I could see one side of Ruby's hair was shorter than the other.

'Go on then.'

'All right then.'

'You wouldn't dare.'

'Yes I would.'

'Bet you wouldn't.'

Ruby turned away and bent down to pick up her two plaits.

'I might've known,' she said bitterly.

I couldn't bear it.

'Here,' I said, thrusting the scissors at her.

'Go on. You do it. Then we'll both be the same.'

Even as I spoke I hoped she would refuse the sacrifice. The scissors chomped sickeningly through my hair. Chomp, crunch, snap, chomp, crunch, snap, saw. My head felt light, the back of my neck shivered.

'Oh dear,' said Ruby.

'What?'

'It's a bit crooked. Hold on.'

Crunch crunch crunch.

'Stop it! I'll be bald in a minute.'

'That's better.'

I looked in the mirror and burst into tears. The face of a medieval peasant from our history book blubbered back at me.

'I look like a serf or a villain. It's sticking up all over the place.'

'That's just the electricity,' said Ruby.

Hers was starting to curl up prettily like a proper haircut. Mine was a ragged brown helmet.

'Do you think we could sell it, like Jo did?' she asked.

The thought of walking into Belinda-Jayne's with our hair in a paper bag defeated us.

'Let's burn it,' said Ruby.

She gathered up our mingled hair from the floor and threw it in the empty grate, which was never used.

'Don't!'

She struck a match and a lock of hair flared up with a horrible burning smell.

'What in heaven's name is going on?'

Percy stood staring at us. The flames sizzled and died.

'What are you trying to do? Set the chimney on fire? Burn your baby brother in his bed? Betty!' he shouted, not caring about waking Peter. 'Betty! Come up here.'

'Oh April, your hair!' Betty burst out crying. 'Whatever have you done? And Ruby! You naughty naughty girls. And what's that dreadful smell of burnt feathers? Oh, how could you?'

A wail came from Peter's room. 'Come on, Ruby, I'm taking you home,' said Percy. 'I don't know what your father will say when he sees you, and at this time of night.'

'It's all his fault,' I said. 'He started it. He cut off one of Ruby's plaits with the breadknife.'

'What?'

'Oh dear,' said Betty, 'I thought he'd turned over a new leaf.'

'I've got my bike. Please don't come with me,' Ruby said.

'You're not going home on your own and that's final. Come on.'

Ruby crammed her hat on and went out with a despairing look at me, leaving me and Betty with the crying baby and a grate of singed hair.

'I can't go to school tomorrow. Everybody will laugh at me.'

'You should have thought of that.'

I could hear her comforting Peter. After a while she came back.

'Perhaps Belinda-Jayne can fit you in after school to tidy it up a bit. Why on earth did Lex cut Ruby's hair off? With a breadknife.' She shuddered.

'Because he hates her.'

She left me with the bleak absence of a denial.

'What happened when you got back last night?' I asked Ruby on the way to school. I was wearing my pixie-hood. I was going to tell Miss Fay I had earache and ask if I could keep it on in class.

'Nothing. Your dad marched straight up to the bar and said to my dad, "What do you mean by treating your daughter like that? You're nothing but a bully and a coward. And letting her run round the village in the dark!" I thought my dad was going to hit him but my mum goes, "I was just putting on my coat to look for her. Ruby, you naughty girl, sneaking out when you're supposed to be in bed," and then she tells your

dad that I cut off my hair myself in a fit of temper. "What fibs
has she been telling you?" she goes, and your dad goes, "I
believe what Ruby told me." Everybody's staring, Mr Vinnegar
and Sack and Mr Annett and some other people.

'Then my dad says, "Get up to bed Ruby. I'll deal with you
in the morning. Thanks for bringing her home anyway," and
my mum goes. "Have a drink, Mr Harlency, on the house,"
and your dad goes, "I'm a bit choosy who I drink with. If you
so much as lay a finger on that child again I'll knock your teeth
down your flaming throat." '

'Blimey. Good old Percy; what happened next?'

'Your dad walked out and my dad came upstairs and belted
me one.' Then she said, scuffing her shoe on the pavement,
'I'm not allowed to come round your house any more, and
you're not allowed to come to tea on my birthday.'

Titchy pulled my hat off as soon as I stepped into the playground.

'April, whatever do you look like!'

'Her mum did it with the garden shears.'

'She looks like something the cat dragged in.'

'Ruby's looks nice though, doesn't it?'

'You look like nothing on earth, April.'

'You could have a perm, then it might not look so bad,'
Veronica said kindly.

It was even worse than I had imagined.

'Shut up, leave her alone. Come on, April.' Ruby put her
arm round me and led me to a corner of the playground past
Mr Reeves and Miss Elsey who were talking together.

'He tempers the wind to the shorn lamb, eh Miss Elsey?'
said Mr Reeves.

'Oh, rather!' Miss Elsey agreed. I could see she didn't know
what he meant either.

In the afternoon Miss Fay read us the tale of Shock-Headed
Peter. I was so tangled up with misery that it felt as if everybody
was laughing at my Peter as well as at me, and my mum for
chopping my hair with the kitchen scissors, although she hadn't

and I wanted to shut myself away safely at home. Except I was in disgrace.

'You ought to go and sit with the boys, April,' Doreen had said. 'Shame really, you used to have such lovely hair.'

Of course she had never thought so when it was long.

I sat dumb with embarrassment in Belinda-Jayne's while Belinda-Jayne, whose name was really Mrs Marshall, clucked and snipped, and Ruby and a row of vultures waited on the wall outside.

'There you are.'

Belinda-Jayne held up a mirror so that I could see the back.

'It looks quite nice,' I said in surprise.

'Your mum's got lovely hair, hasn't she? A nice natural wave to it . . . what are you putting that pixie-hood on for?'

'How could you do this to me, April?' Mr Greenidge stared in horror. 'A woman's crowning glory is her hair.'

'I'm not a woman am I? I'm a girl and girls can have their hair however they like.'

'Oh April, April.'

He lifted the ends of my hair and let it fall, shaking his head. I had been beginning quite to like it, and now I felt ugly again.

'Anyway, it's my hair.'

'You've changed, April. Don't spoil yourself.'

I knew he was remembering the time when we laughed like hyenas. He still wore the slipper on his foot but with a thinner bandage, which showed above his sock like an old man's long underpants. Suddenly he lunged out and grasped my knee, snatching his hand back as the tea-room doorbell jangled.

His face twisted in pain although it was I who could feel the marks left by his fingers.

'It doesn't matter,' he said in a low voice.

'Whatever you do, you won't stop me loving you. And that's the long and short of it.'

I couldn't call for Ruby in the mornings now and had to wait for her outside the Co-op. We parted there in the afternoon, making plans to meet up later if we could. Mr Greenidge and Liesel would be waiting round the corner, or I would see Liesel looped by her lead outside the shop and try to get past without her joyful greeting giving me away.

'Not having a party on your birthday?' he asked.

'No. If Ruby can't come I don't want anybody, and she didn't have a party.'

'Come to tea at Kirriemuir. I'll lay on a spread, birthday cake, anything you like. What do you say? It would be such a treat to share your birthday.'

'But – I always have a birthday cake at home – '

I was appalled at the idea, and how could I tell my parents. I was sure they would feel hurt.

'Crackers, balloons. Liesel in a paper hat. Do say yes. We'll have a lovely party. We could play games. Musical chairs, Hunt the thimble, Blind man's buff, Sardines, Postman's knock.'

'How could we, with just the three of us? It would be silly.'

'I never had a birthday party when I was a little boy,' he said wistfully. I saw a boy with his face pressed to a windowpane looking out, sadly, like an orphan.

'It's very kind of you.'

I was completely trapped. I felt as if I had gorged on party food already.

'I can't ask them.'

'Leave it to me. I'll sort them out. Use all my diplomatic skills.' He was cheerful again. It was impossible, Betty would think I preferred a shop cake to hers. They would think I liked the Greenidges better than my own family. I didn't want to be in a plot with Mr Greenidge.

'I hate my birthday. I don't want a birthday. I don't want a party, just leave me alone.'

I ran away from him.

'April.'

My birthday, endangered by falling on April Fool's Day, bruised by the Bumps at playtime, clouded by Ruby's absence from the tea party and devastated by the loss of the black-and-green propelling pencil Betty and Percy had given me, was made a total disaster by the arrival of Mr Greenidge and Liesel with a huge box of chocolates.

'Come in! April's just about to blow out her candles.'

It was, as Percy might have put it, the icing on the cake.

'A little bird told me it was somebody's birthday.'

I waited, weighed down with dread, for him to ask to see my presents. They had warned me against taking my propelling pencil to school and I had not dared to confess that I had lost it on the way home.

I knew it was expensive. It was beautiful too and I had loved it. I couldn't bear to think of it lying somewhere, lonely, trodden on, or drowned in a drain, or in someone else's pocket, somebody horrible.

I would tell Miss Fay tomorrow and she would ask if anybody had found it, but nobody would own up. I would never get it back. I was in mourning for that propelling pencil, green and black with a gold band and clip and tip, that Percy and Betty had specially chosen for me.

'I expect you had lots of lovely presents, eh?' said Mr Greenidge, chomping cake after I had blown out the candles in a gust of tears, which fortunately I had been able to hide as I bowed my head to cut the cake and make a wish.

'April? Mr Greenidge is talking to you.'

'Yes thank you.'

'Why don't you show them to Mr Greenidge?'

'Ruby gave me this bracelet.'

I held out my wrist to show a circle of the glass beads I had given Ruby for Christmas.

'Very pretty.'

'Show Mr Greenidge your new propelling pencil,' Betty said.

'And I got a compendium of games and a cardigan from Granny and Grandpa and a ball from Peter.'

'Go on, April,' said Percy.

I could see they were anxious in case Mr Greenidge thought they hadn't given me a good present.

'I can't. I left it at school.'

'I hope it's somewhere safe.'

'It's in my desk. It's quite safe.'

172

'Never mind,' Percy said in a disappointed voice, as if I didn't think enough of the pencil to bring it home.

'What's it like?' said Mr Greenidge. 'Very smart, I'll be bound.'

I described the pencil, fighting tears. Everybody knew that if you cried on your birthday you would cry all the year round.

True to my foreboding, nobody put up a hand when Mrs Fay asked if anybody had found my pencil.

'It was very silly of you to bring it to school in the first place,' she said, but she let me go to Mr Reeves's and Miss Elsey's class-rooms to ask if anyone there had found it. They all shook their heads. Somebody was lying.

I was trailing home searching the gutter without hope when 'Pee-wit, pee-wit!'

I turned. Mr Greenidge was hobbling as fast as he could after me. How dare he use our new secret call, the hateful old spy. Liesel dragged him along.

'Wait. I've got something for you!'

'What?' There was only one thing I wanted, I certainly didn't want any more sweets.

'In my pocket.'

'I don't want it.'

'Oh yes you do-o,' he almost sang, looking so pleased with himself. 'Go on, left trouser-pocket.'

Reluctantly, gracelessly, I put my hand in his trouser pocket, and felt something shiny. I pulled it out. My whole body blazed with joy.

'My pencil! Where did you find it?'

It lay in my hand green and black and shining gold.

'I didn't. I bought it. I guessed you had lost it. Our secret, eh?'

'But—'

The happiness drained from me. I stared at the false propelling pencil. Then I realized that I had been saved.

'Well, do I get a kiss to say thank you?'

'Oh, yes.'

He bent down and I put my arms round his neck and kissed

him in the street. I was truly grateful, yet I knew I could never feel the same about the pencil as my own lost one, and it was heavy with secrecy and guilt. Now I would always have to be nice to Mr Greenidge.

'It's time we went back to the orchard. To spring-clean our house,' Ruby said.

'No, don't let's go back there.'

'Why not?'

'I don't know. I just don't want to.'

'But we've got to. It's ours. If we don't, somebody else might find it and take it for their camp. Anyway, we left some of our things there and they've been there all winter.'

'It might have gone. The farmer might have taken it away, or an old tramp might be living there. A murderer might have moved in.'

'Nah.'

'What about that man who got Sorrel Marlowe then?'

'I thought you said that was Rodney Pegg. He lives in London, doesn't he, so he wouldn't be living in an old railway compartment in Stonebridge, would he?'

'Oh, all right then.'

'Look!' I caught Ruby's arm.

The orchard was all white, as if millions of butterflies had settled on its branches.

'It's the garden of Eden,' she said.

We stood hand-in-hand. High above the bird-song a silver aeroplane trailed a white arc that bloomed and expanded into parallel tracks of cloud and dissolved into the blue. The orchard was an open fan of dark spokes frothing into white flounces, then the pattern of the rows of trees was broken as we ran towards the railway carriage through wet grass and buttercups and ladies' smocks, feeling sharp stones in the hidden furrows under our feet.

The camp was intact, untouched, in tendrils of spring growth. Ruby took a duster from her knicker leg and a minia- ture tin of polish, a free sample from a salesman, out of her pocket and a packet of Gold Flake. We sat in the doorway watching blue snakes of smoke coiling in the air while the sun-dried petals slicked to our legs and startled spiders ran to hide in dark corners and cobwebs as thick as wire netting behind us.

Eighteen

Dittany failed to get a maypole made even though she went round to the almshouses seeking an old craftsman, who sent her away with a flea in her ear, so Bobs said. She approached the Forestry Commission but they were no help either. We sat in our desks at school singing the coloured ribbons of the maypole dances and songs about the cuckoo whose voice we could hear through the window of the class-room that was full of the scent of bluebells and the smell of tadpole water. Down the meadows was full of flowers when we went there after school. Ruby's parents seemed to have forgotten that she wasn't allowed to play with me. Sometimes Betty let us take Peter out in his pram. Two or three days could go by before I started worrying about Mr Greenidge, and then I would have to meet him secretly again, with Peter when I could have him.

One Sunday morning as we cycled past Kirriemuir on our way to Sunday school we saw Dr Barker coming out of the gate. The next time I met Mr Greenidge he said, 'Mrs Greenidge is very poorly. It might cheer her up to see a young face about the place.'

I took her a bunch of wild flowers and her eyes filled with tears. She was lying on the wicker couch in the conservatory with her tapestry on a stool beside her. I thought of Beth, when the needle grew too heavy for her fingers, and I was afraid. There were wide pale-blue circles under her eyes and blue veins on her hands. 'Hark at the birds,' she said. Her voice sounded worn out. 'Your hair suits you like that April. It shows the shape of your face.' For the first time I felt that Mrs Greenidge liked me.

'Come and help me make some tea,' said Mr Greenidge.

I was outraged when he embraced me in the kitchen, with Mrs Greenidge so ill.

'Mrs Greenidge isn't going to . . . die, is she?'

'Oh it's been such a long, long time, my darling. Too too long, I've missed holding you in my arms so much. What did you say? Mmm mmm mmm.' He nuzzled my neck.

'Will Mrs Greenidge get better?'

The kettle was screaming.

'Who can say? Poor old girl's getting very frail. Don't forget to warm the teapot.'

I went cold. 'Very frail' was how the murderess had described her crippled husband in *Deathcap Cottage*. Before she poisoned him.

'I bought these specially for you.' He spread out chocolate fingers on a plate.

'Is it her dicky ticker – I mean her heart?'

If Mrs Greenidge died I would have to marry him as soon as I was old enough.

''Fraid so, my dear. Tricky organs, tickers. Now give me a kiss before she starts to wonder what we're up to. Mustn't arouse suspicion, eh?'

I gritted my teeth so that I wouldn't bite him. I could see myself in a bride's long white dress walking down the aisle on his white linen arm. Suppose he had put poison in Mrs Greenidge's tea? No, he couldn't have. But suppose he was secretly giving her a slow poison, deceiving even Dr Barker, and there was really nothing wrong with her heart?'

'Must you light your pipe in here, Clem?' said Mrs Greenidge wearily and I intercepted his look of pure hatred.

Mrs Greenidge did get better. At Whitsun she was strong

enough to walk to the war memorial and sit on a folding stool to see the Morris dancers. People sat on the bridge watching them and the hobby horse pranced and lunged into the crowd standing around, some with pints of beer in the sunshine. Bobs and Dittany were there and I think the white-clothed men, with their ribbons and bells and sticks, their black hats and socks and shiny black shoes, made up for the maypole. One of the dancers bopped Miss Fay on the bonce with a bladder on a stick. Peter stretched out his arms and clapped his little hands at the music. He was wearing a blue-and-white romper suit with embroidered yachts bobbing on blue waves across the yoke. Betty was carrying him. Percy was holding the fort. I saw the Silver boys and waved.

'Wouldn't it be lovely if the Morris Men came to the Copper Kettle?' I said.

'Just what I was thinking.'

They went to the Rising Sun, where Lex had put trestle tables and benches on either side of the porch.

When we got home I said, 'Hey, Dad, when are we going to get the tables and chairs for the garden?'

'All in good time.'

Then Miss Fay actually came into the tea-room with another lady, saying to her, 'I'm afraid it's the best I can offer you, but it's improved slightly since it changed hands.'

'Any port in a storm,' said her friend and asked to be shown to the ladies room. 'This is April, one of my pupils,' Miss Fay told her friend.

I took her out the back.

It was just my luck that a gang of motor-cyclists should roar up and come swaggering in unbuckling helmets and slapping gauntlets.

'What a pleasure to see you here, Miss Fay. What can I do for you?' said Percy.

'Just a pot of coffee for two and some plain cakes, Mr Harlency. I've got a loin of pork in the oven for a late luncheon.'

'Very nice too,' said Percy. 'Coming up.'

The bikers had pushed two tables together and were becoming very rowdy.

'Keep it down lads, eh? There are ladies present,' Percy asked them.

'Oh, I say, keep it down chaps. There are ladies present,' one of them mocked, putting on a posh voice.

'Oh, really? I can't see none,' another of them said. 'Can you?'

'Nah.'

Miss Fay and her friend had gone crimson and were pretending to chat as if they hadn't heard. I was lurking in the kitchen now, dying of shame. A loud belch ripped the air. All the bikers laughed rude, ugly laughs. From the doorway I half expected Miss Fay to stand up and roar, 'Silence! Hands on heads!' It was worse to see her frightened. I had to take plates of egg and chips to the bikers' table and as I put them down among the huge black arms and cigarette smoke, Miss Fay bit into her cake and gobbled like a turkey and put her handkerchief to her face.

'Water. Bring some water quickly,' called her friend. I ran to get it.

Miss Fay removed something from her hanky.

'This is intolerable. A plastic doll. Come, Agnes, we're leaving. I can only apologize for bringing you to this establishment. I'm sorry.'

It was John, a tiny pink baby in a nappy, 3d in Woolworth's. I had been wondering where he'd got to.

Miss Fay looked as if she were going to cry. Her friend looked embarrassed.

'On the house, Miss Fay,' said Percy placatingly.

'I should jolly well think so too. You haven't heard the last of this, not by a long chalk.'

To me she hissed, 'I hope you realize you've let the whole school down, April Harlency.'

John was lying in a wad of cake crumbs. He would need a bath, a good long soak, before I could play with him again. Ruby had his twin, called Lennet.

Three days later we had a visit from two Health Inspectors in disguise. Percy spotted them for wrong 'uns right off. They didn't find anything amiss, but Percy said, 'You can bet your bottom dollar Miss Fay had a finger in this particular individual fruit pie.'

'Rotten old stoolpigeon,' said Betty.

'It's all right for you, you're not in her class,' I made the mistake of saying.

'I think you're forgetting who nearly got us closed down. I hope you realize that Miss Fay could have choked to death?'

'Good riddance to bad rubbish,' I mumbled out of earshot.

Miss Fay had put the flowers they made me take to school on Monday in the waste-paper basket.

'Better luck next time,' Ruby said when I told her what Percy had said. I remembered that Miss Fay's dried fig of hair had been caught in a May-Day net threaded with tiny coloured beads, and I felt sad.

I was lying in bed that night when a thought froze in my blood. What if I *had* killed Miss Fay? What if it had been my fault that Major Morton died? And Professor Scoley? Supposing Mr Greenidge *was* poisoning Mrs Greenidge so that he could marry me? What if even now he was sprinkling rat poison into her cocoa?

I burst into the sitting-room where Betty and Percy were listening to a play.

'We've got to get the police. Get Mr Cox. Mr Greenidge is going to murder Mrs Greenidge.'

'What?'

They looked startled, as if I had broken into their yellow lamplight evening world.

'Come on, back to bed. You've been having another of those nasty dreams, haven't you? What have you been reading now?'

Betty laid aside her knitting with a sigh, a sock on four needles.

'No, it's true. We've got to stop him.'

'Up the wooden hill to Bedfordshire, come on. Besides, we're still waiting for the telephone if you remember. How could we ring the police even if we wanted to?'

'Go round there, to the police station.'

'This has gone far enough. We're trying to listen to a play if you don't mind.'

Back in bed again, I lay in the darkness thinking, supposing I'm really the devil's daughter, and I don't know it? I got up again and switched on the light and searched until I found the palm cross we had been given at Sunday school on Palm Sunday and I stuck a drawing pin through it and hammered it into the wall above my bed with my shoe.

Nineteen

The communist invasion of Stonebridge began while the congregation of St Michael and All Angels was at prayer. The Silvers were having a garden party, and children released from Sunday school watched the convoy of comrades rolling along the High Street through the scents of honeysuckle and manure and of cooking dinners wafting out of doors and windows standing open to let the steam from the kitchen out into the heat of the day. They came in cars and vans and an old green bus.

Mr Silver had invited all our family, but only I was free to go. He had asked Ruby too and she had made the mistake of mentioning it at home. Lex had forbidden her to go anywhere near the Paper Mill: 'I'm not having you hob-nobbing with the likes of them. They ought to go back to Russia were they belong.' She would have to sneak out. Mr Greenidge had been disapproving when I told him about it.

'I'd steer well clear of that lot if I were you.'

I could see that he was jealous because I liked the Silvers.

'The man's a scoundrel. I don't know how he has the nerve to hold a garden party in Stonebridge after that filthy Burgess and Maclean business. Don't know why he doesn't go and join them. Uncle Joe Silver! He's a traitor to his country. Ought to be put against a wall and shot, the lot of them.'

'There are going to be donkey rides and a coconut shy and all sorts of stalls and races.'

'I'm disappointed in you, April. Deeply disappointed. Bitterly disappointed.'

He turned and walked away, exaggerating his limp, stopping to call back to me, 'I suppose you know they murdered their own Royal Family?'

'Yes, Miss Fay told us.'

'Sensible woman, Alice Faye. One of the old school.'

'Her name's Olivia.'

'At least it isn't Olga.'

He stumped off.

'All the crowned heads of the Communist Party will be there, so to speak,' Percy said wistfully.

'I wish we could shut up shop for the afternoon,' Betty said. 'You might even see Paul Robeson, April, Mr Silver told me he's met him. If you do, get me his autograph and tell him I'm a great fan, won't you?'

'How will I know which one's him?'

'Oh, I think he'll stand out from the crowd, in Stonebridge,' said Percy.

'Oh my baby, my curly-headed baby,' Betty sang, into Peter's straight dark quiff.

'Here's Ruby. Have a lovely time and don't forget to say thank you for having me.'

'Yes, yes, spandy nice and Meg has colonge on hers,' said Ruby.

'Cologne,' said Betty.

Joe and Molly Silver were standing at the gate on the stone bridge that crossed the moat to greet their guests under a red flag. Beyond them, the garden had been transformed into a little fairground and we heard the music of a baby merry-go-round. We joined the people strolling around eating ice-cream and candyfloss, sitting in groups on the grass. Wire netting enclosed the garden to prevent any children from falling into the river or the deep pool. Charmaine Vinnegar was led past us on a donkey, splitting the air with hysterical shrieks, her feet almost touching the ground.

'Somebody ought to tell the RSPCA,' said Ruby. 'Look at them!'

They were African men in bright striped robes over striped trousers with round matching hats, and a tall woman in a patterned garment and high head-dress. She was eating pink candyfloss and wore gold sandals. The men's ankles were bare above black polished shoes. I didn't think any of them was Paul Robeson.

'Aren't they lovely?' said Ruby.

Bobs and Dittany came up with two Indian ladies in saris, as pleased with themselves as if they'd caught two rare butterflies. Doreen was looking covetous. She collected dolls in National Costume, but so far she only had a Welsh lady.

'Have you been on a donkey yet?' asked Bobs.

'Not yet. There's so much to do we don't know where to start,' I said.

'I can recommend the toffee apples,' Dittany told us, so we headed in that direction. I won a glass salt-and-pepper set with red tops, on the hoop-la stall.

'I'm going to give it to my mum.'

'Excuse me,' said Ruby, 'but don't you happen to live in a café?'

'Oh yes, never mind.'

It was such a beautiful day that nothing seemed to matter much. We had a go on the roundabout, sitting in a car with our knees sticking up and little Juney going round on a gilded cockerel behind us. Leo Silver, wearing a checked shirt and corduroy trousers, watched us climb out and asked if we wanted any strawberries.

'We've got heaps,' he said. 'Some are a bit squishy though. And cherries. D'you want to come and get some?'

'OK.'

'Are you going in for the races later?' he asked.

'Dunno. Are you?'

'I might.'

'So might we.'

The strawberries were piled on punnets on a trestle table draped with greengrocer's grass and Molly Silver stood behind it now spooning them into frilly paper jelly dishes and frightening off wasps with a flywhisk made from a beaded handled horse's tail. To her right, under the flat blue branches of a cedar tree, a group of coloured musicians in wide-brimmed hats and blue suits with trousers as baggy as a clown's were setting up drums and unpacking brass instruments that flashed in the sun. We saw Mr Reeves with his youngest child on his shoulders holding a balloon like a soap bubble on a string in her hand.

The three of us, Leo, Ruby and I, were at the coconut shy. The man in charge was singing 'I've got a luvverly bunch of coconuts' and Ruby had the ball in her hand, swinging it back to take aim. A hairy tattooed arm closed on her neck from behind, choking her scream, and swinging her off her feet. The ball fell from her hand. A woman shrieked.

'Put her down, you brute.'

Leo rushed at Lex battering him with his fists, trying to grab the arm round Ruby's neck while she kicked and clawed at it and the dirty vest, her face squeezed scarlet.

Lex swiped Leo to the ground with his free hand. 'Bugger off out of it. Four Eyes.' He started walking with the struggling Ruby still dangling.

'Let her go,' I was screaming. Then Joe Silver leaped on Lex from behind, and he let go of Ruby who tore off blindly across the garden. Lex whirled round and Joe smashed his fist onto his chin knocking Lex's head back, and then Molly Silver was between them beating them both with her flywhisk and people were picking Leo up from the grass. I raced after Ruby, dodging through the crowd, jumping bushes and running through flower beds.

'Ruby! Wait!'

She wouldn't stop and I couldn't catch her and she dragged her bike from the hedge and jumped on it and pedalled over the bridge. Lex was charging towards me. I had to stop him. I dragged the gate shut and pulled on it with all my weight from the outside. Joe Silver and several other men came pounding after Lex and if I could hold the gate they could catch him.

Lex wrenched the gate from my hands, bruising them and shoving me into the hedge with its impact and thudded up the lane skittering on loose stones. Ruby was out of sight. The men ran to a halt.

'Where's the little girl?'

'She's gone. She had her bike.'

We saw Lex suddenly fold in half as though he had a stitch and sit down by the side of the lane in the goosegrass and old man's beard.

'Drunken sod. Do we go after him?'

'The kiddy's got away safely at least.'

'For now,' said Joe Silver. 'I'll call round there later. Do you think she's gone home, April?'

I shrugged. 'Search me. I shouldn't think so. She might have gone to my house. I'd better go and look for her.'

Leo had joined us and his father put his arm round him.

'I'm proud of you, my boy. All right, April? I'm sorry your afternoon had to be spoiled.'

'My glasses are broken, Dad.'

'Don't worry, my son. I'll fix them.'

Lex had his head on his knees. He got up and started shambling on up the lane.

'Sure you'll be OK, April? Don't go near that ugly brute. I think I'll give Constable Cox a ring.'

The other two Silver boys and Mr Reeves had arrived now, and I felt so envious of them all as they turned back in a group to return to the party. I was alone on the wrong side of the moat again. Lex ought to be put up against a wall and shot.

Ruby had not gone to the Copper Kettle.

'I'm not having you going anywhere near the Rising Sun. I'm sure Ruby will turn up in her own good time. She's probably feeling embarrassed about what happened,' Betty said. 'Poor kid. Well, it's gone far enough. I'm going to report him if no one else does.'

'Mr Silver's going to ring Constable Cox.'

'Good job too.'

I was secretly relieved to have been forbidden to go looking for Ruby at the Rising Sun because the prospect terrified me. Then as the afternoon wore on into evening I began to worry. By ten o'clock I was demented. I kept getting up from bed to peer out into the moonlight, listening for Ruby's call, and then lying down again with Bobbity. I was on my knees praying that Ruby was not in a dark corner of the cellar, that she was not dead, when I heard footsteps and a knocking on the back door.

I crept half-way down the stairs to listen.

'I'll have my daughter, if you don't mind.' It was Gloria.

'What are you talking about? Ruby isn't here.' Percy.

'You'd better come inside.' Betty.

I shifted down to the foot of the stairs.

'What do you mean, she's not here? She must be.'

'When did you last see her?' Percy.

'She was home at dinner time. Then she ran off to that garden party and my husband went after her to bring her home, but she ran off again, on her bike.'

'You mean to say that you haven't seen your daughter since dinner time and you wait till eleven o'clock at night to come looking for her?' Percy.

'Well, we had a busy night. You know how it is,' Gloria whined.

'No, we don't know how it is,' Betty snapped.

'Well, where is she then? My husband's frantic with worry.'

A bitter laugh. Percy.

'Oh is he? Did he happen to mention what happened at that garden party? Did he tell you what he did to his daughter? That he disgraced her in front of everybody and terrified her out of her wits?' Betty.

'She's a very naughty girl. She was told not to go out and she deliberately disobeyed. I'll tell you something else. That April of yours is a bad influence on Ruby. She—'

'Shut up!' Percy. 'This isn't getting us anywhere. Don't you realize your daughter is *lost*? Out there, somewhere in the dark. Anything could have happened to her.'

'I don't know what her dad will say.'

The door opened on me crouched on the stairs. I expected

to be in trouble for eavesdropping but Betty said, 'April, have you any idea where Ruby could be?'

'No.'

'Liar!' said Gloria. 'I bet you've got her hidden upstairs.'

'Don't you call my daughter a liar.' Betty.

'Would she have gone to any other friend's house?' Percy.

I shook my head.

Gloria dabbed her eyes with a hanky.

'Any secret hideouts or camps? Think.'

'No.'

Suddenly I knew where Ruby was. I would go there first thing in the morning and take some food.

'Come on, we're going to the police,' said Percy.

'How could she do this to us?' wept Gloria.

'You're shivering. Do you want some cocoa?' Betty asked.

'Yes please.'

She tucked the gossamer shawl round my shoulders although it was a warm night when moths bumped against the win- dowpane.

'Are you quite sure you don't know where Ruby could be?'

I almost betrayed Ruby over the steam of my cocoa.

'No. I mean I am quite sure.'

There was that old blanket in the railway carriage, candles and matches. And spiders and possibly ghosts, and a murderer and Rodney Pegg.

'Mum, I know—'

'Know what?' Her voice was sharp.

'I know Ruby wouldn't be in a haystack.'

There had been a case in the local paper of a tramp who had fallen asleep in a haystack and been cooked.

'I certainly hope not.'

I sipped wretchedly, not meeting her eyes. Betty picked up her knitting. After a few moments she clucked, as if she had dropped a stitch.

I tried to stay awake until Percy got back, but I woke to early sunshine and instant recollection of Ruby's escape. I dressed and crept downstairs. They were all in the kitchen, Percy, Betty and Peter. Betty was making tea and toast. How could I get out now?

'What's the time?'

'Six. Jim Cox is organizing search parties.'

'Can I come?'

'No, pet. You stay and help your mother.'

'Will Lex go?'

'That b——. Serve him right if—' He broke off. 'No, I didn't mean that.'

Major Morton. Professor Scoley. Ruby?

'Well, I'm off. Take care of yourselves.' Percy finished his tea and toast and kissed us all.

'Bring her back safely,' said Betty.

Percy nodded and went out.

'Do you want a boiled egg? I'm doing one for Peter.'

The thought of it made my stomach heave. Betty dipped strips of toast into Peter's egg and he sucked them, getting yolk on his chin. I sat, playing with my toast, torn apart by panic and guilt. Gloria was right. I was a liar. All those people out there searching. I was the only one who could tell them the truth, and the only one who could save Ruby from them.

'I'm just going out on my bike.'

'No you're not.'

'I've got to. I've got to go somewhere. To the shop, there's something I need.'

'At half-past six in the morning?'

'I meant later. I promised to get something for Mrs Greenidge.'

'Well you can get it on the way to school, can't you?'

'School? I didn't think I'd be going to school!'

'I just don't know what to do for the best,' said Betty.

'It might be better if I did go to school,' my heart began racing.

'I think I'd rather you stayed at home today. Miss Fay will understand, and Mrs Greenidge.'

'They won't. Nobody can.'

'They'll find Ruby all right. They'll bring her back safely, you'll see.'

Then she suddenly put her arms round me, half-crouching so that our faces were level.

'If you do know something, April, please say, now. Ruby's life could depend on you.'

I was about to speak when someone knocked on the back door, so I never knew what I might have said.

'Perhaps there's some news.' Betty rushed to the door. 'Oh, Bobs, it's you. Come in,' she said flatly.

'We're going out to join the search. I just wondered if April had any ideas where we might look. I mean, Ruby could be trapped somewhere. A silo, the old eel trap in the river . . .'

My dream of Ruby trapped in the burning orchard flashed into my brain.

'April?'

'No.'

If Ruby was found she would get into the most awful trouble with all those people looking for her. And so would I. We would both be sent to an approved school. I had to find her before they did so that we could run away together. Please God don't let Ruby be murdered or trapped by fire before I get there.

'Tell everybody there will be tea and sandwiches here if they want them. I can't think of what else to do . . . oh dear, I just wish they'd hurry up and find her. I can't bear to think of her – out there, somewhere.'

'Will they have bloodhounds?' I asked.

'There may be some police dogs, Alsatians I expect.'

Wet pink tongues beaded with saliva flapping over jagged teeth, panting after a runaway slave. Myself running across the fields pursued by baying dogs, accidentally leading them straight to Ruby's hiding place.

As Bobs left, a policeman and policewoman arrived.

'Could we have a word in private, Mrs Harlency?'

'Oh, my God!'

'No, it's all right. We hope . . .'

'April, take Peter through a minute.'

Peter was crawling on the floor. I captured him by the back of his vest and carried him just out of sight.

'We have to prepare ourselves for the worst, Mrs Harlency. We've found the bicycle.'

I heard Betty gasp and cry out, 'No.'

'Of course it may not necessarily mean anything at this stage. I wonder if we could ask April some questions. I gather that she's the missing child's best friend.'

'That's right. They're inseparable.'

'OK, let's have her in then. We'll be as gentle as possible,' said the policewoman.

'Did you and Ruby have any special places you used to play in? Any hideouts or hidey-holes, a secret camp perhaps? I know when I was a little girl I had a camp in an old hollow tree.'

She could never have squeezed into a hollow tree now.

'One of your school friends said she thought you have a secret . . .'

'What friend?'

'It doesn't matter who it was. All that matters is finding Ruby and bringing her home safely, isn't it?'

'Yes.'

'So why don't you tell us where you think Ruby might be hiding, mmm?'

'I don't know. In the rec maybe, or she could've taken sanctuary in the church. She might have climbed into the belfry and got stuck.'

In the midst of all this drama what could I do but lie to the police, to the kind policewoman?'

'Where was Ruby's bicycle found?' I asked as they were leaving.

'Where do you think it might have been found, April?'.

'How should I know? I don't know! I wish everybody would stop asking me all these questions.'

The baker and the milkman came next and I ran upstairs to pack a few clothes and Bobbity in a carrier bag. I would have to steal food when I got the chance and some money from the till. Ruby's bicycle lay on its side with its wheels spinning. Perhaps she had abandoned it to throw them off the scent, to make it look as if she'd been kidnapped. I hid the bag under my bed and looked round my bedroom through tears. There was my white sugar peepshow Easter egg, piped in pink icing, too precious to eat, and all my treasures that I would never see again.

Mr Greenidge came into the tea-room in his white suit and a panama hat. He had picked a white rose for his lapel as if it were just another sunny day. He looked jaunty. Out on the spree. As if he might start twirling his stick in a tap dance or make Liesel jump through a paper hoop.

'No, I haven't called in for my tiffin, Mrs Harlency. I just dropped in at the Rising Sun to see if there was any news.'

'Well?'

He looked as if he were about to say something important.

'The bicycle has been found.' His voice was solemn as if he were at church.

'We know, the police have been here.'

Mr Greenidge looked disappointed.

'Oh. Well then. Did they have anything to add? Any fresh clues?'

'She hadn't opened up, had she? Gloria?'

Mr Greenidge put his hand on my shoulder.

'Ah well. One must take the charitable view. Somebody has to hold the fort. Life must go on eh? Poor woman's pretty distracted to give her her due. And our little April, this is a dreadful ordeal for her too.'

'Well I'm glad Gloria's keeping the home fires burning pulling pints!' said Betty.

Mr Greenidge's fingers tightened painfully on my bone, transmitting the message right through my body that he knew where Ruby was hiding.

'Fair dos,' he said. 'Worry makes thirsty work.'

I twisted free and looked up into his cold blue eyes, at the beard like a badger shaving brush. A white handkerchief with a blue letter C.

'Best be off. I'll keep you posted if I hear anything. Drop it, Liesel! Drop!' Liesel had Peter's rubber squeaky teddy in her mouth, squeaking feebly.

'Chin up, April.' He squeezed my chin between his forefinger and thumb. 'I only wish I could be out there too.' He tapped his ankle angrily with his stick. 'Makes a chap feel so damn useless.'

There was no way I could make my escape because that day, for the first time, the Copper Kettle was as we had imagined it, full of people, even Mrs Edenbridge-Dwyer popped in, more customers than we could cope with, and Betty rushed off her feet.

To and fro I went between tea-room and kitchen with my stomach quivering like a heap of scrambled egg, serving the customers eating and drinking Ruby's disappearance. Mr Greenidge returned just as the policeman came back into the steamed-up kitchen.

'Afternoon, Inspector. Any joy?'

'Thank you, Mrs Harlency, I could murder a cup.'

'It's a bit weak I'm afraid. We're running out of everything.'

'So long as its warm and wet. Nothing as yet, sir.'

Behind their back Mr Greenidge mouthed a kiss at me.

'Leave me alone. I hate you,' I hissed. He recoiled as though I had spat at him.

'I was just remarking to my lady wife, Mrs Greenidge, that the police have an almost impossible task. There are so many places that a child could hide, aren't there, barns, sheds, a hollow tree, an old railway carriage, a stable loft.'

'What was that you said, sir? An old railway carriage?'

I was out of the house and on my bike, voices shouting behind me, along the High Street, legs hurting, pedalling on, zooming down Lovers Lane. At the bridge I threw my bike in the grass and raced across the meadow, zigzagging through cows, tripping in the rough grass over clumps of thistle and sorrel and cowpats, scrambling up and running on until a red-hot stitch seared my side and I stopped, sobbing, panting, touching my toes to make the stitch go away. Then I saw a cloud, a billowing black-and-grey plume of smoke twisting and spreading in the sky above the orchard.

A hand grasped my shoulder. I turned, into a blur of black

and silver buttons. The Inspector. And then we both saw the men walking forwards in a crooked line across the field. Percy, Tiny Vinnegar, Joe Silver, Mr Drew the Sunday-school teacher, fathers of the children at school, and at the centre of the line was Lex, carrying Ruby on his back.

Her face and arms and legs were black. Her gingham dress was scorched. One bare foot dangled where a laceless plimsoll had fallen off.

'It wasn't me! I didn't tell!' I was running alongside Lex.

'I knew you wouldn't,' Ruby's smudged face said before Percy dragged me violently by the arm and caught me a slap round the head that sent me spinning with shock and grief.

Our house was dreary with a constant grey drizzle of shame and disgrace. I had that foolish feeling all the time, as if everything I did was silly, as if my body and face were naked. After all the tongues and lips and voices attacking me, picking me to pieces, all the questions, I spent most of my time in my bedroom. I tried to read *Valley of Doom*, to blot out my panic with fear but it made it worse. The rattling of the dice in my compendium of games was agonizingly loud as my ears strained to catch words from downstairs about Ruby. About me. The bell on the tea-room door jangled and jangled. It was summer outside and children's careless shouts sounded cruel. A ball thudded heartlessly in the road and soared dully into the blue that I couldn't see. Nobody had said I was a prisoner and yet I knew I was. Even Peter turned away from me. He was grizzly with teething but I felt that he sensed that I was tainted. George Dixon and Julia Lang sang songs for good little children on *Listen With Mother*. 'I'll kill myself,' I vowed. 'Then they'll all be sorry.' I hated them all but what was truly unbearable was the separation from their love. Percy and I avoided each other's eyes because we both knew this, that at the time of Ruby's capture, by hitting me in anger he had turned into Lex for a moment.

On the third day I got up while everybody was still sleeping, after a disturbed night when I had lain awake listening to their voices soothing and shushing Peter. I crept out the back door

194

and got my bike. The latch on the shed was silver with dew. I rode along the quiet High Street to the Rising Sun and leaning my bike against the fuschia hedge, tiptoed round the yard.

'Pee-wit. Pee-wit.'

I stood below Ruby's window calling in a hoarse whisper, 'Ruby! It's me. Wake up.'

I stooped down and found a little piece of gravel and threw it at her window as Ruby would have done. It hit the glass and fell down into silence, and birdsong. I looked around the yard. No piglets. No pullets. A pile of weedy crates, broken brown bottle glass flashing as the sun struck it. I picked up a bigger pebble and flung it harder and a white spiderweb cracked in the glass.

'To whit too whooo,' I tried our old call. 'Ruby! Ruby!'

'You're too late.'

I whirled round to see the postman standing there.

'You've missed them. They've done a flit. Cleared out. Lock stock and barrel.'

Twenty

When I went back to school I took a book to read at playtime. I wouldn't speak to anybody. After a few days Veronica sidled up to me. 'Can I be your best friend now Ruby's gone?'

I looked up from my book. 'If you want. I don't care.'

My parents made me go to tea with the Greenidges. Of course Mr Greenidge had pretended to the police that his mention of a railway carriage had just been 'a shot in the dark'. When he opened the door of Kirriemuir and tried to hug me, I kicked him in the shins and went through to the conservatory knowing that he couldn't tell. Mrs Greenidge was lying on the couch with Liesel at her feet. Liesel lifted her head and wagged her tail but she didn't get up.

'Move, Liesel,' said Mrs Greenidge trying to shift her. 'You're heavy, you silly great salami. I wish she hadn't taken to lying there like a dog on a tombstone. Doesn't do much to keep my spirits up.'

I could see it was meant to be a joke but it wasn't funny so I couldn't even smile.

'Come and sit down, April. How are you? How is your baby brother? I suppose he'll be running about soon.'

'All right,' I said.

Mrs Greenidge took my hand in her purple hand.

'It's very painful isn't it? It's so hard to lose somebody you love.'

At that I felt myself lay my head in her lap, sobbing against the slippery silk while she stroked my hair and underneath my grief was surprise that Mrs Greenidge should be the only one to understand.

I heard the jiggling of teacups as Mr Greenidge put down the tray but I didn't look up.

'There,' said Mrs Greenidge, still stroking my hair. 'That's better. You run along now. Don't worry about tea.'

She gave me her own hanky with a spray of violets in the corner and a purple border, smelling of her turquoise scent.

'April, wait a minute,' Mr Greenidge whispered in the hall, 'wait!'

I ran out into the road and sat on the bridge watching the shallow river swirling round bright stones and endlessly washing the green hair of the water weed. I was empty. Rinsed.

When the post arrived one morning, seeing it was a bill I almost left it on the mat, having learned that presenting my parents with brown envelopes only made them cross. Then I saw something white underneath. It was addressed to me in Ruby's writing. I rushed upstairs and shut my bedroom door.

> The King's Arms
> Market Street
> Maidstone
> Kent

Dear April

Sorry I couldn't say goodbye. I hope you are well and didn't get into too much trouble. I didn't mean to set the camp on fire it was an accident. Write back in invisible ink or a code. In haste.

Love from Ruby.

P.S. Your best friend.

I started to write back at once in the Dancing Men code from the Sherlock Holmes story. It took ages, and it was only after

I had posted it that I realized that Ruby would not be able to read it because I had the book. If they ever gave me any pocket money again, I would save every penny for the fare to Maidstone. After a day or two I told Betty about Ruby's letter and Percy went round to see Constable Cox to give him Lex and Gloria's address, but we never heard what happened. 'They were shamed into flight,' said Betty.

'I wish we'd done more. Poor little Ruby, even Miss Fay was concerned about her.'

Veronica was useless at thinking of things to do and trailed round after me saying, 'What shall we play?'

'I know a game called Lady Marlene,' I said once in desperation.

'How do you play it?'

'You dress up and do ladylike things.'

'Shall we play it then?'

'No.'

Veronica screamed and flapped at Dittany's bees, practically forcing one of them to sting her, and I was pleased when the drake bit her on the leg.

'You're not very kind to poor Veronica, are you?' Betty said one day. Things were almost back to normal at home now.

'She's a bore. She smells of marmite.'

I went upstairs to write another letter to Ruby. I hadn't heard from her for a while.

> ' "One misty morning
> When cloudy was the weather,
> There I met an old man
> Dressed all in leather . . ." '

Mr Greenidge stepped out into my path on the way to school, making me jump.

> ' "Dressed all in leather
> With his cap under his chin.
> How d'you do and how d'you do
> and how d'you do again?" '

'How do you do, April? I don't do very well. Why have you turned against me? You cross the street to avoid me, you hardly speak to me in the tea-room. Please, April. Stop hurting me so.'

'I'll be late for school.'

'Meet me later, please. I beg you.'

'I can't.'

'Please.'

'What about Mrs Greenidge?'

'The old dragon won't know, will she? She's hardly likely to come breathing fire from Lovers Lane in her present state of health.'

'She isn't a dragon. You're an old – werwolf.'

'Werewolf,' corrected Mr Greenidge. 'You don't really think that, do you, April? You don't hate me, do you?'

A dew-drop sparkled on the end of his nose like the diamonds on the gates and fences. He looked so sad that I had to say no. I'd always thought they were called werewolves because they were wolves sometimes.

'Bless you for that, my darling. Run along to school now. I'll see you later. Mind how you go.'

Miss Elsey's playground whistle pierced the mist, and I ran. The Virginia creeper on the Rising Sun was turning scarlet again and the new landlady was sweeping the porch.

'You'll be late. Hurry up or you won't half cop it,' she called out in a friendly way as I ran past.

I couldn't care less. Sometimes out of habit, Miss Fay called out Ruby Richards when she took the register even though Ruby's name had been crossed off. Present, Miss Fay.

I had nothing to say to Mr Greenidge when we met. We walked past the Paper Mill. Leo Silver was balancing along the stone ridge of the waterfall. He saw us and waved, almost overbalancing.

'I'm in quarantine,' he shouted. 'Chicken pox.'

His face was covered in spots.

'Mind you don't fall in, young man,' called Mr Greenidge, and muttered, 'serve him right if he does.'

'Is that your new boyfriend, April? Is that what's been going on behind my back? Have you been consorting with that spotty young hooligan, eh? I warned you against getting mixed up with that lot, didn't I, and look what happened at their so-called garden party.'

'You told the police about the secret camp! You went there spying on me and Ruby. I do hate you and Leo's my friend so there!'

'Hey, hey, now now. I didn't mean it. It's not the boy's fault I suppose. Look what I've got in my pocket for you.'

'No.'

'Three guesses.'

'No, I don't want to.'

'Is it a – toffee? Is it a – propelling pencil perhaps? No. It's a liquorice pipe!'

At the mention of the propelling pencil I had to look at him. He was grinning and dangling a black pipe with pink tobacco.

'Thank you.'

'That's better.'

'Why didn't you bring Liesel?'

'She was reluctant to leave Mrs Greenidge's side. She's been asking after you, you know.'

'Liesel has?'

'Mrs G. My better half.'

'Oh.'

I made Veronica come with me to take Mrs Greenidge a bunch of Michaelmas-daisies the next day. I could tell that she knew that Veronica wasn't really my best friend. Veronica was scared of Liesel, and of Mr Greenidge who was not pleased to see her.

'Do you want to come truffle-hunting with us early tomorrow morning?' said Bobs on Saturday. 'Looking for fungi in the woods.'

'Yes, go, April. Better than moping around like a dying

duck in a thunderstorm. Bring us back some mushrooms for breakfast,' Betty said.

'What about Sunday school?'

'It won't hurt to miss it for once, and it doesn't seem to do you much good. Anyway, you'll probably be back in time,' said Percy.

'I always feel I can worship so much more satisfyingly in the open, when I'm at one with nature, in the fields and pastures and woods, under God's heaven,' said Bobs.

'Same here,' said Betty.

'Fields are pastures,' I said.

'Back in the knife drawer, Miss Sharp,' said Percy. 'They aren't necessarily.'

Peter was banging a saucepan with a wooden spoon, sitting on the floor.

'Definite musical talent. Runs in the family,' Percy raised his voice over the din.

I hated Sunday school without Ruby to get the giggles with. Sometimes I just cycled around until it was time to go home. Doreen threatened to report me to Mr Oswald but she hadn't yet. I went round to Beulah House and had an early breakfast with Bobs and Dittany before we set off. I showed them how to make a cobwebber from a privet stick and they vied with each other to catch the prettiest spiders' webs. We carried a chip basket apiece, mine for mushrooms, Bobs's for edible fungi and Dittany's for poisonous specimens, which they were going to draw and paint for their book. Fairies' bonnets and weeping widows lay in the basket already.

'Guess what? This'll make you laugh. The Village Players are putting on a production of *Miranda* and Dittany's going to play the part of the mermaid. Can't you just see her with her hair all spread out and a gleaming tail?'

'I wish Ruby could see it.'

Bobs sighed and the heavy tail flopped onto the ground with its scales dulled. We held the strands of the barbed wire apart, taking turns to climb through into the mushroom field where cows lay on their folded legs in the long wet grass glittering with a zillion diamonds.

'Look, there are hundreds of mushrooms. We'll get them after we've been to the woods, on the way back,' said Bobs.

'I read a book called *Deathcap Cottage* once, about a woman who poisoned her husband. He was an invalid.'

'Proper little ray of sunshine, isn't she?' said Dittany. 'Come on, race you to the wood.'

I couldn't be bothered. They ran on ahead laughing and jumping over mushrooms. 'Don't touch anything without asking first, and don't put your fingers in your mouth,' Bobs warned.

Boletus. Brackets. Blewits. I soon grew bored. There was the bright green mossy tree stump, with hollow channels from its roots, where Titchy Vinnegar had once said he could magic a beautiful golden fairy mountain if we closed our eyes while he hid behind it. This was Tippetts Wood where Rodney Pegg had got Sorrel Marlowe.

'Can we go now? Haven't you got enough yet?'

'Just a sec while I get this ox-tongue.'

Dead man's fingers. Stinkhorn. Fly agaric. The leaves that we turned up with our boots smelled of mildew. Twigs cracked when nobody had stepped on them.

'I'm going to go and start picking mushrooms.' Although I would be scared to walk through the wood alone.

'OK. We've got enough now for this morning. A goodly haul.'

'Somebody's got there first!'

A bent figure was picking mushrooms into a basket.

'It's Mr Greenidge. He would! Trust him to spoil everything.'

'We're trespassers too,' Dittany reminded us quietly.

'Top o' the morning to you, ladies. I see you've had the same idea as me.' He peered into Bobs's and Dittany's baskets.

'Some of these chappies don't look too appetizing. Wouldn't like to meet one of them on a piece of toast on a dark night.'

'They're not. Deadly poison some of them. That destroying angel for example.'

'Destroying angel?'

Mr Greenidge looked at me. I bent down and started picking mushrooms.

'Well, best get these home for Madam's breakfast. Don't like to leave her alone for too long.'

'How is Mrs Greenidge?

'Poorly, I'm afraid. Very poorly. One does what one can.'

He blew his nose loudly. Dittany's eyes filled with tears.

'We'll bring her a jar of our nettle-flower honey and a pat of Bobs's special damson cheese,' she promised.

'That man's practically a saint,' she said when Mr Greenidge was out of earshot.

A sad and shabby circus set up its Big Top in the recreation ground. A mule was tethered to a spike in the grass, and all the kids hung around hoping it would extend its long black rubber tube, and shrieking when it did. Bad-tempered men and women yelled at you when you tried to go and look into the caravans or the wild animals' cages. We all went to the circus, and Peter screamed at the clowns and I didn't blame him because they were not at all funny. The wild animals looked like old soft toys that sat on a shelf and nobody played with any more, with grey patches where the sawdust might trickle out.

'Bertram Mills it ain't,' said Percy.

It was nothing like the circuses in Enid Blyton's books either.

Veronica was sitting beside me, where Ruby should have been.

'What did you like best?' Betty asked afterwards as we walked, depressed, out of the Big Top across the wet grass. It was getting dark.

'When that elephant went to be excused,' Veronica giggled.

'Ruby was brilliant at acrobats,' I said. 'She could've been an acrobat in a circus if she'd wanted to.'

'I can do the crab,' said Veronica.

'You are a crab,' I said.

'Isn't that Dr Barker's car?' said Betty as we walked past Kirriemuir. 'I do hope Mrs Greenidge hasn't taken a turn for the worse.'

Mrs Vinnegar came hurrying along the road with her grey coat unbuttoned over a stained apron.

'Have you heard? Mrs Greenidge's gorn. I'm just going round to offer my services.' We all stared at her.

Then, 'Gone where?' asked Veronica.

After a silence Betty said, 'Gone to heaven, dear.'

'He killed her. He murdered her,' I said at home.

'Now, April. We know you're upset but I won't have that kind of talk. How can you say such things about your friend?'

'When he's been so good to you.'

'He poisoned her, I know he did.'

'That's enough. Poor Mr Greenidge is heart-broken. He's a widower now so we ought to be specially kind to him, shouldn't we? You run upstairs and write him a nice letter saying how sorry you are. A letter of condolence, it's called.'

'If Ruby was here she'd believe me.'

'Don't you remember that story I told you about the wrong man being hanged? Is that what you want to happen to Mr Greenidge? If it is you're going the right way about it.'

'I can't write a letter. I wouldn't know what to put.'

'Just make him a nice card then. Paint some flowers.'

Two days later Mr Greenidge came into the Copper Kettle with a black armband round the sleeve of his black coat and a black tie. There was a red circle round the iris of one eye, which I couldn't look at. He invited us all to the funeral, thanking me for the beautiful card which meant so much to him.

'We'd be honoured, Mr Greenidge, but I think April's a little young, don't you?' Percy said.

'Mrs Greenidge was very fond of her. I know she would appreciate it if April were to be there to say goodbye.'

I wondered if he really meant that he wanted me to be there.

'She's rather an emotional child. A bit highly strung,' Betty said. 'I really don't think it's a good idea.'

Was I? First I'd heard of it. Miss Fay mocked children whose mothers claimed they were highly strung.

'Very well, you know best. Eleven o'clock on Friday. Afterwards at Kirriemuir.'

'We'll be there. Oh, Mr Greenidge, do you need any help with the – refreshments?'

'Well, I hadn't thought. There seem to be so many things to organize.'

He blew his nose and wiped his eyes.

'Leave it to the Copper Kettle. We'll do you proud. The full monty. On the house, Mr Greenidge, I insist.'

'Percy, you're an officer and a gentleman, sir. Excuse me, don't want to blub—'

He hurried out, harrumphing into his handkerchief.

'Why did you have to say that about "on the house"?' Betty groaned. 'Oh, Percy, it's not that I begrudge – but how on earth can we?'

'We'll manage somehow, won't we, my son?'

Percy threw Peter up in the air and caught him, as Peter laughed wildly. I was crying. The black armband looked so sad. Betty was crying too, Percy and Peter laughing.

Granny Fitz had a Persian lamb coat, but it was at Herne Hill and weighed a ton, far too heavy to post. Betty borrowed a black ottaman-rib coat and hat from Bobs. Peter was taken to Beulah House while Betty and Percy were at the funeral. I was to go there in the dinner hour. Dittany said Peter would earn his keep by being the model for a drawing class. We had one of her sketches of Peter and me up on our wall at home, a birthday present for Percy.

'You know when we met Mr Greenidge picking mushrooms? Well I bet he put some poisonous ones in there and gave them to Mrs Greenidge.'

We were eating parsnip soup in the kitchen of Beulah House. Peter was in an old wooden, worm-eaten high-chair that must have been used for orphans.

'Don't be ridiculous.'

'How can you say such a terrible thing?'

'No, listen.' I had thought about this so much that I was able to be calm and matter-of-fact.

'Remember when he was looking in the basket of poisonous fungi? He seemed very interested in them, didn't he?'

'Well, yes. But anybody would be.'

'You think he's a saint but I know he wanted Mrs Greenidge to die.'

'April!'

'He did, he told me, lots of times.'

'Why on earth would he want her dead?'

'So's he – because – well, he did anyway.'

I couldn't tell them he wanted to marry me.

'Stop it. You don't know what you're saying. It's dreadful, with the poor woman not cold in her grave and the funeral service hardly over.'

'I wouldn't've have believed it of you, April,' said Dittany. She pushed away her soup bowl. 'I'm afraid you have a sick mind.'

Bobs rolled up her napkin and thrust it into her napkin ring as if she was too disgusted to eat any more.

Tears were splashing into my soup.

'I haven't got a sick mind. He did tell me. He wants to marry somebody else.'

'What?'

'Who?'

'I – I don't know.'

A letter had come from Ruby that morning at long last and I held onto it in my pocket. Bobs and Dittany looked at each other and I could see that they had begun to believe me. I felt scared then, at the thought of Mr Greenidge being arrested, in his black armband.

Peter picked up his bowl and turned it upside-down on his head. Bobs and Dittany were not amused. Both the Harlency children were nuisances, I felt, even though Peter was a godson. I was still starving but it didn't seem polite, or highly strung, to ask for more. Hunger was overtaken by anxiety as Bobs and Dittany whispered together at the sink. Not yet cold in her grave. I could see Mrs Greenidge lying on the couch and remembered the silk of her dress darkened by my tears. Mr Greenidge was hanging from a gallows with bulging blue eyes. He was a waxwork in the Chamber of Horrors. I put my head down on the table and wept while Peter shouted and banged his spoon.

'April, dear. What is it? Why are you crying like that? Do be quiet, Peter, there's a darling.'

'I wish Mrs Greenidge wasn't dead.'

'Of course you do. We all do.'

'Don't tell anybody what I said, please. It was a mistake. I don't really think he poisoned her, honestly.'

'There, there, do stop crying. We won't say a word. We'll forget the whole thing.'

But the whole thing couldn't be forgotten. I had already broken off pieces of the deadly fungus of gossip and shared them out among Veronica and other playground confidantes including Doreen who gave a bit to her mother, whose services in laying out Mrs Greenidge had been rejected and who was pleased to scatter the spores upon the wind that blew them through the village until it was infested with the ugly misshapen toadstools of rumour and malice.

They dug Mrs Greenidge up again at the dead of night, a group of men with spades and lanterns and ropes hauling her back from the grave. Mr Oswald, Constable Cox and policemen from Elmford, Mr Seabrook and Dr Barker, and drove her away to the mortuary.

The verdict was death by natural causes. The dicky ticker.

Twenty-One

So I stand in the churchyard of St Michael and All Angels and think, Liesel should be there too, asleep on the bottom of the bed, but she couldn't be, in body at least, because Mr Greenidge had her put to sleep soon after Mrs Greenidge's second burial. Betty broke the news to me when I got back from my grandparents' where I had been sent to stay for a few days. Why didn't he give her to me if he didn't want her? I would have looked after her, and loved her again. Although I was not present at Mrs Greenidge's disinterment I have imagined it often enough to believe now that I witnessed it from the shadows of a tree threshing restlessly in the moonlight.

Across the churchyard I see two graves that I remember now, that we used to like, lying like stone Egyptian mummies or greyhounds in the grass, so old that all their lettering has long since been obliterated. As I walk over to look at them again I see it. The name jumps out at me, blinding me, hitting me in the heart.

RUBY COPPARD
1944–1994
ADORED WIFE OF ROBERT
MOTHER OF PETER AND APRIL
AND GRANDMOTHER

She came back. She was within two hours' reach and I missed her by just two years. I am kneeling with my arms around the stone and I hit my forehead hard against it and my tears fall on the names Ruby and Peter and April. Ruby. Sent to bed too early under that lumpy green quilt, that sharp granite quilt, when she should be out playing with her red hair flying in the sun that frazzles rainbows in its aureole. There was a funeral here, my best friend's funeral, and I should have been there. At my mother's funeral, as the cars drove slowly up the street of terraced houses, I saw through the window of the undertaker's limousine a woman cross herself, a blessing from a stranger. The chiselled letters are cold and salty as I kiss them. Peter and April. How could she, oh how could she do that to me?

At last I look up and see, through my dishevelled hair, a man carrying a bunch of dahlias walking along the grass path between the graves. He might be a boy I used to know. I go to the church to hide, half-expecting it to be locked but the iron latch lifts. Blue light is falling through the memorial window to twin airmen lost in the sky during the war, as it used to, and there is the marble plaque in the wall that says 'And God Shall Wipe Away All Tears From Their Eyes', that always made me want to cry, and the painted organ pipes, the blue light burning above the Lady Chapel. The velvet vestry curtains part and a young man is walking down the aisle towards me. I feel exposed and wonder if he saw me weeping on Ruby's grave, and almost duck into a pew and bow my head, but I stand there until he comes up to me, in his grey silky shirt front with a wisp of white collar, and realize that I have a hank of feathery grasses wound round my fingers, and my face is probably filthy. He will think I'm mad, and wonder if he should call the police or social services. I try to put him at his ease.

'You must think I'm mad, out there like Nebuchadnezzar in the grass, but the thing is – I . . .'

'Sorry?'

'You know, Nebuchadnezzar the King of the Jews? Bought his wife a pair of shoes?'

Now he'll think I'm an anti-Semitic loony.

'I beg your pardon?' he says.

Pardon Mrs Arden, me chicken's in your garden.

'Are you in some sort of trouble? Can I help at all?'

His grey watered-silk eyes are kind but he is just a boy. To his left, a screen displays a collage made by Sunday-school children. There is a table of paperback books below the blue Mothers' Union banner with white fleur-de-lys.

'No. I don't think so. But thank you. You see, I've just found, I used to live here, and I've just come across the grave of my oldest, my dearest, my best . . .'

I run out of the church. Where the light streams through stained glass as it did onto the landing at Kirriemuir when you could change the day to gold, emerald, sapphire or ruby red by holding a sweet paper up to your eye.

I am sitting on the bench outside when I hear the iron key turn in the lock and his footsteps on the stone flags, hesitating. I could look up from the mirror of my compact but I deny him the chance to comfort me, a hard-faced woman with a mascaraed tissue crumpled in her lap applying lipstick in the cruel sunshine.

I walk past cottages leaning against each other in gardens of flowers and beans and sun-split speckled tomatoes on withered vines, past the war memorial by the river and white Beulah House with its dovecot and campanile, past the school playground with a bleached mitten unravelling on a spike of the fence, and I see Ruby everywhere. On her bicycle, by the fuchsia hedge of the Rising Sun, red and purple, and the leaves of the virginia creeper hang limply in the heat.

The gravel of Kirriemuir has been laid to lawn, the hedge has gone and a child's bicycle lies on its side on the grass. Sometimes, in memory, that pink quilted bed is as innocuous as a rose, and I think, what Mr Greenidge did wasn't really so bad. I am as sure that he loved me as I am certain that Rodney Pegg used his bicycle for excursions to the country to prey on little girls. And then I remembered how Mr Greenidge corroded my childhood with fear and anxiety and deceit. I still dream sometimes that Liesel is alive again.

The post office is gone and the Co-op has been converted

into somebody's front room, but amazingly, Belinda-Jayne is still there and the other shops under different names, except for Boddy's where a descendant of T. D. Boddy is still butchering and purveying. The village is so little changed and yet the last establishment I expect to find is the Copper Kettle.

The kettle is boiling over with pansies and trailing geraniums, the tea-room has grown a shop on its left-hand side. A wooden sign says ANTIQUES BYGONES KITCHENALIA. I stand, empty as a sieve sluiced with tears, and stare. Kitchenalia. There is a tub of wooden rolling pins, our Kitchmagig potato masher. Utensils with scorched handles of yellow banded in green, rusted bun tins that print fancy leaves on the bottoms of your fairy cakes, boxes of steel knives and forks and spoons, a St Ivel cream-cheese glass painted with blue flowers, a yellow kitchen cabinet with sliding glass doors, pale-blue Pyrex pudding dishes, a Chad Valley swan and a big tin Triang tortoise. There is the enamel Forestry Commission sign with painted flames that used to hang above the fire brooms in Tippetts Wood. I cannot bear to look inside the tea-room itself. I might catch some stranger by the arm and say, 'We used to have little pink-shaded lamps and fresh flowers on every table and fairy-lights.' People are rummaging through the boxes outside the shop, I know what they're up to, with their Kitchenalia, purchasing pieces of our lives. They are trying to buy their way into the past they think we had, they want to be snug and safe down Rabbit Lane. A thousand bus tickets faded to the colours of old ration books won't get them there and they can force all the carrots in the world through a Mouli grater, but they'll never find their way into the burrow where Bobbity and Sandy live.

Walking back to the station I pass or am passed by various imposters who imagine that they live here, but I know that the real people of Stonebridge are all about me, in Brownie uniforms or their mothers' shoes, wearing rhubarb leaves as sunhats and painting their lips red with a Smartie, pursuing their concerns as they always do. They are fishing for crayfish or preparing for a Grand Dance at the Village Hall. They are shopping at the Co-op and sewing run-and-fell seams under the tutelage of Miss Fay, whose dancing shoes are waiting in her desk, and piercing the grass with the steel tips of flimsy easels. They are racing along the High Street in a box on wheels and sitting on the bridge swinging their legs over the river shouting out rude comments to passers-by. Had yer eyeful, or d'you want the ha'penny change?

Whatever became of those glass salt-and-pepper pots with red bakelite caps that I won at the Silvers' garden party? Hoopla – they may be kitchenalia now, but Leo is standing on the ridge of the waterfall waving, 'I'm in quarantine', invulnerable to the bomb that blew him to pieces on a photographic assignment to Cambodia for his newspaper. A balloon floats past like a soap bubble on a string.

Up Station Hill under the overhanging trees with the rough hempen smell of a sack on my face. Ruby missed Charmaine Vinnegar's wedding to John Cheeseman and the birth of Charmaine's pigeon pair, Pearl and Dean, a few months later. We thought they might have the reception at the Copper Kettle but the Vinnegars hired the village hall, luckily as it turned out, because a prawn cocktail fight broke out and Constable Cox was called. Anyway, we didn't have a licence.

I wrote to Ruby about it but my letter came back marked 'Gone Away'. It was not long after that that Percy and Betty, both of them broken with tears, told me that we were so badly in debt that we had to go back to London and lodge at the Drovers Tavern until we got back on our feet and found a tenancy somewhere.

Ruby and I lost touch.

I am sitting on the station opposite the platform where Professor Linus Scoley descended from the train. The booking hall is closed. I had to come in the side entrance, and I neither know nor care when there will be a train. White bindweed is tumbling down the fence behind me and the little pink convolvulus running around the iron feet of the bench. The advertisement for Virol has gone, undoubtedly sold as an amusing rusty Bygone. I press the calyx of a white bindweed bloom to feel the flower jump out and smell the rank green scent. Grandmother, grandmother, pop out of bed. Why did Ruby never try to contact me when we were older? There aren't so many Harlencys in the London phone book that she couldn't have located me, through Peter, after I had married and changed my name for a while. Did she write to the Copper Kettle and were her letters returned, or did she think that I just hadn't bothered to reply to her or that I had found a new best friend? Perhaps, as I did, she thought we had all the time in the world to find each other again.

Robert Coppard. I picture a big, gentle man with hair the colour of copper-beech leaves in a work shirt washing putty from his hands at a kitchen sink. He gives his children the left-over putty which they sniff, loving its smell, and roll into silver-grey balls and slap between their hands to make imprints of their small palms laced with the lines of destiny. A teller of tales. Or perhaps he is an artist rinsing clay from his fingers, while in his studio a head of Ruby wrapped in wet cloths waits for resurrection, a sculpture that will transcend the standard stone bed spread with a green marble quilt.

I was talked into marrying a man I did not love quite enough and we had a cottage in Dulwich Village with a white picket fence and hollyhocks. We divorced after seventeen years of amicable childless marriage jogging along in dullish tracksuits. Last year on the afternoon of the fifth of November, it was wet and already almost dark at three o'clock and when I was shopping in Superdrug, the shining coloured and sparkling Christmas gifts suddenly looked garish and tawdry in the fluorescent light and a male voice was slurping and droning 'In the bleak midwinter', and it felt like the end of the world.

Further up the road a council mini-van stopped outside a video shop and the sliding door opened and six or seven boys climbed out; and it was the bleakest thing. I knew that some at least of those boys did not want to be choosing videos on the afternoon of November the fifth and were taking them back to a house where who knows what goes on, and although they were dressed in padded jackets with flashes of neon pink and green, and trainers, their eyes were the eyes of the orphans of Beulah House. I walked on past Woolworth's which was boxed in with silver scaffolding and I saw him, my husband Colin, pushing a striped double buggy skilfully through the shoppers, and it was as if one of the silver scaffolding poles rammed me in the heart.

It was Peter, our proper little Bobby Buster, our cuddly Jim whom everybody wanted to eat, who did the decent thing and gave Percy and Betty four lovely grandchildren.

A train is coming up the line like a zipper knitting together the two lines of the track behind it, taking me back through the white and green and purple July to London. As I stare out of the window at the clustering suburbs I see, in the backyard of a warehouse, leaning against a wall, a row of tall coloured carpets exposed to the weather and in the sunshine they have the soft smudgy radiance of assorted chalks or pastels in the hues of hollyhocks and I feel a spasm of joy through my grief for Ruby.

Jaz is going out as I come in. She is wearing tailored shorts, subject to that law of nature which ordains that small broad-shouldered girls with pointy calves and noses must accentuate them with hems above the knee and mushroom-shaped hair-styles, and it strikes me as strange that she believes me to be a minor character in her drama while I think that she is a bit player in mine; nevertheless affection for her engulfs me in the hall.

'You decided not to stay then. How was your friend? The cats have been fine.'

'She was fine. Lovely.'

'You look a bit – I don't know. I think you've caught the sun perhaps.'

'Anyway, thanks and have a nice time wherever you're going. You all take care, y'hear.'

Bobs and Dittany's *Fungi of the Kentish Woods, Fields and Hedgerow* is in my bookcase next to their pale-blue privately printed poems *Dog's Mercury*. Polysyllabic Dittany Codrington and brisker Bobs Rix. The coloured plates have retained their delicate and vivid colours. Had I been the destroying angel in a cotton frock and wellingtons?

Lex and Gloria's crime was that they were given a work of art and they treated it as if it was worthless with no reverence for the care that had gone into it, all that precision stippling and the rainbows in the pigtails that ended in two paint brushes of wet red hair in the rain. Ruby dips a plait into the paint water in Art and scatters an arc of tinted droplets over the blue absorbent sugar paper to the annoyance of Miss Fay, Miss Fay in her kilt with its Cairngorm pin and her criss-cross dancing shoes, after the death of Major Morton. In remembering the past one inevitably makes elisions and takes meteorological liberties: drops stitches, embroiders and unpicks. It was true that I had, as I told Jaz, kept a journal for many years but, looking back, I must admit that many of my childish entries read only 'wrote my diary'. A bowl of purple plums blooms on my table. I was unable to walk past the greengrocer's sign that said Kentish plums.

Ruby and I lost touch. In half a century we never celebrated her birthday together. Now I have to think about Ruby's extraordinary present to me, the names of her two children, and how to honour it; and as I sit in the sun in the ravaged garden in the scent of crimson roses watching the cats, I take the point of Miss Fay's most important lesson at last: kilt up your skirts, plump up your pumps and on with the dance.

COLOPHON

Shena Mackay was born in Scotland and published her first novel at the age of 20. She is the editor of *Such Devoted Sisters*, and author of two novels, *A Bowl of Cherries* and *Dunedin*, and a collection of short stories, *Dreams of Dead Women's Handbags*. She lives in London.

The text was composed by Intype, London. The front and back matter were done by Moyer Bell. The display faces are Melior and Bembo.

The book was printed by Royal Book, Inc. of Norwich, Connecticut on elemental chlorine and acid free recycled paper with soy based ink.